Polterguys

Polterguys, Volume 1

Sonia Rogers

Published by Blue Beagle Publishing, 2019.

This is a work of fiction. Similarities to real people, places, or events are entirely coincidental.

POLTERGUYS

To the best aunt a girl could ever ask for.

I know you'll never see this, but you were one of my biggest fans, and this book would have ranked up there with one of your favorites (except for the curse words - haha).

I love you, Aunt Joyce, more than you know.

Ed Ward — Paranormal Investigator

I deal in ghosts, ghouls, and goblins.

Got a pest the exterminator won't deal with?

Call me — the Poltergeist Guy!

Chapter 1

The thirty-second commercial played on an old thirteen-inch black and white TV I'd found while dumpster diving behind an electronics store. The bright red background on the single slide showed up as gray, but I could still read the black words against the lighter color, despite the wavery lines running up the screen.

I mouthed along as my recorded speech twanged its way through the words I'd written myself.

Cringing a little at how I sounded on the shitty little speaker, I couldn't help but be reminded of that kid on the old TV show. You know the one I mean - the suspender-wearing nerd with the nasally, annoying patter.

I comforted myself with the thought that anyone watching my ad would most likely be a) half-asleep at 2:13 a.m. or b) so frightened they wouldn't notice I sounded like I had the world's worst head cold.

When the phone rang at 2:14, I let out a little squeal of happiness. Uh, I mean, I let out a masculine war whoop of domination. The commercial worked! I was officially in the ghost hunting business!

Clearing my throat and running a hand over my thinning hair as if the person on the other end of the call could see it, I lifted the receiver and answered the phone with a jaunty – yet official-sounding - greeting, "Poltergeist Guys. This is Ed. What's ruining your night?"

Heavy breathing filled my ear. I could almost feel the moisture from the guy's hot breath. Great. My very first call was a crank. Feeling a little deflated, I hung up and wiped my ear on my shoulder, wondering if the guys that starred in the ghost hunting shows ever had to deal with prank calls.

Before I could let go of the handset, the phone rang again. I ran through my spiel a second time, although not quite as cheerfully, "Poltergeist Guys. This is Ed. What's causing your problem?"

The same hot breath came through the speaker. I slammed the receiver down on the old office phone, enjoying the muffled jangling sound it made.

Feeling nostalgic, I lifted the handset and slammed it down again. Then, just for fun, I did it one last time.

All this new technology had taken away one of the most effective tools of phone use. Punching the end button on a cell phone with your finger – even if you did it forcefully – just disconnected the call with a whimper. How were you supposed to let the person on the other end know you were upset? With an old-school phone like mine, they could *hear* the bang when you hung up.

The phone rang again. I picked it up and started my pitch for the third time, hoping for someone besides the pervert. I'd expected a fair share of prank calls in this line of work, but I still needed to answer in case a real client was on the other end.

Cell phones, in my opinion, had the only advantage over the old house phones in that respect – they came with caller ID. Well, plus the fact you weren't chained to one spot as you talked.

Gritting my teeth and speaking through the false smile I planted on my face in order to keep my tone business-like, I uttered, "Poltergeist Guys. This is—"

Before I could finish, the same jerk-off started his obnoxious act again, but this time, I heard a faint wheeze being added to the charming sound of some perv getting his jollies.

Still and all, I needed clients for my new business, and what if the guy just suffered from asthma? I decided to give him the benefit of the doubt for a few more seconds. "Hello? Is someone there?"

Faintly, between gasps for air, the voice on the other end whimpered, "Help...meeee..."

I sat straight up in my office chair. Okay, my 'office chair' was a really wobbly old kitchen chair I found on the side of the road, but I could still sit on the thing. Don't get all judge-y on me.

Leaning forward, pen I'd stolen from the bank in hand, I touched it to the pad of paper. It wasn't really a pad, just loose-leaf notebook paper I'd found on clearance at the local dollar store. There were notepads there, too, but not for the whopping twenty-five cents the loose-leaf paper had been clearanced out at.

Eventually, I'd have the kind of money again to spend on things like fancy-dancy stationery, but until I found some suckers – uh, clients, every penny counted.

"How can I help you? Is it a ghost?"

"...trapped..." The breathing smoothed out just enough to let the single word slip through the phone line. Now we were getting somewhere. My instincts were right!

With a renewed sense of business-like enthusiasm, I asked, "Trapped where?"

Wait, the guy was trapped? Or did he think he trapped a ghost?

"Sir, should I call the police for you?"

"...don't...cops..."

"Sir? Has a ghost trapped you somewhere? Are you in danger?"

The breathing faded like the phone had drifted away from his face. Desperate to keep him on the line, I spoke louder, "Sir? Are you there? I'll be happy to help, but I need to know where you are!"

Click.

Dammit. I threw the pen across the room, then jumped up and chased after it. I'd only gotten the chance to steal the one, and if there were any other calls, I'd need it.

While I searched for the writing instrument in the dark corner of my office - okay, fine, the dark corner of my unfinished basement, the only place in the house my wife would let me set up, but hey, people have home offices, right? - a thought occurred to me. I had a computer expert at my fingertips, one that owed me more than a few favors.

I pulled my crappy flip phone out of my pocket and punched the little phone picture next to his name, certain he'd be awake.

After the third call, he groggily answered, "What the fuck do you want, dude?"

Trying to sound authoritative, I snapped, "Language!"

Alvin sounded a little more awake when he sputtered, "You ain't my fucking dad, Ed! I'm going back to sleep."

Before he could hang up, I asked, "Okay *Alvin*, that's fine. Go back to sleep. Just don't be surprised when I tell your mother what you're *really* doing in your room when she thinks you're watching educational videos."

That got his attention. And a few more curse words thrown at me.

"Dude, what do you want? And don't call me Alvin. Call me Ghosty, or Ghost."

I rolled my eyes at the name. "Listen, *Ghost*, I need to find an address from a phone call. Is that something you can do? You know what? Never mind, I'm sure it's above your skill set. I'll find someone else."

"Of course, I can do that! Geez, dude, what the fuck? That's child's play!"

Smirking into the phone, I knew I had him hooked. Teasing a teenager by suggesting they can't do a task is like dangling the proverbial carrot in front of a donkey. And Alvin could be kind of an ass sometimes.

"See you in my office," I demanded, pressing the button to end the call, then picking up and slamming the handset of the house phone with a pling that made me smile.

A few seconds later, the thump of bare feet coming down the steps announced Alvin's entrance. Rubbing his eyes with one hand, he held a laptop in the other.

Did I mention the kid is my step-son?

"Don't wake up your mother," I cautioned, but it was too late. He'd already reached the bottom of the stairs, shoving at the hank of blond hair hanging in his face, only for it to fall right back into his eyes. "You need a haircut. Maybe we should go get you one tomorrow."

Ghost muttered a few words I couldn't make out. Probably just as well.

The kid and I had a checkered past of sorts. We tolerated each other for the sake of his mother, my wife Masha, but we'd never been what you call close. More like two planets circling the same sun.

Ghosty_boy69 - what a dumb name! - gently set his laptop on my desk. The computer had been a gift from his grandfather, and probably cost more than all my office equipment combined, especially since I'd scrounged the table out of a dumpster behind a Chinese restaurant downtown. So what if it smelled like soy sauce and ginger? Even if my stomach did growl a little every time I sat down at it.

Let me tell you, I had a hell of a time getting that table home in my little Pacer, but after I strapped it to the roof with the legs pointing toward the sky, the trip went faster. Anyway, it was only a little wobbly, and it did exactly what a table is intended for – hold my stuff.

I watched Alvin check out my office space as though he'd never been in the basement before. Heck, I guess it might have been his first time down there, considering his mother waited on him hand and foot. Turning in a small circle, he looked at the rusty metal shelving filled with over-stuffed cardboard boxes, the gym equipment with forgotten athletic clothes draped over the dusty handles, the washer and dryer sitting quietly in a dark corner, finally turning back to my secondhand table and chair sitting in the middle.

He sneered, "Dude, this place is a dump."

Before I could come up with a witty reply, the phone rang again. We both stared at the old-school phone, me with pride, and Ghost with an unbelieving look.

Smugly, I picked up the receiver and said, "Poltergeist Guys. This is Ed. Got ghosts?"

The same guy said hello in his heavy-breathing language. Covering the mouthpiece, I whispered, "This is him. This is the address I need."

Pulling the phone back up, I spoke to Heavy Breather Guy, "Hi, again. Still need help?"

"...trapped...help..."

Trying to sound professional, I chirped, "I'll be happy to help you, sir. I just need to know where to go. Can you give me your address?"

Alvin – er, Ghost – bent over the wobbly table and tapped away on his computer while I spoke. I gave him a rolling motion with my hand to tell him to hurry.

"...need..."

"Need what, sir? You're going to have to give me a little more to work with."

Ghost muttered, "Almost," while still tapping keys.

"...help..."

"Sir, did you say your home is haunted? That's great! I can help you with that! I just need to know where to go."

Ghost triumphantly threw his hands in the air, "Got it!"

I leaned over to look at the screen, then swiveled my head up to glare at him. His elation fizzled when he looked back down at the computer.

"That's our address *here*, boy genius."

I shoved the irritation I felt back down into my bowels. I mean, someone could be dying here, and I needed the kid's skills with the computer to find the guy.

I thought seriously about popping him on the back of the head – you know, jokingly, of course - but our relationship was already shaky at best, and I figured killing him wouldn't improve it much. Plus, his mother – my wife Masha – she's kind of scary when she gets mad. Oh, and her father? He's scary when he isn't mad, if you know what I mean.

Boris Bykov, my father-in-law, is a large Russian bear posing as a man. He's the kind of guy who speaks softly and carries a big stick. And by that, I mean he literally carries a stick with him everywhere. He calls it a cane, but I've never seen him use it for help walking. Then again, I've never seen him hit anyone with it either, but I'm not about to take the chance that the first time I see it will be just before I see stars and then the black veil of unconsciousness.

Either way, I skipped smacking the kid on the back of the head and went back to the phone call, while Al- dammit – I mean, *Ghost* – I rolled my eyes again at the stupid name - started his process all over again.

"Sir, are you still there?"

Nothing but empty air answered. On the bright side, the guy hadn't hung up, so maybe we could still get an address. Gently, I set the receiver on my stack of blank paper and turned back to the kid, who was punching keys like Liberace on his glitzy grand piano.

While he worked, I assessed the teen. I'd never heard a whisper of the name of his biological father in five years of marriage to his mother, although it was obvious the kid inherited the unknown father's looks. While Masha and Boris had dark complexions and darker personalities, Ghost had pale skin, hazel eyes, and blond hair. The kid's body didn't resemble the rest of his family either. Tall, thin, and kind of gangly, he towered over his mother and grandfather who were shorter and more solidly built.

Don't get me wrong. I'm not saying my wife has a bad figure, but she's not a willowy model by any means. She's more of an Oprah-Winfrey-in-mid-weight-swing kind of woman. Luckily, I like a woman with a little meat on her bones.

Born in the United States, Alvin never learned to speak Russian. Masha rarely spoke her native language at home, preferring to perfect her English. It needed a lot of perfection, in my opinion, but I didn't have the courage to tell her that to her face,

In fact, there were only two times my wife ever spoke her native language: when she talked to her father, and when I screwed up. And unfortunately, I tend to screw up a lot.

Over the years, though, I've discovered if I ignore the venomous looks accompanying the foreign words being flung in my direction, I can pretend they're Russian terms of endearment. Sort of.

Either way, Alvin, Ghost, whatever you want to call him, bore no resemblance to the rest of his family. He reminded me of someone else though, now that he was finally growing into his adult look. Maybe an actor, one with blond hair and a cleft in his chin. In fact, if you squinted your eyes so you couldn't see the zits dotting his forehead, he kind of looked like that guy in all the movies. You know, whatshisname-

"Okay, this time I really found it!" Ghost grinned with satisfaction, jerking me out of my thoughts. Absently placing the handset back on the cradle, I leaned back so I could see the map on the screen. I couldn't help but suck in a deep breath when I saw the origin of the phone call.

"Is that—"

Ghost shoved blond hair out of his face and grinned, "Yup. Graystone Cemetery."

"So...someone is making a phone call from the cemetery?"

Fully awake now, the teenager bounced on the balls of his feet with excitement and managed to roll his eyes at the same time, "Dude, it's a cell phone! They go everywhere! Not like the dinosaur you've got with the cord plugged into the wall!"

Armed with the address, I didn't need the kid anymore. "Thanks for the help. Go on back to bed. You can still get a couple more hours of sleep before school."

Planting his feet and crossing his arms, the kid set his jaw. "No way, dude. You dragged me into this. I'm going with you. I can be your helper, or whatever. I took CPR in health class last semester. The guy might need it from the way he sounds."

I started to tell him to stay home. Masha would kill me if she discovered I took her only son out in the middle of the night, even for a business call. Okay, especially for a business call, since she hadn't bothered to hide her displeasure when I'd announced I would be starting my own business chasing imaginary ghosts rather than go to work for her father.

Then it dawned on me.

I was going to a cemetery.

At night.

Alone.

No, I needed to be the adult here. The kid had school. "No. You've only got a few weeks of school left. If you miss class, your mother will have my hide. Go back to bed."

Ghosty_boy69 gave me a devilish grin and answered, "If you don't let me go with you, I'll tell Ded you woke me up in the middle of the night to hack into the phone company." I shuddered at the words, making the kid's smile grow even bigger.

Ded was short for Dedushka, the Russian name for Grandfather, but it still sent a shiver down my spine every time I heard Ghost use the nickname. It sounded a little too close to Boris's black personality for my comfort.

My reluctant father-in-law hadn't liked me from the very first. For one thing, there was no mistaking me for a nice Russian boy, even though it only took one look at Alvin for it to be obvious Masha had no interest in nice boys from her homeland. Having a baby out of wedlock with a foreigner had been a forgivable offense, it seemed, since it produced his grandson and only heir.

Marrying an American hadn't been quite as justifiable, though, especially one with a checkered past like mine. I've always felt like I'm the Johnny Cash (without the talent) in the relationship, compared to her June Carter. I'm a mess that's in love with a beautiful, talented woman, which means I have to work twice as hard to keep her affection.

At the beginning of our budding relationship, Boris tried everything to break us up, even going so far as to attempt bribery. Five years of marriage later, on days when my wife is in the foulest of moods, sometimes I wish I'd taken his money and run.

"Fine," I grumbled, knowing when I'd been beaten. "you can come with me. But just this once."

Ghost pounded his way back up the wooden stairs to get his shoes, with me frantically yell/whispering – yellspering? -after him to keep it down. While he was gone, I started loading up supplies.

There wasn't much to pocket. Most of the nicer things I used to own, well, I'd sold off a lot in order to pay the bills once my inheritance ran out.

I inventoried my few possessions: a Swiss Army knife missing most of the gadgets, a heavy-duty flashlight that may or may not have been stolen from my last short-lived job as a house inspector, and last, but most importantly, my proudest tool – an EMF meter with EVP detection that I bought on Amazon.

Well, the kid had ordered it once I explained what I wanted. I couldn't remember what the initials stood for, but if I ran into any *real* ghosts, I doubted it would do any good anyway.

Turning the meter on to be sure the batteries worked, even though I put brand new ones in an hour earlier – you know, just in case - I smiled at the electronic glow it emitted.

It looked fancy. It looked official. And with a five-star rating on Amazon, I was cautiously optimistic the thing was real. Or at least, it *looked* real enough to convince clients.

Pushing the button to turn off my new toy and save the batteries, I slid the little box into the pocket of my jacket and put my tennis shoes on. Ghost pounded down the stairs again, making enough noise to wake the dead, and I winced at the thunder of his feet on the wooden steps, hoping Masha had taken a sleeping pill before going to bed.

The phone rang again just as we reached the door leading out of the walk-out basement. I dashed back over to my table to answer.

Expecting the heavy-breathing caller again, I dispensed with the formalities and just answered with my own out-of-breath, "Hello?"

A faint, feminine voice replied, "Hello? Is this Poltergeist Guys?"

Clearing my throat, trying to catch my breath, and still sound business-like all at the same time, which was difficult enough to do without Ghost standing behind me whispering, "Come on, dude! Let's go!", I answered, "Yes, ma'am. You've reached Ed Ward, Paranormal Investigator. What's interrupting your life?"

I know, I know, I'm still working on the right tagline. Don't judge.

The woman on the other end spoke softly, her voice trembling, "I just saw your commercial. I'm havin' some problems with a ghost. Can you help?"

Wow! Two jobs on the same night! My chest swelled with pride as I gave Ghost a giddy smile. Grabbing my stolen pen, I pulled a sheet of paper across the table, ready to take notes.

Ghost tapped my shoulder, prancing around like a little kid who needed to pee. "Dude, we going or not?"

I waved him off like a fly. The kid sighed dramatically and produced a set of earplugs, jamming them into his ears while managing to glare at me at the same time.

"Okay, ma'am. What's your name and address? And when's the best time to come by?"

The woman's voice sounded a little stronger when she said, "I'm Louise Woodall, but you can call me Lou. My address is—"

The phone beeped in my ear, drowning out her words. Holy crap. Another call. I might need to put in another phone line at this rate!

"Ma'am, can you repeat your address? I'm afraid I missed it."

Waving at Ghost, who was gracelessly dancing to music I thankfully couldn't hear, I finally got his attention and pointed at his computer, then at the phone, then back to the computer. He pulled one bud out of his ear. I could hear bass thumping as he stared at me with the confused, yet irritated expression only teens are able to master.

"Address," I mouthed. A fleeting expression of understanding crossed his face, then switched back to confusion again as he turned the laptop to show me the map still displayed on the screen.

Covering the mouthpiece to mute my words, I rolled my hand to tell him to hurry and hissed, "Get *her* address! I can't hear her!"

Eyes widening with comprehension, Ghost started hitting keys again, the loose earbud hanging from his chest blurting out something resembling music, which only added to my hearing problems.

"...so how long 'til you get here?"

Beep. Thump thump thump. Tap tap tap. Beep. Tap. Thump.

Scrunching my eyes tight and crossing my fingers, hoping she didn't say screw it and hang up, I tried again, "I'm so sorry, ma'am. Can you give me your address one last time?" Inspiration struck, and I quickly added, "I'm afraid there's a lot of action going on here in the office, and I'm having trouble hearing you."

"One! Eight! Three! Two! Century! Lane!" Her little-old-woman voice cracked on the Lane part, and I felt terrible for making her do it. At least I got the address.

Prodding Ghost in the ribs, I drew a line across my neck to tell him to stop. He gave me a blank stare, so I closed the laptop lid on his fingers, provoking an "Ow, dude!" along with a scowl.

"We can be there in an hour, Ms. Woodall. Will that be too late for you?" She sighed, the sound drifting through the phone lines and into my ear, reminding me of my grandmother and how much I missed her guilt trips.

"I don't sleep much. I'll be waitin'." With a click, she hung up.

The phone shrieked the second I pushed the button on the cradle down, almost making me drop the receiver from the shock of the sudden, shrill noise.

I let go of the button, switching over to the other line to hear the first caller again.

"We're on our way, Heavy Breather Man. Hang on." His moan sounded so pitiful, I couldn't help but feel sorry for the guy, and I gently hung up the phone.

Looking at Ghost, I asked, "You ready?"

The earbuds were back in place. Ghost was dancing – at least, I think that's what you call it - in his own little discotheque and couldn't hear me. I poked him in the ribs a second time.

"Dude!" Pulling a single bud out, Al- I mean, Ghost spat, "What the fuck, dude? Stop poking me!"

Well, I *had* to poke him again after he said that, just to make sure he knew he wasn't the boss of me.

"Head for the car, Ghosty_boy69. We've got two jobs!"

And just like that, Poltergeist Guys was open for business.

Chapter 2

I suppose you're wondering, 'Why ghost hunting, Ed? Especially if you don't believe in ghosts?"

I guess this is as good a place as any to back up and tell you about it.

Okay, here goes: My name is Edward Wardlaw Ward, heir to the Pizazz toy fortune. I doubt if you've heard of my grandfather, Wardlaw Ward, but I'm sure you remember the Pizazz toys he invented that were so popular in the seventies.

You do remember them, don't you? The combination of frisbees and lawn darts that swept the nation like the Tasmanian Devil in a full frenzy?

I can barely remember when they were at the height of their popularity, but I do remember my grandfather being gone a lot back then.

Oh, did I mention I lived with my grandparents?

My mom crapped out on me right after I turned three. I guess she decided a kid took too much effort and responsibility. She dumped me off at my paternal grandparents' home and took off for parts unknown.

Now, here's the crazy part. I've never met my dad, even though I lived with his parents for the bulk of my life. I heard a lot of different stories about him over the years, including:

"He joined a motorcycle gang and followed them to Mexico. Don't bother looking for him, they killed him over a stolen handlebar incident."

"He went to find himself in Africa. He'll be back once he knows who he is."

"That worthless sonuvabitch is no son of mine! He's dead to me!"

The last one was my grandfather, the man I consider my real dad. Pops taught me how to fish, how to treat a woman, and most of all, he taught me life isn't always rosy.

See, the Pizazz toys, while everyone loved and wanted one, caused a few injuries. Turns out having a frisbee with a metal spike hanging from the bottom might be a *little* dangerous if it's flying full-speed toward your head.

Pops yanked them off the market and paid for the injuries they'd caused, but the bulk of the money earned from the toy had already been squirreled away. Back then, people weren't quite as sue-happy as they are now, and so he kept most of his fortune, although you'd never know it by the way they lived.

Anyway, when he passed away, I inherited the bulk of his estate, including the money he'd never touched. Well, except to buy my grandmother a top-of-the-line kitchen and a few trinkets.

He only bought one thing for himself with all that money, a car he spotted on the floor of the only car dealership in town, paying cash for it.

I know, I know, I promised to tell you how I got into the ghost hunting business. I'm getting there. This is all important background stuff explaining how I ended up starting a business as a joke. Sort of.

Now, where was I? Oh, yeah, my cheap grandfather.

I remember visiting with him a few days before he died. My no-nonsense, giant father-figure lay in a hospital bed at a nursing home, ready to be reunited with my grandmother again.

I'd put off going as long as I could. I wanted to see him, just not there in that hellhole.

Frail, wheelchair-bound senior citizens crowded the dimly lit hallways. Some of them knew who they were, while others wailed in misery, wishing they could forget.

The scent of yeast and shit permeated everything, even the sterile equipment, and over it all hung the unspoken aura of death.

Pop's nurse came into the room right after I got there. Bending over the bed to take his blood pressure, the sight distracted me to the point that I almost missed what he was saying.

The emaciated man lying there didn't resemble the hero who'd raised me, but when he spoke, the voice still belonged to him.

The deep, rumbling voice that terrified me when I'd done something wrong as a child didn't boom the way it used to, but the intensity hadn't changed.

"Eddie, you need to promise me something."

I swallowed. Hard. Keeping promises didn't come easily to me back then. "Sure, Pops, just name it."

He coughed, and the effort took something out of him. Weakly, he reached out and took my hand, squeezing as hard as he could. "Take care of my baby, would you?"

I knew what he meant. He wanted me to keep his pride and joy, the car he'd bought brand new from the showroom floor, the only opulence he'd shown with all his money – a 1976 AMC Pacer.

Have you ever seen one? Probably not. They faded away almost as fast as the Pizazz toy, but to him, that one purchase meant he'd made it in life. It was the one trophy he could polish up and show off to the world.

"Of course, I'll take care of her, Pops. I'll wash and wax her once a week, change the oil, heck, I'll even take her on a few dates!"

The old man twisted his face into something resembling a smile before he started coughing, his body wracked with the fierceness of it. When the spasm finally finished, he let out a feeble laugh and said, "Don't lie to me, boy. You couldn't get a girl to date you even with all the money you're about to inherit."

I grinned, despite the hurtful words. I knew he didn't mean it.

"You gonna come back and haunt me if I don't take care of her?"

Weakly, he smiled, the last familiar vestige of his old self. "I'm gonna haunt you no matter what. Now, go away. I need to rest."

That was the last time I saw him, alive *or* dead.

I'm going to skip all the sad stuff about the funeral and the terrible years that followed.

Let's just say a young man in his twenties should not inherit more money than he knows what to do with. He might go on a long, *long* drinking binge when he realizes he has no family left in the world to care for him. He might not bother getting a job, since he doesn't need the money. He might fall into a depression, resulting in his living in his car.

And if he's lucky, he might eventually end up meeting the girl of his dreams. One sensible and strong enough to pull him out of his funk and back into reality.

I'm not a huge fan of country music, but the night I met Masha, the speakers at the grocery store were softly playing a Johnny and June Carter Cash duet about a town called Jackson. I know, pretty corny, right? But the silly song was zinging through my blood, and something about her caught my attention, even as I tossed a couple of frozen dinners on top of the beer.

I saw the look of derision that crossed her face as she passed by and saw the contents of my cart, and for the first time since Pops died, I truly felt ashamed of myself for drinking so much.

Leaving my cart in the middle of the frozen food aisle, I chased after her as she turned the corner to the bread section. Even after all this time, I can't explain the impulse to talk to the strange woman who caught my attention with a dirty look.

Maybe I just wanted to explain myself to her, convince her that I wasn't a bad person despite the cases of beer. Or maybe I just needed someone to give me a reason to live.

"Hey! Excuse me! Miss? Can I ask you a question?"

She stopped pushing the cart but refused to look my way, focusing on the pile of French bread sitting on the shelves.

I rushed over before she could start moving again, grabbing her cart and breathing heavily as I coolly asked, "Uh, do you know where the asparagus is at?"

I almost slunk away in a cloud of embarrassment when I heard what my steamed-over brain had put together to impress her. But I stayed put.

"Is row one, maybe."

That Russian accent pierced the fog in my brain and forced it to think about something besides getting drunk for the first time in ages.

The woman was the perfect package – dark hair, darker, unreadable eyes, the kind of body a man could get hold of, and a voice I could listen to all day.

"Listen, uh, I don't even really like asparagus. I just wanted to meet you."

I took my hand off the cart and awkwardly let it hang in the air between us. She looked down at it, then back up at my face before putting a loaf of bread in her cart.

"Okay," she said, as she began to walk away.

I started to let her go. I mean, obviously, she had no interest in me. But something wouldn't let me. Some kind of deep-seated longing woke up inside me and screamed for me to try again.

Rushing back and grabbing my cart, I spun it around and chased after her, despite the fact that I couldn't breathe by the time I got back to her. The

Russian beauty refused to look my way as sweat ran down my forehead and into my eyes, making me ram her cart on accident.

"M-my name is Ed." I sucked in a painful breath, "Ed W-ward."

Johnny and June Carter Cash faded away, and The Pina Colada song faded in. "Do you like Pina C-coladas?" I heaved out a few words before I had to stop and take another gasping mouthful of air. She looked at me, and for the first time, a smile graced her face.

"Ed is funny," she pronounced, and just like that, I knew I'd found the woman of my dreams.

I'm going to do you a favor and skip forward again. You really don't want to hear about the hot sex and all that, right? Because it was really, *really* hot. In fact, one time we- well, I better not.

Okay, so long story short: We got married, and I used my inheritance to keep my wife happy. With memories of growing up poor in Russia still vividly in her mind, I could have gotten away with buying *way* less than I did, but her happy smile might have made me go a little overboard.

Are you still wondering what this has to do with me starting a ghostbusting business? We're almost there, I promise.

I'll skip forward another few years. A year of dating, five years of marriage, six years of me being mostly sober. During those six years, two of them were spent helping Masha get her dream business of selling makeup going, and all of them included me spending money like it would never end.

Except it did.

Masha's measly income selling eye shadow and lipstick didn't bring in enough money to pay the bills, so for the first time in my life, I needed to go to work. With no job history, and even fewer skills, I was stuck with entry-level positions doing manual labor.

I tried different jobs, but nothing fit my personality or my lifestyle.

A butcher shop gave me the chance to learn the profession. Being surrounded by the dead meat made me queasy, so I quit after an hour.

I tried being a house inspector. That one seemed kind of promising, and I stayed a whole week – until I came face-to-face with a massive rat snake in the attic of the house I was inspecting.

I even did a short stint as a plumber's apprentice. That is, until we had to clean out a septic tank and I puked all over the homeowner's shoes.

So, with less than a hundred bucks to my name, I wandered into the living room one night when Alvin was watching an old movie on TV. I can't remember the name of it, but the plot consisted of this guy whose ghost buddies who would haunt a house, then he would come in and 'clear' the house of spirits – for a hefty fee, of course.

A smidgen of an idea bloomed. What if I could do the same thing? I mean, I wouldn't have to deal with any actual ghosts because if they actually existed, Pops would have come back to haunt me like he promised.

The idea grew over the next few days, even as Masha kept pushing me to work at her father's Cadillac dealership, selling expensive cars to old people.

Finally, I snapped.

"I'm not going to work for your father, Masha! Boris hates me! He makes me miserable enough with his daily, early-morning visits! Why would I want to spend my entire day with him?"

Masha's accent got thicker the madder she was, and I could barely understand her as she shouted, "Not to be proud, Ed! You work!"

It was time to play my trump card. Forcing a smile on my face, I reached out and put my arms around her stiff body. "Masha, honey, I'm going to start my own business. You'll see, this is gonna earn way more money than I'd make working for your dad."

Masha wiggled her way out of my grasp, crossing her arms as she snapped, "What is business?"

Smiling proudly, I announced out loud for the first time, "I'm going to start a ghost hunting business."

With a confused look, my wife asked, "What is ghost hunting?"

I launched into a long, mostly-bullshit explanation of how I would be helping people by ridding them of the spirits haunting them, leaving out the part that I didn't believe in ghosts. I mean, every marriage needs some secrets, right?

Masha's scowl deepened as I talked. When I finished, she spoke through taut lips, "Is not good to bother such things. Masha forbids."

Well, that just strengthened my resolve. As much as I loved my wife, no one forbade Edward Wardlaw Ward from doing something! I knew I would pay for my rebellion for a while, but damned if I was going to become a car salesman. Talk about low-lifes!

Anyway, *that's* how I started my own business hunting ghosts, despite my wife's extreme displeasure.

Chapter 3

Everybody caught up now? Okay, where was I before I started giving the history lesson?

Oh, yeah, we were leaving for our very first job as ghost hunters.

I eyed Masha's pink Mercedes parked in the driveway, and for a split second considered taking it instead of my car. Then I decided I would be in more than enough trouble over taking Alvin out in the middle of the night. Taking her kid out would make her mad. Taking her car out – for the job she forbade me to do - might end up with me losing some precious body parts.

Once I made the decision that I was pretty attached to everything on my body, I only had one option - my trusty old steed. I'd kept my promise to Pops that I would keep her – although admittedly, I hadn't taken care of her as well as I should have.

The side panels were rusted, there were rips in the vinyl seats, I needed to buy new tires and windshield wipers, and most importantly, the engine needed expensive repairs I couldn't afford.

The worst part, though? The smell. Over the years, the back seat had become a repository for everything from mostly-empty fast food bags to discarded jackets to things that just kind of appeared, leaving a sharp, cheesy odor that never went away, even after spraying an entire can of air freshener. I didn't really notice it anymore, but Ghost wrinkled his nose every time his mother forced him to hitch a ride with me.

Masha called my classic car a rolling aquarium because of all the windows. Regardless of her contempt, I had been through a lot with my trusty little baby, and eventually, I planned to keep my promise to the old man and restore her to her former glory.

Meanwhile, I turned the key in the ignition. Nothing.

Gently giving the dash a loving pat, I murmured, "Come on baby, don't do this to me now. I need you." I shot a glance at Ghost to see if he'd noticed my little pep talk, but the kid was dancing in his disco again, feet tapping the rusty floorboards and his hands making some kind of strange movements, like learning sign language for a deaf giant had become his newest passion.

Satisfied he wasn't paying attention, I crooned, "Papa needs a new pair of shoes, baby. You can do this." I turned the key again, and with a groan, she started up, backfiring twice before the motor smoothed out into the normal rattly-shivery-shaky sound.

Now we were getting somewhere. With one last nervous glance up at the bedroom window to be sure the backfires hadn't woken Masha, I put the car in reverse and pulled out of the driveway.

Graystone Cemetery wasn't far, but with my Pacer running more-or-less on pure gas fumes, I sent up a little prayer we could get to both jobs before I had to put the two singles in my wallet into the gas tank. Sliding the gearshift into neutral at the top of every hill to save gas, we coasted rather than drove most of the way there.

Ghost gave me a few funny looks when he noticed me changing gears like my baby had suddenly become a stick shift, but his earbuds stayed firmly in place, which I took as a good sign.

When we reached the small, historic cemetery at the edge of town, three things immediately caught my attention.

The first was that the tombstones were covered in a dense fog that made the scene look even creepier than a- well, than a graveyard at night.

The second thing I noticed was the tiny church with a light shining through the world's smallest stained-glass window.

Then I saw an expensive sports car parked inside the cemetery itself, nearly hidden by shadow and fog, and I almost giggled. If Heavy Breather Guy could afford to drive *that*, then he had the money to pay for my services.

With that thought in mind, I turned my attention back to the mini-church with the miniscule window. I haven't been in a lot of churches in my life, but the few I *have* been in were large and ornate, nothing like this dollhouse version. This ancient building barely qualified as a structure, much less a house of worship.

When I say the building was tiny, I mean exceptionally small – as in, it looked to be about the size of a guard shack. Just big enough to hold a couple of people and maybe a pulpit, if the preacher sucked in his gut to squeeze behind it. In fact, emptied of contents, the church could have been mistaken for an upright coffin built to hold the world's largest man.

Either way, between the fog, the deserted sports car, and the light coming from a church that shouldn't be having services at three o'clock in the morning, the joy I felt imagining my future income faded away, replaced by a lingering eeriness.

I patted my leg to check for the familiar lump of my pocket knife when it suddenly occurred to me that we might be walking into a trap. Didn't Satanists use real churches for their evil rituals? We could be walking into some crazy cult ceremony. Or worse.

What if the phone calls were meant to lure us here to be sacrificed in a devil-worshipping service? Then again, wouldn't a sacrifice need one of those big pentagrams for the victim to lie in? There was no way of that happening in *this* dinky church, I reassured myself.

After a few seconds of unconvincingly convincing myself that we hadn't been lured here to be killed, I shut the engine off, mentally kicking myself for letting it run so long. Eyeballing the fuel gauge splitting the E, praying it would move even the tiniest bit, I winced as she sputtered a few times before finally giving up the ghost, wondering how far the gas in those little spurts might have taken us.

In the darkness of the car, I debated my choice of trade for a second before I gave myself another mental kick. I'd started this business on a lark, based on hours of research watching ghost hunting shows and laughing at the fakeness of them all, but now someone might actually need our help. It was time to man up and do something about it.

Or we could just call the cops and go home. The thought was appealing. The idea of going inside sounded less and less like a good idea.

No. For once in my life, I needed to finish what I started. We were going in.

Maybe.

Dammit, we were definitely going into that church and rescuing the man who'd sounded so pitiful on the phone.

Maybe I could let the kid decide. If he was too nervous to go inside, then I could just call the cops and still get him home in plenty of time for school. I mean, forcing him to do something against his will wouldn't be very fatherly of me, now, would it?

I tried to hide the nervousness, but my voice cracked anyway as I asked, "Well, what do you think?"

Fingers and toes still tapping away, Ghost stared out the window without answering. Finally, he turned my way, yelling over music I couldn't hear, "Dude, we gonna get out, or what?"

An unexpected surge of irritation at his lack of fear went through me. Jerking the nearest earbud out of his ear and eliciting an "Ow!" out of him, I hissed, "Shut that off! If we're gonna do this, I need you to be on high alert."

"Fine. Fucking chill," he mumbled, shutting off the noise blaring out of the earbud without looking down, his glare never leaving mine.

"Language!" I growled, then opened the door and stepped out, waiting for the inevitable, "You're not my dad!"

Surprisingly, he muttered a surly, "Whatever," instead, as he got out and came around to meet me at the front of the car. I kind of wanted to dance a little jig at the progress but held it back. Baby steps.

As I stood in the dark, gravel parking lot of the cemetery, though, I started shivering. Something in the air just invited fear, but I couldn't quite put my finger on the source, exactly. Sure, the location didn't help, but it was more than that. It almost felt like the air was conducting electricity, the combined power of the two forces eroding the exposed skin on my body and leaving my raw nerves exposed to the toxic atmosphere.

A nasty giggle floated toward us from the fog-covered headstones. My muscles bunched up involuntarily, and it took everything I had not to jump back into the car and leave right then. Forcing my nerves under control, I cleared my throat and whispered, "Let's check the church first. The light's on. Our client is probably in there."

Shadow hid most of Ghost's face, making it look skeletal. Eyes darting nervously between me and the cemetery shrouded in fog, he yelped, "Dude, this place is kinda creepy. It reminds me of- never mind. Maybe I should just wait for you in the car."

I should have felt better since he was finally showing the same anxiety I felt, but instead, it just pissed me off. Gritting my teeth, I suppressed the urge

– again - to pop him in the back of the head, wondering if *real* fathers ever felt that way.

Forgetting about my own fear in my irritation with his, I reminded myself that even though he stood taller than me, inside the giant, clumsy body he was still just a kid. Slowly, and more-or-less patiently, I prompted, "You were begging to come with me just a few minutes ago, remember?" Mocking him, I repeated his earlier words, "I know CPR."

"I didn't beg," he grumbled, heading toward the church as I scrambled to catch up with his freakishly long steps. I'm not sure how he managed to make stomping sounds as he walked through the damp grass, but somehow, he did, and I grabbed his arm to stop the noise, pulling him around to face me.

In the dim, multicolored light seeping through the angel depicted on the stained-glass window – at least, I think it was an angel - I could see his eyes rolling up into his head as he whined, "Dude! *Now* what?"

I thought about giving him a good, hard shake, but I settled for gritting my teeth. "Get yourself under control, kid. We don't know what we're walking into. I'll go in first," I whispered, half-hoping he would rebel at my fatherly protectiveness and rush into the building ahead of me. "I think I see something moving inside."

In an exaggerated motion, he waved his long arm in a circle like he was pitching a softball, and I wondered if maybe I should have insisted we put him in sports after we got married, rather than letting him play video games so much. Maybe that would have taught him some respect and—

"Good idea. I mean, since you're so prepared and all." Sarcasm dripped off his tongue like a toothless old man drooling over corn on the cob.

Teenagers. Can't live with 'em, can't ship 'em off to boarding school after their grandfather screams at you in Russian and waves his big, scary stick at you just for suggesting it.

Ignoring the remark, I made my way to the entrance of the church, the kid's breath hot on my neck. I wanted to make a smart-ass comment about his bravery as he stepped on my heels but bit my tongue. Even a sarcastic, angry teenager was better company than none.

The wooden door of the building stood slightly ajar, and I pushed it gently, hearing the heavy iron hinges creak loudly in the silence. A shuffling sound drifted out of the opening, and I paused, blindly searching in my pants for the knife I'd foolishly dropped back into the pocket.

While I fumbled frantically for my only weapon, I felt a shove in the middle of my back. I'm not saying the kid pushed me on purpose, but to the best of my knowledge, he *was* the only person behind me. I lost my balance, falling straight down onto the floor of the tiny church. Lucky for me, my face stopped the fall by hitting the wooden planks of the floor. With a tiny pop, my nose started gushing blood.

"Oops, sorry, dude," Ghost exaggerated the apology, making me think he didn't really mean it. As he stepped over my prone body, his tone changed to one of amazement. "Dude, get up. You are *not* gonna believe this!"

I pushed myself to a sitting position, woozily trying to balance while I blinked to clear my vision. With one hand covering the faucet coming out of my nose and the other hand on the floor holding me mostly upright, my eyes lined up with something no man should ever see.

Inches in front of me sat a man tied to a chair. His bare, hairy legs rested on either side of my head, and his stomach *almost* covered the G-string thong underwear that appeared to be forty sizes too small. All I could think about was getting something to cover him up with. A blanket, maybe, or some of that old-timey underwear that would cover him from neck to knee. Anything, really, to hide the sight of his manhood struggling to break free from the tiny cloth that almost-but-not-quite covered it.

Frantically trying to talk around the silk tie protruding from his mouth, the naked man struggled against the ropes, giving me a show I hadn't paid to see. Desperate to look at anything but the bushy, squirming crotch that was way too close for comfort, I pointed my blood-covered face toward the kid, only to see him bent over at the waist, gagging.

"Uhhhh...that's just nasty, dude! Someone needs to teach him about manscaping!"

I had no idea what manscaping was, but unless it involved a way to cover up nakedness, I didn't really care. Painfully, still trying to look anywhere but at the scene in front of me, I dragged myself to my feet. Maybe we'd stumbled into some kind of kinky love tryst.

Feeling a bit lightheaded from the blood loss, I might have misunderstood what the guy said when I yanked the tie out of his mouth and down around his neck.

"Garbage bout!"

Ignoring the nonsense, I tried to loosen the bonds around the hands that were tied together behind the chair, but with one hand still pinching the bridge of my gushing nose, getting the knots loose was near impossible. Giving up, I drooped to the floor, turning to make sure my back was to the guy, and called for Ghost.

"Get over here and untie him!" Ghost started mimicking my voice as he came closer, which to be fair, kind of resembled the Squidward character on that dumb kid's cartoon.

I wasn't exactly in a laughing mood, though. I mean, here I was most likely dying from blood loss and this guy needed to be released. Tilting my head back to try and stop the life-threatening flow of blood, I had to trust the kid would do as I asked.

The man in the chair started letting out some familiar-sounding moans between deep breaths. Letting go of my aching nose, I said, "Sorry it took us so long to get here."

Heavy Breather Man looked confused and mumbled a bit, squirming around in his chair.

Ghost's gangly fingers weren't having any more luck with the knots than mine did. After several minutes of trying, he turned to ask, "What's the deal, yo? I can't get them loose."

A lightbulb went off and I suggested, "Maybe if I drip some of the blood from my nose on them, the moisture will loosen the knots."

Ghost gave me a scathing look. "Dude, there's like three drops of blood on your shirt. You're fine."

I looked down at my whitish t-shirt. Okay, fine, maybe my nose wasn't *gushing*, but I definitely had some red on there. I stood up without answering, determined I wouldn't give the kid the satisfaction of knowing I might have overreacted a *tiny* bit.

Heavy Breather began spouting nonsense again.

"Which spell...can't..."

I ignored his ranting as I fumbled in my pocket for my knife. I didn't really feel like chatting, and I couldn't understand most of what he said anyway.

As I struggled with the cursed knots, the man's words ran laps in my head. 'Which spell.' Which spell. Witch spell! Holy shit!

I leaned over his shoulder, trying to focus on his gut, rather than the massive amount of pubic hair I could still see poking out of the uh, underwear beneath it.

"Are you saying witch? Like Samantha and Endora on the old TV show?"

Ghost looked at me like I'd suddenly started speaking Klingon. "Who?"

The man in the chair nodded his head frantically. I gave Ghost a smug look and said, "*He* knew what I meant."

Ghost scrunched up his face. "Dude, are you talking about witches like Sabrina the Teenage Witch? Or do you mean wizards like Harry Potter? There's a difference, you know."

Heavy Breather started shaking suddenly, the tremors increasing until the chair joined in and began jitterbugging across the floor. He sputtered, "S-S-Ssss...witch!"

I thought he was just answering the question until a flash of movement made me look up. A black-clad form rose above the kid's head. Since I knew Ghost stood well over six-foot-tall, this thing had to be either hovering in the air behind him or standing on something. Hoping for the latter, I slowly straightened to see exactly what new kind of horror had appeared. At least this one had clothes on.

Ghost gave me a funny look and asked, "What?"

I shook my head, unable to take my eyes off the thing that was *definitely* hovering in the air above my step-kid.

Everything slowed down as I raised an arm and pointed, the open knife still clutched in my frozen hand. A weapon is only a weapon if you know how to use it, and at that moment, I couldn't have picked my nose with the damn thing.

The guy in the chair let out a noise that sounded like air squeaking out of a balloon, his rattling chair drumming out a rhythm until it finally fell over with a crash. He must have hit his head or something because the weird whistling sound stopped as quickly as it started.

I'm not exactly sure what happened to him, because I couldn't look away from the witch – holy crap, a freaking witch! – hovering behind the kid. She held a black stick pointed at Ghost's head. Was that a wand? Did witches really carry wands? I couldn't get past the fact that witches were real. My overloaded brain didn't have the capacity to add magic wands to the equation.

Ghost looked down at the unconscious man, then back at my thousand-yard-stare. "Dude, it's behind me, isn't it?" He asked the question as emotionlessly as if he were asking me to pass the orange juice, but I could see excitement glittering in his eyes.

In slow motion, my head raised, but even with the incomplete nod, Ghost got the idea. Spinning around, his long, gangly arms whipping like a plane's propeller at startup, he shouted, "Not today, Satan!"

The woman hanging in the air laughed, a screeching, ear-splitting chuckle, and Ghost's bony shoulders rose and fell as he shrugged. With my own body frozen in place, I watched him pull something from his pocket as the witch began chanting strange words, her wand still pointing at Ghost.

A flash lit the room, and with a screech, the witch fled the church through the open front door. Ghost turned to me with a grin, cell phone in hand.

"Dude! I got her picture! *That's* going on Instagram!"

Trying to prove I was just as cool-headed as the next guy, I numbly held my trembling hand out for a wavery high five, jerking it down when I remembered I still had the knife in it. "Nice work, Al- uh, Ghosty."

Robotically, I closed the knife and put it away. My brain felt like a shoe tumbling around in an empty clothes dryer. My whole world had just been upended, and the kid was acting like we were at an amusement park.

I just wanted to get out of the creepy cemetery church and away from the crazy witchy woman. We could head over to the other call, the one with the sweet old woman who sounded like my grandmother. Maybe she would have some cookies or coffee—

"Dude. Dude! Ed!"

Ghost's voice broke into my thoughts of treats and sweet, sweet coffee. Adrenalin had stolen all my energy, leaving me feeling like a pillow that had been punched one too many times, and I yawned, exhaling my "What?" with it.

"This guy is coming around. Let's get him untied and get out of here before that thing comes back."

Using some holy oil we found behind the tiny pulpit — at least, I hope it was holy oil, it smelled more like *un*holy oil - we managed to work the knots loose. The witch must have cast some spell binding his mouth along with his hands and feet because he started talking a mile a minute as soon as the rope fell away.

"I'm lucky you guys came along when you did. You didn't call the cops, did you? Can you believe that crazy witch? She lured me in here with the offer of hot, kinky sex, tied me to the chair, muttered something about revenge, and then left. I've been here for hours! What a bitch!"

I kept waiting for him to mention the fact that a freaking *witch* had just fled the room – a *witch*! I mean, come *on*! Was I the only one who didn't realize witches were a real thing?

Maybe he had some kind of role-playing witch fetish because the mostly-nude man calmly kept on chattering while pulling his clothes out of a hidden door at the bottom of the small pulpit. Thankfully, he put his pants on first, hiding the hairy image of his crotch. Unfortunately, the picture was etched into my brain forever, anyway.

"I'll never answer another ad on Craigslist for a hot, sexy, witch again, I can tell you that! Every once in a while, you come across a crazy, but she took the cake! She said I belonged to some ring of perverts. Can you believe that? Like she was some kind of jacked-up cop or something. She couldn't have been a cop, though, because she didn't have handcuffs! Well, maybe she did, but I never saw them. She wasn't even hot! What the hell? You saw her, right? She looked every bit of two-hundred-years old! Isn't there some kind of law against that? You know, truth in advertising, or whatever? Well, I should get home. My wife is probably wondering where I am. What time is it, anyway?"

I took advantage of the break in his monologue to blurt out, "It's 3:15, but- I don't understand. Was she really a witch? I mean, I used to date a girl in high school who practiced the Wiccan religion, but I never saw her fly in the air like that."

Heavy Breather paused in the middle of buttoning his shirt and stared at me in disbelief. "Why would I answer an ad for a hot sexy witch if she wasn't one?"

"But witches aren't real..." I weakly said.

Giving Ghost a look that said, "Can you believe this guy?" our client asked, "Can you believe this guy?" Turning back to me, he looked carefully at my face for any signs of humor before saying, "You really don't know? Are you new to town or something?"

Smoothing the silk shirt over his belly, his face changed to one of surprise as he continued, "You really don't know about them, do you? You should get out more. You're missing all the fun."

Finally dressed, the man sat back into the chair he'd just been released from to put on his leather loafers. Stunned at what he'd just said, I asked, "Okay, assuming you aren't messing with me, how did you know to call my number for help? If you were already here, there's no way you saw my ad on tv."

Giving me a strange look, he said, "What're you talking about? My phone's been in my pants this whole time. Here, see?" He pulled a smartphone from his pocket and turned the screen toward me.

A vivid picture of him wearing the questionable underwear glared at me. I was going to need some serious brain bleach to get rid of that image. As he shoved the phone back in his pocket without looking at it, I hoped his wife not only saw the picture but that she had a good lawyer on retainer.

My over-stuffed brain had too many lines of thought going to process them properly. Witches were real? How could I have lived here my whole life and not known? Was I the only person in town unaware of that fact?

Holy crap, did that mean other things were real, too? Ghosts? Vampires? Werewolves? Wait! Maybe the boogeyman really *was* hiding under my bed all those times I heard noises, not mice like Pops said!

Springfield didn't exactly qualify as a small town, but it wasn't a big city, either. Hiding something like the fact that witches were real seemed impossible, but apparently, I'd just been sleepwalking my whole life. I looked at Ghost to gauge his reaction to this whole thing. He raised his hands in an I-don't-know gesture, but I could see excitement twinkling in his eyes like he'd just reached a new level on the video game called life.

The sound of the wooden door creaking dragged me back to the present. I tried to chase after our disgusting client to ask more questions but tripped over the chair and sprawled to the floor. His expensive sports car fired up, growling at us through the fog before the crunch of tires on the gravel signaled his departure, along with bits of rock thrown at the church.

Stumbling to my feet, using the edge of the chair to heave myself up, I breathlessly asked the kid, "If the phone was in his pants, then who the hell called?"

Shrugging, his eyes still gleaming with excitement, the kid answered, "I don't know, dude, but you're late for your next appointment. This is some crazy shit! I can't wait to tell Inkspot!"

How the hell had he gone from being frightened to acting as though casting out a witch to save a mostly-nude man so we could go talk to a woman about a ghost was just a normal part of life? Did he know about the witches?

I opened my mouth to ask him, but he had already plugged in his earbuds, bouncing his way out of the tiny church without waiting for me.

Feeling a little down that our first customer – well, sort of our first customer – didn't even offer to pay us for rescuing his sorry ass, I scuffled the few steps back out of the church, pulling the door closed behind me. Ghost waited next to the car, dancing his strange, awkward dance again, and I had to admit, I was a little jealous of how quickly he'd absorbed his fear. Me, on the other hand- well, my legs were still trembling as I opened the car door and I knew I wouldn't be able to write it off as dancing.

After a couple of tries, I finally managed to shove the key in the ignition, then leaned back against the seat with my eyes closed to try and calm down as I waited for the kid to notice me. The blessed quiet ended as quickly as it began.

The car door creaked open and I listened as Ghost attempted to cram his long legs into the passenger side. I waited to open my eyes again until I heard him slam the door shut. Pulling out the earbud closest to me, the kid dropped it against his chest, the strange, electronic sounds forming a backdrop to his question, "Dude, we going or not?"

Shrugging, I held up two fingers, crossed. "Hope so."

I turned the key.

Nothing.

Dammit.

Sitting in the mostly-silent car, Ghost's weird music pulsing from his dangling earbud, I reached out to try again when a strange screeching sound came from the darkness outside.

Suddenly, a black form burst out of the fog and rushed at the windshield, swooping up at the last second and missing us by scant centimeters. I might have let out my own little screech. And possibly peed a little.

"The phone!" I screamed at Ghost. "Get the phone out again! Hurry!"

I turned the key in the ignition. The engine moaned and went silent. I let out a matching moan.

The witch came back for a second sweep as I twisted the key a third time, doing a drum beat on the gas pedal with my foot for good measure.

Ghost kept trying to drag his phone out of his pocket, but between the tight confines of the car, the seatbelt, and his abnormally long legs, well, he was doing a lot of squirming and not a lot of anything else. Nothing helpful, anyway.

I patted the dash, mumbled a few sweet nothings, and tried the key one last time, praying to whatever god is in charge of cars, and my trusty little Pacer's engine started! I threw her in reverse just as I heard a thump on the roof.

Dammit.

I hit the gas and lurched back out of the parking spot. The bitch – uh, I mean witch, let loose a deafening rainstorm of stones on the roof. Inside the car, a fine mist of dirt began raining down on us, and the old glue holding the headliner up gave away. Suddenly, we were covered with a blanket of grubby flannel.

Coughing from the dust storm inside the car, I threw the gearshift into drive by feel alone. With one hand on the steering wheel and the other holding the liner up so I could sort of see, I hit the gas again and took off, barely missing the corner of the church. One more punch on the top of the car and the witch rolled off the roof and down the back glass into the darkness.

I crossed my fingers that she hit the ground hard enough to knock her witchy ass out, but with the headliner covering most of the rear windows, I couldn't tell for sure. Ghost was hacking like an asthmatic with his head stuck inside a used vacuum bag, but he managed to yank the rotten liner the rest of the way off the roof, tossing the flannel cloth into the back seat with all the other junk and stirring up another dust storm inside the car. At least he finally found a good use for those long arms of his.

The car sputtered, and I had just enough time to remember the lack of gas before the motor smoothed out. Taking my foot off the pedal, I babied my baby the few blocks to the nearest gas station.

Well, almost.

The Pacer died exactly one block before we reached the convenience store, the fumes we'd been driving on finally wafting away.

Ghost gave me a look. "Dude, seriously? We're out of gas?"

I didn't bother to respond to the stupid question. Instead, I glared at him in the dim light from the dashboard and grumbled, "Get out."

Alvin glared right back. "Dude. I'm not pushing this piece of crap. No way, no how."

I sat up straight in my seat and gave him what I hoped was a supervisory look.

"Yes. You are. You're the helper, remember? Pushing the car falls under the helper's duties."

Crossing his arms and leaning back against the torn seat, the teenager smiled arrogantly. "Sure, I'll get out and push. But I wonder what Ded will say when I tell him in the morning." As if to emphasize his arrogant attitude, a clap of thunder boomed overhead, and it started raining.

And that's how I ended up pushing my car to the gas station during a thunderstorm, while Alvin – my helper - sat in the driver's seat, laughing and steering my dead vehicle without getting a single drop of rain on his skinny ass. At least the power steering wasn't working. I hoped his arms hurt.

Chapter 4

Exhausted and soaked when we finally reached the pump, I leaned against the car to catch my breath before heading inside to hand the clerk my measly two bucks. Consoling myself while I tried to breathe by counting the last five minutes as exercise, I mentally high-fived myself. After all, I broke a sweat, right? At least, I think I did. The moisture might have been from the rain.

No, it was sweat, I'm sure of it.

Al- Ghost, dry as a bone, stepped out and pulled his phone from his pocket. Holding it up to the gas pump, he performed some kind of weird voodoo with it, then gave me a smug grin and said, "Go ahead and fill it up. I already paid."

I shook my head, humiliated. "No. I've got a couple of bucks. I'll put that in. Once we get to this other customer, she'll pay me. I'm sure of it."

Ghost rolled his eyes. "Dude. Just fill the damn thing up. You think Ded wants to get out in the middle of the night and come get me because you ran your POS car out of gas? Besides, it's going on the credit card he gave me for emergencies. I think this counts."

Knowing the kid was right didn't make me feel any better. The last thing I needed was a half-asleep, angry Russian grandfather showing up to get his only grandson, giving him yet another reason to hate me.

"Fine," I grumbled. "But I'm giving you the money back as soon as I get paid."

Shrugging, he sauntered inside without answering. While the gas pumped, I called Mrs. Woodall, hoping she hadn't fallen asleep waiting for us. She answered on the first ring.

"Hello?" The frail and tired-sounding voice reminded me of my grandmother again.

"I'm so sorry we're late, Mrs. Woodall. We're on our way to your house right now."

With a sigh that sounded more like a yawn, she said, "Call me Lou. Come on by, I'll get a fresh pot of coffee goin.'"

With the promise of coffee waiting, I topped off the tank, then headed inside to use the bathroom and clean up a little. Ghost met me at the entrance, where the smell of bacon and bread hit me in the face like a slap from an angry woman.

"Dude, they have an amazing deli in there. I bought us some breakfast sandwiches."

The feeling of pride that the kid thought of me for a change quickly evaporated into shame when I realized I should have been the one buying breakfast. I nodded, refusing to meet his eyes as I pushed past him.

I used up every single paper towel in the holder trying to dry myself off in the dim light of the bathroom, then shrugged at my soggy image in the broken mirror. I looked more like a bum leaving a homeless shelter than a man who owned his own business, but then again, wasn't that one of the reasons I wanted to do a job like this in the first place? So I didn't have to push a desk and dress like all the other zombies in the workplace?

With one last swipe at my dripping hair, I checked my watch. Four o'clock in the morning. If Ghost wasn't home by the time Masha went to get him up for school, there would be hell to pay. And by that, I mean *I* would be the one paying for it while Masha simmered in a stew of rage directed toward me and my new business. We needed to get a move on.

At least the rain had stopped by the time I got back outside. My Pacer smelled like bacon-y heaven when I opened the door, and my stomach let out a growl of approval. My baby started first try, and I gave her a little pat on the dashboard. "Good girl," I purred, as I put her in gear and headed for Mrs. Woodall's house.

Ghost shoved a warm, wrapped package at me, and one-handed, I proceeded to demolish the breakfast sandwich in three bites, ripping the corner of the wrapper off with my teeth on the last one.

As I tried to pull the damp, wax-lined paper out of my mouth while turning into the client's driveway, a familiar-looking black form swooped down and landed on the hood of my car, making me slam on the brakes. Sucking in a breath of surprise, the bit of paper flew into the back of my throat, choking me.

Shit. The witch was back.

"Dude, seriously?" I had no idea if the kid meant my choking fit or the witch's persistence. Either way, I didn't have the time – or the breath - to answer.

I wheezed, trying to force air past the paper blocking my throat. The witch threw her head back and laughed at my predicament. I reversed my efforts and coughed, trying to dislodge the wrapper, and banged my head against the steering wheel. The witch laughed that much harder, her evil cackles loud enough to hear through the glass.

Ghost let out a string of curses as he squirmed around in the seat trying to get his phone out, but as he finally pulled the thing from his pocket, the witch let out a screech and flew straight up, disappearing from sight.

The thump on the roof of the car a second later announced her whereabouts.

"Dammit," Ghost cursed. "What do we do now, Ed?"

I couldn't have answered if I'd wanted to. With my index finger shoved all the way to the back of my mouth, I'd finally managed to push the paper away from my esophagus when a flash from outside the car caught my attention. The heavy boom accompanying the bright light startled – oh, who am I kidding? – petrified me enough that I sucked the paper back into my throat.

I started choking all over again as I chased the wrapper with my finger, gagging as I did. I don't know if you've ever choked and gagged at the same time, but let me tell you, it's not fun. In fact, it's kind of painful.

Someone wrenched open my door and shoved me up against the steering wheel, forcing my finger even farther down my throat and making me heave harder. I had a feeling the breakfast sandwich wouldn't taste as good the second time, and as I yanked the spit-covered digit out of my mouth, the same someone began thumping the middle of my back with way too much enthusiasm.

The little old woman's voice didn't sound so frail anymore as she shouted, "Come on, boy, spit it out! Did ya see that thing on your car? Good thing I keep m'shotgun next to the front door! I'm a damn good shot, too. I'm pretty sure I winged 'er. Sam taught me howta shoot years ago. Said ever' woman needed to know how ta protect herself, an' I guess he was right, 'though I hate to admit it."

The pounding stopped long enough for her to ask, "You okay, Mr. Ward? Least, I hope you're Mr. Ward. Hopefully, I didn't just save the life of a burglar comin' to rob and rape me."

Pausing to let out a cackle, she continued, "I'm just kiddin'. I know who y'are. Sam told me."

I took the opportunity to shove my wet finger back into my mouth while she talked and finally got hold of the paper, pulling out the soggy wad and promptly shoving it into the ashtray. Looking at the old woman for the first time, I rasped out, "Sam?"

"Oh, that's my dead husband. He's the ghost I called y'about." Turning away from the car, she shouted, "Yes, Sam, I told them about ya. They know. I said, they know!" Looking at me with a wry grin, the old woman said, "He always was harda hearing. Being dead ain't seemed to change that any."

Ghost asked, "Your husband is the ghost? Dude, that's so cool!"

Primly, she replied, "First of all, I'm not a dude. Do I need ta lift my skirt ta prove it?" Ghost's eyes widened, and he shook his head no, youthful cheeks flaming red.

"Secondly, I don't really think it's 'cool' that my husband's a ghost. I'd much prefer 'im to be alive."

Ghost gaped, realizing his massive faux-pas. He twisted uncomfortably in his seat under her glare before she switched gears suddenly and smiled.

Formally, she asked, "Now, shall we go inside and drink some coffee while I tell you about Sam?"

Picking up the shotgun leaning against the car, she turned and trotted spryly toward the house, the hem of her nightgown whipping around her knees, only pausing long enough to ask, "You comin' or not, boys?"

After a quick look at Ghost, who stared after the old woman with something like shock and awe on his face, we got out of the car, stopping to look at a black spot on the driveway. It could have been oil, I guess, but I had the feeling it was the blood of a witch.

And that's the true story of how we met Lou, shotgun-toting wife of Sam the ghost.

Chapter 5

The house was typical of a lower-middle-class family whose children had grown up and flown the nest, leaving nothing behind but memories and elderly parents living on fixed incomes. Small but cozy, the tiny living room's walls showcased proud family pictures strewn amidst school images of three children who grew up before my eyes as I made a circle. Lou stood in the doorway on the far side of the room, her three children hanging on the wall beside her, pigtails, crewcuts, and missing teeth smiling for all eternity next to her head.

"Come on in the kitchen, boys. I hate this room."

Hesitantly, I asked, "Uh, shouldn't we wait here for the cops?"

The old woman gave me a puzzled look, clearly not understanding why the police might show up. "Why would the cops be here? You call 911 or somethin'?"

"Uh, that shotgun was kind of loud. Won't your neighbors call?"

Throwing her head back, she laughed. Through giggles that sounded more like they should be coming from the picture of the pig-tailed girl on the wall, she answered, "Nah, they've heard it before. Sometimes, I use it to scare off kids if I think they're up to no good. You know, shootin' over their heads. 'Sides, even if someone did call, in this neighborhood, it'd take 'em a couple hours to get here. We ain't exactly in the hood, as the kids call it, but we ain't in Beverly Hills neither. Now, come on. I got a fresh pot of coffee ready."

We followed her into a kitchen about the same size as the small living room. The smell of coffee and cinnamon wafted out to greet us, reminding me yet again of my own childhood memories.

In the center of the room, a well-used metal table from the fifties stood, worn yellow-patterned laminate on top and surrounded by four equally-worn plastic-covered metal chairs.

As opposed to the formal room at the front door, it was obvious that Lou did most of her living in this room. Open shelving stood against one wall, crammed full of canned goods with knickknacks haphazardly shoved around and on the food. The refrigerator door was hidden by magnets holding pictures, postcards, and childish drawings yellowed with age.

A small antique writing desk and chair sat in the corner, clear but for a stack of open mail neatly piled next to a calculator. It was a nice workspace and all, if you like that kind of thing, but I'll bet she didn't work nearly as hard at getting it as I did mine.

Lou shuffled around the small room with ease, deftly producing coffee cups from hooks attached to the bottom of the cabinet. Her flannel nightgown swayed and swirled as she moved, reminding me of something from back in my drinking days. I tried to pull the memory up, but it faded away before I could remember what it was.

Instead, I assessed our newest client. Other than the nightgown, she could have been ready to go shopping. Her white hair was perfectly in place, and the bright red lipstick she wore made me wonder if she'd been to one of Masha's many makeup parties.

Her small frame shouldn't have been threatening, but after seeing her handle the shotgun, I had a feeling the little package could hold a lot of dynamite, something I hoped I never saw directed at me.

Her speech reminded me of just how Midwestern we were, but despite that, she had an intelligence in her eyes that made me think she could hold her own with the elite of the town if given half a chance.

Like my grandmother, she oozed equal parts motherliness and the demand for respect. I liked her already.

Lou brought the mugs to the table in one trip without spilling a drop. "Hope ya drink it black, boys," she said, hiking up her nightie and sliding into one of the chairs. "I don't believe in addin' nothin' to the nectar of the gods."

Grinning, she turned her head and shouted, "Yes, Sam, I stole your line. I *said*, I *know* I stole your line!"

Meeting my eyes, she explained, "He always called coffee the nectar of the gods. Makes 'im mad when I use his stuff and don't give 'im credit."

Ghost had been uncharacteristically quiet, and she turned to look at him with a grin. "Cat got your tongue, boy?"

"No- yeah- what?"

I couldn't help but smile. Seeing Alvin so uncomfortable almost made everything we'd gone through worth it.

"You hard'a hearin' too? I asked if the cat got your tongue."

"What- what cat?"

Rolling her eyes and cackling like the witch had just moments earlier, the old woman turned her gaze to me as she jerked her head toward Ghost. "He yours?"

I confirmed, "Step-son. He's been helping me tonight."

With a nod, she turned her head again and semi-yelled, "He said it's his step-son! You know, like Ella's boy! The one she's always complainin' about!"

When it looked like she was done speaking to her dead husband, I asked, "So, do you talk to him all the time?"

Taking a sip from her mug before answering, Lou leaned back against her chair. "He don't give me much choice. Talks to me all night and day. If I don't answer 'im, he gets mad and starts poundin' on doors and throwin' my favorite knickknacks."

As she spoke, I remembered my handy-dandy little gadget. Since the old woman seemed pretty sane, other than talking to her husband the ghost, that is, it seemed like a good opportunity to test out my new toy. Pulling the EMF meter from my pocket, I pushed the button to turn it on. Lights and sirens started going off, making me jump, and I fumbled with it to find the silence button.

Once I finally shut the damn alarm off, the old woman stared at me curiously and asked, "What's that doo-dad?"

Trying to sound professional, I answered, "It's an EMF meter with EVP detection. Tells me if there are any spirits in the house. Very delicate instrument."

Her eyes narrowing, she pounded the table hard enough to make the coffee shiver in the cups as she asked, "I already told ya there was a ghost here. You callin' me a liar, boy?"

The sudden movement under my elbow made me drop the meter on the table. Before I could move, it bounced back up and fell to the floor, the lights going dark.

Dammit!

I shoved my head underneath the table to grab my expensive little toy but fumbled, my fingers accidentally pushing it closer to where the old woman sat. Bent double, with my head near the floor, I answered through the blood pounding in my head, "No, ma'am. If I can pick up activity on here, though, we'll have proof you aren't crazy."

"Now you're calling me *crazy*?" She pounded the table with her fists again.

The second blow so close to my head made me instinctively look up. The old woman sat with her legs apart, nightgown pulled up to her hips for comfort, and her massive granny panties were staring me in the face. G-String Guy immediately moved to second place on my list of Things I Never Wanted To See.

Gulping, I scrambled backward to get my burning eyeballs out of the line of sight but hit my head on the metal corner of the table hard enough to see stars made of tiny little granny panties circling my head.

Snorting laughter, she asked, "Y'okay there, son? I was just messin' with ya. Didn't mean ta make ya hurt yourself."

I pulled myself up above the table and shook my head to dispel the image of her dancing underwear before answering, "Yes, ma'am, I'm fine."

"What's with all this ma'am busi- hang on. Of *course*, he's talkin' ta me, Sam! You see any other women in here? I know the boy has got some long hair, but even with them cataracts you had before you died, you can see well enough to tell he's a boy!"

She turned back to me and finished her sentence as though she hadn't just rambled off something to her dead husband, "I told ya ta call me Lou. Forget that ma'am business."

I nodded, "Yes, ma- okay, Lou, if you insist. Now, what are you wanting to do about your ghost problem?"

Her eyes narrowed in anger and my head started spinning at the carousel of emotions. The woman could change moods faster than a machine gun could shoot bullets. I tightened my grip on the EMF meter as she sharply asked, "What problem?"

"Well, ma- uh, Lou, you called, so I'm assuming you want us to get rid of your ghost. Send Sam into the light, or whatever you want to call it."

Ghost, trying to be helpful, chimed in, "We can blast him into the next life!"

Lou shot him a dirty look that she then shifted over to me. Before I could blink, she shoved her chair back, stood up, leaned over the table, and poked her finger in my face as she angrily shouted, "I don't want ta get rid o' Sam! What's wrong with you? We been married for forty-two years! Why on *earth* would I want ta get *rid* of him?"

I tried to push myself away from the finger in my face, but with my back already against the chair, and with the way my night had been going, I figured it would probably tip over if I tried to shove it away from the table. Ghost, sounding incredibly adult-like for once, gently asked, "How can we help you then, Mrs. Woodall?"

Sighing, she moved her finger out of my face and held it straight up to let Ghost know he needed to wait for his answer. Turning her head, she shouted, "No, Sam, they aren't gonna send ya to the afterlife. I won't let 'em. Okay? Sam- Sam, *don't do it*! You know that's my favorite!"

On the shelf over the window, a figurine rose by itself, hovered in the air for a second, then magically dashed itself to the ground.

The old woman's voice broke as she yelled, "Dammit, Sam! You know how much I loved that little cow! The kids gave it to me for Christmas when they were little! Keep it up, and I *will* let 'em send you away! You hear me, you ol' coot?"

I shot a look at Ghost and realized we must be wearing the same expression – one of flabbergasted astonishment. Huh. Guess I didn't need my fancy meter after all.

A tear ran down the old woman's face as she pulled a broom and dustpan out from beside the refrigerator and cleaned up the broken cow.

Muttering to herself as though she'd forgotten we were there, she tossed the broken figurine into the trash can and neatly put away the cleaning supplies before wiping her cheeks and sitting back down at the table.

"Can ya help me figure out a way to make 'im stop breakin' stuff? That's all I want. That, and for someone to believe me. Sam won't make a peep when the kids are here – y'know, on those rare occasions when they come to visit their poor old widowed mama – he says he don't wanna scare 'em, so when I try to tell 'em what's goin' on, they think I've lost my ever-lovin' mind. And of course, *he* thinks that's hilarious. So, can ya help me or not?"

Taking a deep breath, I pushed the unneeded EMF meter across the table to Ghost before answering, "Ma'am- sorry- Lou, I don't see any way we can prevent Sam from breaking anything else without sending him to the afterlife."

The old woman's face fell, and I quickly continued, "but let me try something. Is he still here in the room?"

Nodding, she waved at the empty air beside her. "Right here somewhere, I imagine. I can hear 'im mumblin.'"

Feeling vaguely like I was talking to the invisible friend of a child, I slowly and carefully spoke to the empty spot, "Now, Sam, we seem to have a problem here—"

Lou interrupted, "He can't hear ya. He's deaf as a board. You'll hafta speak up."

Repeating myself, I yelled, "I can send you to the afterlife, Sam. Is that what you want?" Pulling a soggy piece of business-card-sized notebook paper with my info printed somewhat neatly across it out of my shirt pocket, I waved it in the air to dry, then shoved the piece of paper across the table to the old woman.

"You see that, Sam? That's my – ahem - business card. If you break one more thing, Lou is going to call me, and I'm going to come back and send you away. If you want to stay here with your wife, all you have to do is control your temper and not break anything. Do we have a deal?"

I left out the fact that I had no idea how to send him to the afterlife. While wondering if ghosts could read minds, I raised an eyebrow and looked over at Lou to see what her dead husband said.

Nodding firmly, she said, "He says he'll try."

Gingerly, I held my hand out over empty space and gave two firm shakes, feeling like a fool. Lou giggled. "He's laughin' at ya 'cause he can't shake hands, but you gotta deal anyway."

Ghost had been staring out the window while I 'negotiated' with the ghost, but he turned back to me and said, "It's getting light out. Mama will be waking up soon. We should probably go, dude."

I tried to suppress a shudder at the thought of Masha discovering I'd kept her baby out all night. Her wrath would eclipse the witch's fury, making the attack earlier seem like little more than a mosquito's annoying buzz. But before we could go, there was a tiny little matter left to deal with.

Rising, I looked at Lou as I said, "He's right. We should go. There's just the tiny little matter of payment."

Lou blinked. Then blinked again.

"Payment?"

Uncomfortable, but knowing I needed to prove to my wife that my business would make money, I pressed on, "Yes, ma'am. The fee for a house call is fifty dollars. Since I didn't need to terminate the ghost, I won't charge you for that."

The old woman's voice deepened with self-righteousness as she rose to her feet and crossed her arms over her chest. "Fifty dollars for comin' to help an old widow woman in distress? A poor woman livin' on a fixed income?"

Stuttering, I tried to explain, "Well, Lou, it's just that this is a business, and—"

"And nothin'!" The tone – and decibel - of her voice rose until she was almost shouting, "I can't believe you're gonna try and fleece an old woman outta her hard-earned social security! A woman who called you, desperate for help!"

I looked at Ghost for backup, but he was studiously examining a hangnail on his pinky finger. Holding my hands up in defeat, I called out, "Okay, okay! There's no charge for tonight. We'll call it a new customer special."

Rolling her eyes, the old woman began to laugh.

"Wow. You're pretty easy. How do you spect to run a business if you let your customers run over ya like that? I'm just messin' with ya, boy."

Taking the head off an old cookie jar shaped like a politically incorrect cook, she pulled out a crumpled wad of bills and peeled off fifty dollars. As soon as my greedy little hands closed around the money, she said, "Now, there's just the matter of me takin' out that thing that was chasin' ya. Whaddaya think – fifty bucks for savin' your life? That sound 'bout right?"

Feeling like I might cry, I pushed the money back toward her, but she started laughing again. "You really *are* easy, aincha?" I looked over at Ghost, who had given up on the pretense of checking his fingernail and had his head on the table, shoulders shaking with laughter. Taking a step toward him, I finally let myself do what I'd wanted to do all night and popped him on his too-long hair as I growled, "Let's go."

Following us to the front door, Lou kept up a spiel of cheerful chatter, "Sam says if ya need some help with ghosts, he'll be happy ta act as a consultant."

Loudly, she said, "Yes, Sam! I just told 'em!" Lowering her voice again, she continued, "And if you need some help gettin' somebody ta pay—" she patted the shotgun next to the door, "I'll be more than happy ta help y'out with that. You'd be surprised how fast people will ante up the cash when there's a shotgun pointed at 'em."

Ghost walked out to the car, trying to plug in his earbuds, but he was laughing so hard, he couldn't keep his head still enough.

I hung back behind to say, "I might take you and Sam up on your offer, Lou. After all, having an 'in' from the afterlife could be useful."

As she closed the door, her shouting could be heard through the solid wood, "*Yes*, Sam, he said he might need your help! I'll let ya know if he calls."

With one last glance at the oily-looking splotch on the driveway, I got into the car. Ghost had already crammed himself into the seat, moving and grooving to some 'music' I'm pretty sure I would hate. Feeling grateful, and a little guilty at the same time that the subject of gas money wasn't brought up, I drove us home with nothing but the sound of tapping fingers and my car's engine to keep me awake.

Chapter 6

The peaceful silence ended when we opened the front door. Masha stood waiting for us in full-blown-angry-Russian-mother mode.

"Where have you been? Why you have Masha's son out all night?"

Ghost slipped past me and headed out of the room, leaving me to my own devices. "Traitor," I breathed out, knowing he couldn't hear me anyway with his earbuds in.

"Masha, honey, I had a job last night! Look, I made some money for us!" I dug the fifty bucks out of my pocket. Snatching the bills from my hand, she held them up in the air for examination like a master jeweler checking a diamond for the four K's.

"Is not enough. Why you take Alvin? He needs sleep!"

She tucked the folded bills into her bra.

Dammit. There went my tiny profit.

"Masha, honey," I crooned the words, knowing the best way to calm her down was to promise more money. My wife had her priorities, and at the moment, finances were at the top of the list.

Before my inheritance ran out, it hadn't been an issue, but I knew I needed to make this new business profitable or she would leave me faster than I could say, "Deposit this."

I may be a loser at life, but I'm not stupid. I'm a middle-aged man with a combover and no skills. Five years ago, I married way above my station in life. Masha loves me, I know that, because she married me before I told her about my inheritance.

The problem is my wife expects a certain level of responsibility from me that I've never had to deal with. Money's part of it, sure, but she thinks I'm stirring up trouble by becoming a ghost hunter. If she had her way, I'd be working for her father, pushing used cars on old people and bringing home a steady paycheck from the Cadillac dealership.

Like I said, Masha loves me, but I knew when I started this new venture that it would take a while for her to warm up to it. Besides, I needed to grow up and provide for my family. Prove myself to myself, so to speak. And, if we're being completely honest here, maybe bringing in some money would get Boris off my back finally.

In the meantime, I needed to soothe my angry wife. "Masha, sweetheart, I love you so much! Do you want to go upstairs? I'll rub you all over with oil and give you a massage…"

"So you fall asleep in middle? Again? No, Masha does not think so. Besides, Papa will be here soon. You will explain to him why you keep Alvin out all night."

Shit. She'd already told her dad. It was a lot easier to calm Masha down than Boris.

I watched her storm into the kitchen, my tired brain trying to figure out the best way to keep from getting disappeared by an angry Russian man who carried his weapon by his side. An angry Russian who didn't like me anyway and would love to get rid of me.

See, I have this theory that Boris is in the Russian mob, that the Cadillac dealership is a cover for his real job of assassin. With that in mind, I do my best to toe the line where he's concerned.

I followed my wife into the kitchen, knowing sleep had just dropped down a spot on my list of things to do. Pouring a cup of coffee so I could stay awake until I had a chance to 'talk' to Boris, I carried it to the table and sat down across from Masha, who was tapping her foot and glaring at the empty spot where the microwave used to be.

Ah, crap. She was going to bring up 'the incident'. Again. I took a sip of the coffee, burning my tongue in the process, and closed my eyes, waiting.

The Russian accent got a little thicker as she reminded me, "Still no microwave."

"Masha, honey, it was an accident! I told you what happened!"

"You put phone in microwave to cook!"

"I dropped it in the toilet! Alvin told me that would dry it out."

Rolling her eyes, she threw out a few Russian endearments under her breath, then through gritted teeth, continued, "You promise Masha new microwave!"

"I just gave you fifty bucks! That's enough for a new microwave at Wal-mart."

Snorting, she sneered, "Not enough. Masha want nice microwave like old one. If you work for Papa—"

Trying to keep my voice nonchalant yet firm, I interrupted her, "Masha, honey, I just started my business. You have to give me a little time to start making money."

Spitting out a few more Russian endearments, she stood and slammed her hands on the table, spilling my coffee. Closing my eyes, I reassured myself for the thousandth time that the words meant she loved me.

"I borrow money from Papa for bills. You have one month to get business making money. And not to take Alvin with you again."

Knowing she wouldn't be satisfied with anything except acquiescence, I nodded my head, but she wasn't done yet. "And buy new microwave!"

"Yes, sweetheart. I'll go check my messages now. Maybe I have another job waiting."

Leaving the cup of coffee where it sat, I hurried out of the room. Masha was still glaring at the spot where her new microwave should already be when I shot one last glance back into the room. Dragging myself down the stairs to the basement, I found Alvin – Ghost – waiting for me.

Leaning forward like I might start spilling state secrets, he asked, "Dude, how bad was it?" I shrugged. "You know your mom. She says you can't go out with me anymore."

His jaw dropped for a split second before he said, "Dude! I had so much fun! She can't fucking tell me I can't go anymore!"

Donning my dad posture, I mumbled, "Language," absently as I looked at the answering machine. The light was blinking faster than my accelerated pulse.

Forgetting the dad stuff, I looked at Ghost, smiling proudly. "More calls! Yes!"

Ghost grinned back, showing the rarely-seen real smile of a teenager in captivity, "Dude! I know! I was waiting on you to get down here to listen to them!"

Carefully sitting on my wobbly chair, I pulled my stack of loose-leaf paper closer and readied my stolen pen, preparing for the plethora of jobs.

This was going to work! I could feel it! Masha would get her microwave and I might actually pull this off!

Pressing the button on the answering machine, I held my pen over the paper, leaving dots of ink where my trembling hand touched it. The first three calls were hang-ups.

"Okay," I muttered. "Maybe they just needed time to get up the nerve to talk to me." Looking over at Ghost, I quipped, "Fourth time's the charm."

Crossing his fingers, he gave me a hopeful look.

The fourth call wasn't the charm. Some weirdo started spewing hate speech, so I punched the erase button and waited for the next call to start.

"Mr. Ward, this is Candy with the Colonial Collection Agency. We've been trying to reach you—"

I kept my eyes directed away from Ghost as I scrambled to shut the bill collector's message down and start the next one.

"Yes, uh, my name is Grady and uh, I think I have a poltergeist in my house." I tightened my grip on the pen and got ready to write, my face stretched to the breaking point with a smile to rival that of any Miss America.

"- I, uh, my number is—"

Click.

"What the hell?" I pressed rewind and listened to the message again. Nope. Not a misfunction of my old, worn out machine. The call ended before he could give me the phone number. Frustrated, I slammed my open palm down on the table. Hitting my desk did nothing but make the phone's bell rattle and hurt my hand, but I felt a little better after doing it. Carefully writing down the caller's name with my still-tingly hand, I used the other to punch the button for the next message.

"Uh, me again, Grady. Uh, the poltergeist keeps hanging up—"

Excitedly, I waited for the next message. There were only two left.

"Uh, 555-1868. Call me. Uh, it's uh—"

I carefully wrote the number down next to the name and waited for the last message.

"I am trying to reach Ed Ward. I have a problem I think you might be able to help me with. If you could call me back at 555-1200, I would appreciate it. Oh, my name is Riley. Riley James. Please, if I don't answer, leave a message. I really need to talk to you as soon as possible."

My sore hand trembled a bit when I reached for the phone, but not necessarily from the smack on the table. Riley James oozed wealth, her cultured, educated voice that of a woman who moved comfortably in the upper echelons of society. If we could get into *that* market- well, Masha would get her new microwave in record time.

Riley James answered before the phone finished the first ring, "Good morning, Mr. Ward. I appreciate your calling back so promptly."

I tried to keep the sound of sweaty palms out of my voice when I said, "Good morning. Thanks for calling Poltergeist Guys. What's plaguing you today?"

Ooh, that was a good one! I was so busy writing the tagline down that I almost missed what she said.

"My mother is Louise Woodall, Mr. Ward. I believe you went to her home earlier?"

Crap. Visions of money flowing into my bank account like a river dried up faster than Shit Creek in a drought.

"Y-yes, ma'am, I did. She was having some problems with your deceased father haunting her. Is there an issue? She seemed to be pleased with the results of our visit when we left."

With a heavy sigh, Lou's daughter asked, "Could we please meet in person, Mr. Ward? I have a proposition I'd like to discuss with you."

Masha's voice floated down the stairs just then, "Alvin! Is time for school! Come along, my baby boy!"

With a roll of his eyes, Ghost shoved himself off the stool and whispered, "Text me when you find out what's going on."

I waved him away before Masha came down looking for him, nodding as I waved. I probably should have mentioned that I had no idea how to text, but he'd get over it. Returning to my call, I concentrated on keeping my tone as business-like as possible. Even so, my voice cracked, and I faked a cough to keep up the façade.

"Of course! Ahem. Excuse me, little dust in my throat. Just let me know when and where. I'll be happy to meet you.

"How does right now sound? I can meet you at the coffee shop on Third and Roosevelt."

The front door slammed as I confirmed the meeting. Good. Hopefully, I could get out of the house before Boris came for his daily visit.

Cracking open the door leading out of the basement, I checked for Masha's car. Gone. Perfect! I raced for the Pacer, noting the dents in the roof as I opened the door. Just as I slipped into the driver's seat, Boris pulled into the driveway behind me, blocking my little car with his Cadillac. Gripping the steering wheel with both hands, I rested my head between them and waited.

Before I could close my eyes and pretend to be hibernating, Boris strode up, wearing the malevolent look he'd perfected over the years – the one meant to invoke terror in the hearts of his enemies. Or rather, enemy. To my knowledge, I was the only person he felt the need to use the look on. And for the record, it worked.

When he reached the open car door, stick planted between his legs to make sure I saw the damn thing, I looked up and gave him a cheesy grin.

"Mornin', Boris."

"So you say."

Boris spoke with a thicker accent than Masha. A man of few words, at least where I was concerned, he did his best to avoid talking to me at all when possible.

On the few occasions Masha thought something was important enough that we needed to speak, Boris would always reluctantly comply with his only daughter's wishes. I'm not going to lie, I didn't want to talk to my father-in-law any more than he wanted to speak to me, but knowing how *much* he hated it – well, it gave me a little charge when I saw anger flashing across his face at being forced to do so.

"So... what's up?" I didn't know for sure what Masha said about my late-night adventures with Ghosty_boy69, and I wasn't about to tip my hand. Over the years, I'd learned the hard way to play dumb with Boris.

Without a word, he stood there staring at me like I was some new strain of manure he'd discovered on the bottom of his shoe, and I started getting antsy. I had a meeting to get to, and I didn't have time for my father-in-law's intimidation games. Especially when they worked.

"You have boy out all night?"

Okay, that was all he knew, or he would have started with it. Better to go ahead and tell him the truth rather than try to stumble through a lie when I was already so tired.

"I did. I'm sure Masha told you I started a new business, and Ghos- er, Alvin, helped me out last night. I actually have a meeting right now—"

"You pay boy."

It wasn't a question.

And now I knew the real reason for our 'chat'. Things were about to get sticky. Clearing my throat and playing stupid, I lied, "Uh, no, not yet. I was planning on it, but Masha took the money we earned last night and—"

Boris interrupted me again, one of his favorite tactics for control of the conversation.

"Nyet. Boy will be partner. How much?"

"How much- what?"

"How much you pay boy?"

Truth be told, I hadn't really planned to put Ghost on the payroll, but then again, having a computer expert - hacker, whatever - on board wasn't the worst idea.

Either way, it wasn't any of my father-in-law's business. Drawing myself upright, I huffed, "I think that's between me and Alvin. We'll sort out the details."

"Boy gets half."

"What? No way. Ten percent."

My father-in-law gave me an evil smile. Well, it looked evil to me. Haggling with a car salesman is a dangerous pursuit. Maybe that's why he chose the profession- he just liked the thrill of driving a hard bargain. Regardless, he seemed to be enjoying this negotiation a little too much for my tastes.

"Forty percent."

I wasn't about to give the kid almost half of everything I made – assuming I managed to make any money at all. I hesitated for a second, trying to figure out a way to argue with his numbers.

That's when I came up with a brilliant idea.

I reached down and started the car, implying how much of a hurry I was in and wincing a little when she backfired. Over the rough sound of the motor, I yelled, "Can't do it, my man. I'm actually on my way to meet an investor right now. Best I can do is a quarter of the profits."

"One third." Boris raised the stick and pounded it on the ground. I couldn't hear the thump of the solid wood against the pavement over the engine, but the meaning was clear, and I tried not to let him see me gulp.

"Fine," I yelled back, anxious to get out from under his stare. "One third! Now, can you please move your car so I can go to my meeting?"

He stood there for another moment, just long enough to make sure I knew he won the argument, then slowly made his way to the Cadillac, moving it into Masha's spot.

I made sure to give him a big smile and a wave as I pulled out, wishing I had the courage to give him a one-fingered wave. He glared in return.

In the history of shitty in-laws, I think it's a testament to my love for Masha that I deal with her father as well as I do. Of course, she doesn't see it that way. I'm not deferential enough for her, or something like that. I'm not sure. I usually stop listening when she starts yammering on about me and Boris.

Anyway, I was thinking so hard about my love for my wife and my equal dislike for her father that I drove right past the coffee shop, making me even later for my meeting. I decided to leave that part out when I apologized. Boris deserved to get the blame for every single minute of my tardiness.

I hurried into the coffee shop, where the bittersweet scent of coffee, the smell of yeasty baked goods, and the sourness of cheap perfume and body odor smacked me in the face like a pissed-off woman without a drink to throw.

I spotted my uptown client right away. It wasn't too hard. In a building full of poor college students and starving artists attempting to make themselves look sophisticated and suave by drinking expensive coffees while sitting at tall tables and browsing the free internet, she stood out like a freshly-minted penny in a jar of old change.

Tall and slender, auburn hair perfectly in place, and dressed in clothes that looked tailor-made just for her, she gazed around the room with a secretive smile, as if she were amused at all the pretentiousness oozing from the wanna-be's. She gave off an aura that made me pretty sure she would be more comfortable at a country club soiree than in a coffee shop like this one.

Since she'd gone through all the trouble of coming so far from the country club at the edge of the city, I checked myself over to be sure I was presentable. Smoothing my thinning hair over the bald spot on the back of my head, I started across the room, installing my best 'nice to meet you' smile as I dodged small tables and power cords.

Crap, I'd forgotten to bring the sheet of paper with her information on it. I had no idea what her name was. Something unusual, something fitting for a woman of her caliber, as though Lou had known her child would go places the instant she laid eyes on the new baby. I scratched my head, messing up the 'do I'd just fixed.

It was too late to do anything about it, I realized. Seeing me head her way, she rose to her feet, hand extended, and I got my first full glimpse of her face as she did. My heart stopped. Not literally- I'd be dead if that happened, ha-ha, but the woman standing in front of me with the grim smile on her face was the most stunning thing I'd ever seen in my life.

Light brown hair with glints of copper shot through it, brilliant gray eyes that hinted at the intelligence behind them, and lips that looked so soft and inviting, it took everything I had to keep from touching her mouth to see if they felt like the whipped icing they reminded me of.

"Mr. Ward," she purred. "It's nice to meet you. My mother spoke highly of you."

Words suddenly lost all meaning as I stared into her eyes, and I stuttered out a response.

"I-I- uh, uh huh."

Obviously used to men acting like complete jackasses around her, she took hold of my hand and shook it for me, pretending to ignore my limp wrist and sweaty palm. After, she pulled her hand away and surreptitiously lifted her napkin from the table to wipe my disgusting fluids away. What a classy lady.

Sitting back in her seat, she made herself comfortable, waving at the empty chair across from her, as though she were a queen who expected me to follow her commands without question. I sat, feeling rumpled and unworthy.

"Would you like a drink?"

With the vague notion that coffee would at least give my trembling hands something to hold onto, I managed something of a nod.

Raising her hand in the air, the queen snapped her fingers, something I'd never seen in a coffee shop before. Even though there weren't any waiters, the kid behind the counter rushed over to help, despite the line of customers already waiting.

Pushing a twenty at him, she nodded in my general direction. With glazed eyes glued to the beauty in front of him, the kid growled out of the side of his mouth, "Whatcha want, man?"

I cleared my throat and in a voice that came out way too loud, said, "Just coffee. Black."

Reluctantly, the kid left, only to return in seconds with a cup that slopped its contents onto the table as he shoved it in my direction. His eyes never left the woman sitting across from me. I'm pretty sure he was storing up images for the best fantasy ever when he cooed, "Can I get anything else for you, ma'am?"

She darted a glance at his chest, then gave him a smile that would fuel his wet dreams for months to come. "No thank you, Jess. That will do. Thank you so much. And, keep the change."

As though he'd forgotten the money clutched in his damp hand, the barista gave a start. Shoving the money in his apron pocket, he stared at her with moonstruck eyes until she coughed gently and said, "Jess? I believe you have other customers waiting."

Once the kid reluctantly went back to the counter, she set me back in her sights. There was no sign of the beautiful smile that Jess received when she snapped, "Mr. Ward. I asked you to come here because I'm worried about my mother."

Remembering how well Lou handled the shotgun when she shot the witch, I said, "Uh, I'm pretty sure your mom is perfectly capable of taking care of herself."

She shook her head and said, "I'm talking about the delusions that my father is haunting her. If you were there for more than a minute, I know you saw her talking to herself, thinking he's back from the dead." She shifted in her seat, and for just a second, I forgot I was married and dreamed of being her chair.

"- charlatan, but I—"

"Wait, what? Did you just call me a charlatan? I'm not sure what that means, but it doesn't sound good."

Closing those beautiful gray eyes for just a second, I could see her collecting her thoughts before she replied, "Mr. Ward—"

"Ed, please."

She sighed and started again, "Mr. Ward. I don't believe in ghosts or ghouls or goblins or things that go bump in the night. Therefore, logic dictates that you are a charlatan, taking people's hard-earned money to relieve them of something that doesn't exist. Surely you can see my viewpoint."

I thought about explaining everything we'd seen that night, how I hadn't really believed in that stuff either until I saw it with my own eyes, but I knew it was a waste of time to try and tell her. She wouldn't believe me. She'd already made up her mind, and anything I said would be nothing but a fairy tale because people like her didn't live in the same world I did.

She lost some of her beauty in that moment. It was one thing not to believe me, someone she'd just met, but to just automatically assume her mother had lost her mind? That diminished her in my eyes. Anyone who talked to Lou for longer than a minute could see she wasn't crazy.

Well, yeah, the thought had wormed its way through my brain when I first met her, but I'd stuck around long enough to see Sam in action. Maybe the snobby woman glaring at me needed to spend a little time with her mother instead of sitting on her throne of ice and judging from afar.

Now that I'd caught a glimpse of the beauty queen's inner workings, I wasn't quite as star-struck, so I cleared my throat and got back to business.

"So, what's your proposition, then? If you don't believe in what I do, what could you possibly have to talk to me about?"

I felt a little calmer, but her name still hadn't come to me. I figured I could fake my way through the rest of the meeting, but then she threw me a ringer.

"Do you know who my husband is, Mr. Ward?"

Crap.

Truthfully, I shook my head no.

"My husband is going to be the next mayor of this city. Surely you've seen the billboards around town?"

I shook my head again. "I don't get out much."

Sighing, she continued, "Regardless, Randall *will* be the next mayor, and I can't have my mother wandering around telling people that she's being haunted by my dead father, that she talks to him on a regular basis. Do you understand what I'm trying to say here? Can you understand what my husband's opponents would do with something like that?"

I'd just about had enough of her condescending attitude. Her beauty faded by the second until finally, trying to stay polite for Lou's sake, I snapped, "Could you just stop pussy-footing around and tell me what it is you want from me?"

She reached into her purse and extracted an envelope. Little sparks were flying out of her not-quite-as-pretty eyes as she shoved it across the table toward me, and I wondered if she'd inherited that temper from Sam. She wasn't used to being treated like one of the – shudder – working class, and her voice lost all softness when she said, "I'm going to put my mother in a hospital, one where they specialize in mental disorders. I need you to erase my mother's name from your records and forget her. I can't let it get out that she called in some idiot to exorcise the "ghost" from her house." She actually used air quotes to emphasize ghost, like I might be too stupid to grasp her innuendos.

The last of my good mood disintegrated. I was exhausted, I was cranky, and I wasn't sure how the sweet little old lady I'd met earlier had raised this she-devil, but in my admittedly un-expert opinion, the old woman didn't have anything wrong with her except for the fact that she had a bitch for a daughter.

Standing, I shoved the envelope back across the table, feeling a little twinge of longing when it left my hand. "I don't need your hush money. I have no problem erasing your mother's name from my records, but I'm telling you that you're making a mistake by putting her into a mental institution. She's perfectly sane."

She smirked, and I wondered why I ever thought she was pretty. Picking up the envelope, she dangled it in front of me. "This will buy a lot of late-night television ads, Mr. Ward. I suggest you take it. I would hate for you to have your business license revoked. You *do* have a business license, don't you?"

I did not, in fact, have a business license yet, but her snotty little remark gave me the feeling that she already knew that, and I wondered just what else she knew about me. Feeling like she had me wedged into an uncomfortable corner, I did the only thing I could do.

I wish I could say I took the envelope and ripped both it and the money inside to shreds, but I'm not that brave – or that strong. Nope. Shame-faced, I took the damn envelope and shoved it into my jacket pocket.

As I strode away, dodging tables and power cords, I heard her call out across the room, "Remember, this is none of your concern anymore, Mr. Ward! Stay away from my mother!"

Eyes from every corner of the coffee shop lifted and stared, and it dawned on me how her words must have sounded to a room full of strangers.

"I'm not a pervert!" I yelled, shoving the door of the coffee shop open and feeling exactly like one.

I climbed into my car, coughing a little as more dust from the roof puffed up when I sat down. I turned the key, hoping the she-devil had rushed back to the good side of town already.

Nothing.

Already embarrassed and ashamed, I turned the key to the off position and leaned back against the seat, closing my eyes. I craved sleep like a dieter craves chocolate cake, but I had to warn Lou about her daughter's evil plan.

I opened my eyes and tried the car again, patting the dash with one hand and whispering to her while crossing my toes for luck. The Pacer started with a puff of smoke and a backfire, and we were off.

I was three blocks from Lou's house when the cop lit up and pulled me over.

Chapter 7

Wearily I rolled down my window, staring out the windshield in resignation as the officer approached my car.

I caught a glimpse of his blue uniform from the corner of my eye as he put a hand on the roof of the car, leaned down, and asked the age-old chestnut, "Do you know why I pulled you over?"

I stared straight ahead, suddenly worried my drooping, red eyes might be misconstrued as something other than lack of sleep.

The horizon tilted, then righted itself when I shook my head, and I wondered if the cop would still take me to jail if I passed out and cracked my head on the steering wheel.

"Sir, I pulled you over because it should be illegal to drive a piece of shit car like this."

Wait, what?

I turned my head slowly, partially to keep the horizon from tipping again, but mostly because I expected the worst. Because, you know, the day was going so well already.

To my surprise, my old high school buddy Bob Jenkins stood there grinning at me. In my drinking days, he'd pulled me out of a couple of jams, not to mention a few ditches. I'd only seen him once since then, at my wedding, and I'm pretty sure he only came to see if I was falling-down drunk at the ceremony.

We played football together for five years, eighth grade through our senior year of high school. Bob helped me pass my math classes, and I helped him remember the football plays that never seemed to stick.

Having a car – okay, Pops' Pacer, but he let me drive it whenever I wanted - I toted Bob around when he needed rides, and in return, he introduced me to the parties where the cool kids hung out. For a while, we were as close as brothers, if not closer. At least, until we graduated, and Bob took off for the bright lights of Columbia on a football scholarship.

And me? I could have gone with him, but I didn't need no education! I was gonna be rich! So, with a manly handshake, we went our separate ways.

Eventually, Bob came back to town, but I'd already started my downhill spiral of drinking. Our few meetings since then had been sparse and usually involved me needing help. Good old Bobby did his best to help me out whenever he could-

Bob's voice dragged me out of the past and back to the present. "How the hell are ya, Eddie?"

Shocked and happy to have something go my way for once, I grinned back, "Bobby! You old sonofabitch! What's going on?"

Ignoring the question, my old buddy pulled his sunglasses down so I could see the sobriety in his eyes as he asked, "Ed, man, who did you piss off?"

The lack of sleep had rusted the gears in my brain. Still laughing a little, it took a second for the abrupt change of topic to soak in enough to turn the gears and force the question into focus.

"What?"

"The chief of police himself sent me out here to watch for you specifically. I don't know why, he just said if I saw you, to turn you around and send you home. So, who did you piss off?"

A whole paparazzi's worth of flashbulbs went off in my brain, and I suddenly remembered the name of Lou's daughter. Riley James. Squinting up at my old buddy the cop, I asked my own question in return, "Is there somebody with the last name of James running for mayor?"

Officer Bob whistled. "Holy shit, Ed! What have you gotten yourself into? You don't want to mess with Randall James, he's got his finger on everything in the city."

I scrunched up my face as I said, "It's not him so much as his wife."

Bob let out a bellow of laughter as he stuck his hand through the open window and slapped my shoulder, rattling my teeth.

"Damn, Ed! You sure know how to pick 'em! Does this mean you finally divorced that crazy Russian woman you were so hung up on?"

I tried to laugh along with his banter while rubbing the sore spot he left on my shoulder, but a ray of truth suddenly shot through my brain, sobering me up in a hurry.

Riley James had contacts in high places. She must have sent a message to the chief of police *before* the meeting with me.

Most likely, poor Lou had been whisked out of her house and into the mental facility minutes after hanging up the phone with her daughter. I had to give her credit, Riley James moved fast. But money and reputation always seem to make things happen in a hurry.

Looking up at my old friend, I asked, "Can you do a wellness check on somebody?" Bob's eyes narrowed as he suspiciously asked, "Would this be for the person I'm supposed to stop you from seeing?"

Nodding frantically, I gripped the steering wheel with both hands until my knuckles turned white. I stared at the tendons showing through the skin, not trusting myself to look up as I pleaded, "Look, Bob, you know me. I promise I'll go home if you'll just go check on the old woman. I just want to make sure she's home and okay. I swear I'll leave and won't cause any trouble if you'll just do that for me."

I could hear the indecision in his voice as he said, "That's all you want? You just want to make sure the old lady is okay? You swear on your football trophy?"

I felt a wave of relief go through me. That high school football trophy meant enough to me that I still kept it prominently displayed above the fireplace in my house, much to Masha's dismay. "Is ugly and old! Take it to basement!" I heard the same thing every week when she dusted the mantle.

That trophy represented the one thing in my life I had done right. The winning touchdown that took us to state, run by yours truly, made me that hometown hero every high school football player dreamed of being. Sometimes, it feels like I've spent my whole damn life trying to recapture the pride that trophy represented.

"I swear on my trophy, Bob."

With a handshake and a harsh warning to stay put, he got in his cruiser and drove away.

The thump of his hand on the roof of the car scared me awake a little while later, my sleeping body reflexively putting my hands up to defend myself.

"What?"

My old friend laughed, but quickly stopped when he saw the worried questions in my eyes. Shaking his head, he said, "There's nobody home. I knocked on the door, but no answer. I even peeked in a few windows since you seemed so concerned, but the place is empty. It was kinda weird though. I thought I heard somethin' inside." Shrugging, he continued, "Guess the old lady musta left a radio on or something before she left."

"Sam," I muttered. "He's there by himself."

Bob gave me a confused look. To keep from being tossed into a room next to Lou – although the idea of a long, medicated sleep sounded pretty good right then - I waved away the unspoken question.

"It's all good. Thanks, Bob. I'm going home now. It's been a long night."

"Well, if you decide to try and sneak into the old woman's house again before five, could you bring me some donuts and a coffee before I send you back home?"

Too tired to laugh, I pledged, "Deal."

The engine on my Pacer dragged a little when I turned the key but smoothed out pretty quickly as I pulled away. Waving goodbye to Bob out the open window, I left it down as I drove, the chilly morning air keeping me awake long enough to get home. I don't remember those few minutes of driving, but I remember the feeling of sweet relief when I made it into the bedroom at home.

A feeling that faded away as I looked at the bedspread. The frou-frou comforter wasn't my style, but Masha loved all things frilly and girly. If sleeping under a pink blanket made her happy, I would willingly curl up underneath it.

As I stared at it from the doorway, though, my fatigued mind started playing tricks on me, giving me a double vision kind of déjà vu. The flowers seemed familiar – not because I'd looked at them every night for a year - but because they reminded me of something else... another floral bedspread in another room. The jukebox in my head tinkled out a few notes to go along with the memory, but not enough to figure out the song.

I shook my head. I was too tired to think, much less stay awake long enough to try and remember something that most likely didn't have any significance.

It can't be anything important or I'd remember it, I told myself as I stripped down and crawled under the covers.

In a matter of seconds, I fell into the deep sleep of the exhausted, forgetting about the strange feeling as my body succumbed to sweet unconsciousness.

I was right in the middle of a hot dream about Masha and me finally getting some sexy time together when something woke me up so fast, I forgot to breathe for a second.

Alvin sat on the edge of the bed staring at me. In the dim lighting of the room, he resembled the nickname he insisted I call him, his pale hair and face only adding to the illusion. When I finally realized he was a living person, and not some angry spirit come to exact revenge on me, I sucked in a deep breath and rolled over on my side, trying to hide the physical remnant of my dream.

Wishing it had been his mother coming in to wake me up so we could re-enact the Pizza Boy and The Princess dream, I grumbled, "What?"

"Dude, what were you dreaming about? You were moaning and groaning like crazy."

Ignoring the question, I sat up - making sure to bunch the blankets over my lap - and asked, "What time is it?"

"Four o'clock. What happened today, dude?"

"Look, kid. Go make me a pot of coffee while I pee. I'll fill you in." Squinting at the dark window, I asked, "Is it raining?"

"Cats and dogs, dude. Cats and dogs. Okay, hurry up and get downstairs. I'll make your coffee, but then you have to tell me everything. Damn, I can't wait for school to be over."

The sweet smell of warm coffee beans tickled my nose before I reached the bottom of the staircase. Stumbling my way to the kitchen, I dazedly poured a cup while Ghost bounced excitedly from foot to foot like a kindergartener that waited too long to tell the teacher he needed to pee.

"Come on, come on! What happened?"

Holding up a finger, I took a sip of coffee, feeling the warmth and caffeine disperse throughout my body. Instant calm didn't follow the single sip, but I felt like maybe I could face the day – well, night, I guess. Four hours of sleep wasn't much, but it would have to do.

Glancing out the window as I crossed by it to get to the table, I saw only dark gray skies and sheets of rain. The nasty weather had set in for a while.

I took another drink of coffee before taking pity on the kid. Over the next ten minutes, I filled him in on everything that happened while he was gone. Except for the part about the sexy dream, because, you know, his mom and all.

Eyes wide, he asked, "So how much?"

"How much what?"

The kid rolled his eyes. If the powers-that-be ever decided to add an Olympic category for eye-rolling, Alvin Vincent Bykov would make America proud. "Dude! The envelope! How much money did she give you?"

"Huh. I never looked. I was so tired, I forgot about it after I left the coffee shop. I think it's still in my jacket pocket."

A nasty thought wormed its way through the valleys of my brain just then. In my fatigue, I'd stripped off my clothes – including the jacket I'd been wearing - when I crawled into bed, sleeping in just my underwear, but I should've tripped over them when I stumbled out of bed. Shit. Masha must have done laundry while I slept.

A sick feeling went through me, landing in my stomach. I didn't mind sharing the money with my wife, but it would have been kind of nice to invest in some new things for the business – maybe a new answering machine, or a real desk. Or, you know, a shotgun.

Frowning, I asked, "Where's your mother?"

Ghost shrugged. "She sent me a text saying she was shopping for a new microwave, so I rode home with Inkspot."

The sickness in my gut increased, but I paused to ask, "You have a friend named Inkspot?" I waved off the answer. Inkspot wasn't any worse than Ghosty_boy69.

Jumping up from my chair, I ran to the basement. My clothes from the night before were folded neatly on top of the dryer. I checked the trash can. Empty. I hobbled back up the stairs, huffing and puffing, using the handrail to pull myself up.

When I came back into the kitchen, Ghost was staring at me like he'd seen a – well, a ghost, I guess. "Dude! Did you lose the money?"

Still trying to catch my breath, I wheezed, "Did your mother say where she was going shopping?"

Ghost shook his head and lifted his phone from the table, double-checking the message. "Nope. Just says 'Shopping for microwave. Love, Mama.' Do you think she found the money?"

A sudden, foggy memory pushed its way into the forefront of my mind. My head falling to my chest and the corner of the envelope irritating my chin as I dozed in the Pacer, waiting for Bob to come back. I must have taken it out of my pocket and put it somewhere in the car!

"Be right back," I muttered, as I raced out the back door and into the driving rain. By the time I made it back into the house, I no longer needed a shower, but I held the soggy envelope in the air triumphantly.

"Found it!"

"Dude, how much did she give you? And is that what they call hush money?"

The whole end of the envelope ripped when I tried to open the flap, and the stack of hundred-dollar bills fell from my shaking hands and to the floor with a solid thump. I picked up the brick of soggy money and began trying to separate the loose bills – something that's not easy to do when your fingers are cold, wet, and trembling. If all those bills were hundreds, this was more money than I'd seen in one place since I first got my inheritance.

Just then, the chunk of a car door closing filtered through the sound of rain, followed closely by the lighter thump of the trunk. Masha was home, and if she saw the stack of bills, they would disappear faster than a magician could say, 'Abra—'

Before I could even think about finding a hiding spot, the steady thrum of rain grew in volume, then dimmed again as the back door slammed shut. Ghost's eyes were huge as he waved to get my attention.

"Dude! Toss it here!" Pulling the hoodie away from his scrawny chest, he gestured toward the pocket opening across his abdomen. For a split second, I thought about how stupid I would be to give the teenager the wad of money, but Masha calling from the mudroom changed my mind in a hurry.

Al- Ghost caught the sodden brick almost languidly when I tossed it to him, as though he'd been practicing the fine art of catching wet money his whole life.

"Alvin! Where are you?" Shoving the money inside his pocket, Ghost called back, "I'm here, Mama. Do you need help?"

A giant box with legs squelched its way into the kitchen, wet, size seven footsteps following behind. Masha peeked around the corner of the cardboard to shoot a disdainful look at me, her hair hanging in strings over her unhappy face. Dumping the new microwave on the counter with a mushy thump and a disconcerting clang, she called over her shoulder, "Please to clean up, Ed."

Alvin shot me a knowing look and jumped up. "I'll do it, Mama. Ed has business waiting in his office."

My wife snorted like an angry bull ready to tear apart the inside of a china shop, and I knew exactly where the china shop resided. I needed to make a quick exit, and the kid had just handed my excuse to me.

Smoothly, I shoved my chair back from the table, knocking it over. The noise drew Masha's attention and she gave me an appraising look.

"Why you wet?"

Ghost jumped to my rescue. I kept waiting for the punchline, but he seemed sincere when he said, "Mama, you won't believe what Ed did for me. I forgot something in his car earlier, and he went out into this rain to get it for me. Wasn't that nice of him?" Lifting his ever-present earbuds, he spoke loud enough for the neighbors to hear, "Thanks, Ed. I appreciate you getting my earbuds out of your car. That was cool of you."

Masha stared at the pair of us in disbelief. With good reason. Alvin and I had forged an unspoken agreement over the years. Our lukewarm relationship had been founded on his refuting all my attempts at being fatherly, and to tell the truth, after so many rejections, I'd quit putting a whole lot of effort into it. Between his resistance and my indifference, this was the first time in all the years I'd been around that he'd spoken so kindly of me. Gulping, I forced a smile on my face for Masha's sake and muttered, "Welcome, kid."

She held the look of suspicious disbelief for another second before deciding that questioning the anomaly wasn't worth the effort. With one last scrutinizing look at my innocent-ish face, she went to work ripping the wet cardboard box away from the new microwave.

Alvin scurried into the mudroom, returning with a mop. Wildly shoving it around the wet floor like a janitor at the end of his shift, he gave me a look intending to convey meaning, and said, "Hey, Ed, can you put this mop back in the *broom closet* on the way downstairs?"

I had no idea what the look or the emphasis on his words meant. Then it dawned on my tired brain. The broom closet. He must have stashed the money there.

Masha was busy pulling accessories out of the box and didn't seem to notice the inflection he'd placed on the words. In fact, I'm not sure she knew we were in the room anymore.

I gave a short nod to let the kid know I understood his code, then took the mop out of his hands and headed for the mudroom. As soon as I opened the broom closet, I saw the torn envelope poking out from the shelf above my head. I stretched up on my tiptoes to reach it, cursing the kid's freakish height as I did.

When I managed to grasp the edge of the envelope with my fingertips, my calves cramped. I yanked the money toward me. Bills began fluttering through the air like prisoners trying to escape the confines of their envelope cell. I scrambled to capture them before Masha came looking for me, banging my head against the door frame in the process.

The familiar sound of Masha's squeaky footsteps across the damp floor of the kitchen grew louder. I held my breath as Ghost half-yelled, his voice laced with panic, "Mama, how does this thing work? I can't get it to turn on." Her accented voice answered, the words drowned out by the squeaks heading back into the kitchen. Taking advantage of the distraction, I tip-toed toward the basement stairs, clutching the money in my damp shirt.

As soon as I closed the basement door, I leaned back and heaved a sigh of relief. I needed to find a place to stash the money. Masha rarely came downstairs except to do laundry, but if she even remotely suspected I had money hidden away, you could bet your bottom dollar she'd be searching the house from top to bottom.

And don't get me wrong, I believe in 'What's yours is mine and what's mine is yours' in the marital sense, but after years of being married, I knew how my wife worked. One big haul like the one in my hand and she would expect more of the same. I needed to pass the money to her slowly, like a paycheck. That is, if I kept it. I still felt funny about having it, and until I talked to Lou, the money needed to remain more secret than the location of Hoffa's body.

As I debated the best place to hide the sodden brick, the vague memory of an item on an old honey-do list popped into my head. I made my way to the wall vent Masha had ordered me to secure a few years ago when she still used the workout equipment in the corner.

The cover did exactly what it was supposed to do - sit perfectly over the hole in the wall, but for some reason, no one had ever secured the damn thing. The metal grate fell on Masha's head one day while she was walking on her treadmill, making her lose her balance and slide off the back, a scene that amused me *way* more than it did her.

She used the machine for a few months after her fall, but now the treadmill sat dusty and unused in the corner, ever since Dr. Oz mentioned something about them being bad for your health. At any time, though, Ellen or Dr. Phil might suggest differently, and Masha would begin working out again.

It wasn't a perfect hiding spot, but it would do temporarily until I could come up with something better. And it had the added bonus of acting as a dryer for the cash.

Feeling like a criminal, I shoved the money in and replaced the grate just as I heard Ghost stomping his way down the stairs, calling back to his mother, "No, it's okay, Mama. I'll bring the laundry up. That way you don't have to walk all the way down here."

Shooting a look at the closed door to be sure his mother hadn't followed him, Ghost hissed, "Did you hide it?"

I gave a quick nod and hurried over to my desk, sitting carefully in my crappy chair just as Masha opened the basement door and began descending the stairs.

Ghost rushed over to the dryer and hurriedly began dragging clothes out, shoving them into a waiting basket.

Masha was not a stupid woman, and Alvin's 'help' had raised her antennae. Closing my eyes, I rolled them in secret before opening them again, pretending to take notes. As Alvin chattered on about his day at school, my wife meandered over to my desk and examined the paper in my hands.

"What is this," she demanded, sounding a little like her father. Okay, a lot like her father.

"Possible customers," I said, trying not to sound too proud of myself. "In fact, I have to call one of them right now to set up an appointment."

With a snort of derision, Masha snatched the basket of clean laundry from Alvin's hands and headed up the stairs. "Not to forget to pay my son," she intoned at the base of the steps before making her way up, slamming the door behind her. Shit. Was there anything she and Boris didn't share?

"What's she talking about?" Al- Ghost asked, genuine confusion on his face. So, Boris hadn't told *him* about our little deal yet. Part of me really, *really* wanted to tell the kid that we had agreed on ten percent for his share, but Boris trusted me about as much as I trusted him, and I knew he would tell the kid the truth the first chance he got.

"I struck an agreement with your grandfather. You'll continue working for me, and in return, you make twenty-five percent of the profits." The thump of the old man's stick reverberated in my head, and I corrected myself quickly, "No, wait, that's not right. You get a third."

The teenager's eyes were shining with greed when he asked, "Dude, does that mean I get a third of whatever's in the envelope?"

I shook my head no. "I don't even know if I'm going to keep that money yet. I don't want to betray Lou. Besides, if you go flashing money around, your mom will figure out I have it, and you know what that means."

With a little laugh, Ghost answered, "Means neither of us gets to keep it. Mine will go into my college account, and yours will go in her pocket. I love my mom, but I think she might love money just a tiny bit more than she does me."

"And I come in at fourth place: money, you, Boris, and finally me. Although her car might edge me out."

Giving me a funny look, Ghost asked, "Dude, you sure about that? 'Cause I don't think she would've stuck around all these years if she didn't love you."

I knew Masha loved me, but I wasn't sure I ranked as high as the kid seemed to think – at least, not at the moment. Married couples tend to go through cycles of highs and lows, and at the moment, my marriage was swinging at the bottom of a low arc. If I could get my business making some steady cash, the cycle might turn my way again. At least, I hoped so.

I let out a sigh and cracked my knuckles. "Either way, we need to get to work."

I'd almost forgotten about the other phone call. The message from Riley James – and everything that followed - had shoved the other possible job out of my mind. Hopefully, this client would be more pleasant. As much as I hated to admit it though, odds weren't good that this client would pay as well.

Speaking of the money, I still hadn't gotten a chance to count it. The safest measure would be to wait until Masha left the house again before I tried. Besides, having a little hidey-hole that nobody else knew about wasn't a bad idea.

I mean, I trusted the kid – sort of - but what if he wanted to buy a girly magazine or something? That would be considered contributing to the delinquency of a minor if I gave him access to something like that, wouldn't it?

Decision made, I went to call the number I'd written down. I could barely read my own writing. Was it always this bad? Geesh. Maybe I needed to check into getting some glasses. Squinting, the name Grady wavered into mostly-clear view.

"Hello, is this Grady?"

"Uh, yeah. Uh, is this the ghost guy?"

Smoothly, I answered, "Poltergeist Guys. What's eating you?" Yikes. Scratch *that* tagline off the list.

"Huh?"

"Let me start over. Hi! This is Ed Ward from Poltergeist Guys, returning Grady's call. Is this Grady I'm speaking to?"

"Yeah, uh, so I called because I think I uh, have a poltergeist. He uh, he's breaking into my house and stuff."

"Well, sir, I'd be happy to come by and take a look. When would be a good time for you?"

"Uh, whenever. I'm uh, not currently working. That's uh, that's how I realized I have a poltergeist."

I gave the kid a victorious look. Another customer! "So, would tomorrow evening around eight be okay, then?"

"Yeah, okay. Cool. See you then."

Click.

Ignoring the look of confusion on Ghost's face, I threw my arms in the air to crow about the new client when I remembered I had no idea where Grady lived. I smacked myself on the forehead and called the number back before the kid could say anything.

"Uh, hello?"

"Yes, Grady? This is Ed Ward again. I need to get your address."

The man on the other end of the line let out a dull chuckle, "Uh, you don't already know?"

I pulled the receiver away from my ear and stared at it as though the idiot on the other end could see my scowl. After taking a deep breath, I put it back against my head.

"Sir," I explained, "I'm not a psychic. If you don't tell me your address, I don't know where you live."

"Oooooh."

For a second, I wondered if this guy was for real. Nobody could be this intellectually challenged, could they? He began rattling off numbers before I had a chance to think about it too much, and by the time he finished, I'd forgotten about it.

I barely finished writing the address down on the paper before Ghost whispered, "Got it."

"Okay, then Grady, I'll see you tomorrow."

He hung up without another word. I looked at Ghost, who was bouncing up and down like a kid who had just finished his third soda in as many minutes. "Dude, come on, why are we waiting? Let's go right now!"

I shook my head and gestured for him to take a seat. The bouncing was getting on my nerves, and we needed to talk, as much as I didn't want to.

Damn, damn, damn.

Chapter 8

"Look, kid, we need to talk about this whole business thing. Basically, I've been forced into making you a partner."

Ghost stood up slowly, a hurt look on his face. "Dude, if you don't want my help, fine. I thought I was doing you a favor, but hey, I don't need your pity job."

Dammit.

I tried to figure out how to pry my size ten from my mouth. For the first time in the six years I'd known him, we were actually getting along. And to be honest about it, I kind of enjoyed having him around now that he'd stopped treating me like an unwanted rash. I rushed to fix the damage I'd inadvertently created.

"No! That's not what I meant! Dammit! Sit back down!"

Before he could give me a 'You're not my dad', I kept talking, "I meant I would have offered you the job anyway, but your grandfather beat me to it. I think the two of us make a pretty good team."

In what I can only assume was shock, the kid forgot to say dude when he asked, "You do?"

With an emphatic nod, I continued, "Look, I know I've never been much of a father-figure to you—"

I ignored the raised eyebrows and pursed lips.

"-but I think we could, you know, like, start over or something. Be friends, or at least friendly to one another."

"Friends." Ghost said the word slowly, as though he were musing over the idea of being buddies with someone he'd hated for a good chunk of his life.

I thought back to some of the 'pranks' he'd pulled since I'd come into the picture. The dead snake I found in my sock drawer the day after I moved in with them. The shaving-cream-filled shoes after I'd left them outside one night. Finding my keys in the bottom of the toilet, the giant, red X over my face on our wedding picture, the razor blade that had been carefully glued into my hairbrush. The kid hadn't pulled any punches in the past when it came to his feelings for me.

I nodded, willing to overlook the indiscretions, and mentally crossing my fingers that he believed the sincerity in my tone.

Clearing my throat, I continued, "I pushed the job back until tomorrow because I thought maybe we could hash out an agreement – you know, like a real business. And I guess we'll have to get a business license if we're going to be all legal and stuff."

I couldn't think of anything else to say, so I sat back in my chair, listening to the old wood creak as I waited for Ghost's answer. I mean, he was only going to be into the business for thirty percent, so it's not like he would want to make any big changes or anything. Things would just go along like they were now, and we would-

"I want to change the name."

Of all the things I'd thought he might say, that wasn't one of them.

"What? No, we're not going to change the name. It took me a long time to come up with that. It's a great name."

"Dude, seriously, you need something trendier, a name that's more up-to-date."

I crossed my arms. "No. I'm not changing the name."

The kid crossed his. "Just think about it. I mean, we could call it Spook Seekers or Ed's Ghost Hunters."

The idea of having my name in the business hadn't occurred to me, and as much as I hated to admit it, I kind of liked the idea.

Sighing, I uncrossed my arms and picked up my pen, doing my best to seem unconcerned. "Okay, we'll toss a few around, but if I don't like any of them, we're using Poltergeist Guys."

"Deal," Ghost grinned.

Faster than I could write them down, he listed off, "Ghost Getters, GitRGone, Scary Savers, We Got Spirit."

"Those are terrible," I laughed. "How long have you been holding on to these names?"

The kid shrugged. "That's just off the top of my head."

"How about Poltergeist Guys?" I gave him a smarmy look as I said it.

Ghost shot back, "How about Boogeyman Boys?"

I groaned, "If we're going to go with a stupid name, we might as well call it Ghost Shmost."

"Okay, if you don't like any of those, how about The Exorcisers?"

I was starting to get into the spirit of the game. "How about, "Phantom F.A.R.T.'s? You know, for Fast Action Response Team. I mean, people would remember the name!"

Ghost started laughing as he said, "Our tag line could be 'Nothing can withstand our strength.'"

I dropped the pen, giving up all pretense of being serious.

"Casper's Trappers."

"Haunted Helpers."

"Spirits Away."

"How about After Life Assurance? You know, make it sound like we're business-like and all."

I shook my head at him. "That's pretty good, and this has been fun and all, but I'm still going to call it Poltergeist Guys."

The kid pouted, reminding me of when he was younger and didn't get his way. "Aw, come on, dude! Lighten up and have some fun for once! I mean, Poltergeist Guys is okay and all, I'm just saying you could come up with something that's not so- awkward."

Well, that hurt.

"What do you mean, awkward? What's wrong with it? It tells people we're on the hunt for ghosts!"

Shaking his head, Ghost said, "Dude, come on. It's hard to say and it sounds like one of those old movies from the fifties."

"What's wrong with that? I used to watch those when I was a kid. Well, after my grandparents went to bed. Grandma would have died if she knew I watched that stuff."

Ghost started laughing.

"What's so funny?" I demanded, not seeing anything funny at all in what I'd said.

"We could call it 'Stay Dead, Grandma.'"

I snorted, swallowing the laugh that desperately wanted to come out. Struggling to keep a straight face, I spoke through tight lips, "No. Poltergeist Guys. I've already started advertising it that way."

Still chuckling over his hilarious name for my business, the kid held his hands up in the air, palms out. "Okay, okay, I get it. One more suggestion, and if you don't like it, I'll stop, alright?"

It was my turn to pout. "Fine."

"What about Polterguys? It's easier to say and still gets the meaning across."

"No," I frowned. "It stays Poltergeist Guys."

The kid's eyes narrowed as he pressed his lips together in frustration. "Fine," he said curtly. "What else do you want to talk about? 'Cause if we aren't going out tonight, I might go hang with Inkspot."

I closed my eyes to hide the frustration I'm sure showed on my face. Using one of my favorite tactics for dealing with Masha, I opened them again – keeping them as wide and innocent as possible – as I gave Ghost a friendly smile.

"Since you're so good on the computer, do you think you could check and see if we can file for a business license online? You know, hack them, or whatever it is you do."

The kid blinked. Then blinked again. "Dude, do you know what hacking is? Wait, never mind. Why do you hate technology so much?"

I shrugged. "What's to like about it? There's nothing wrong with the way things were before all this computer stuff came along. I grew up without any of it, and I came out okay. Besides, you kids with your phones and your laptops – you're all going to be screwed when someone finally shuts down the electrical grid for good."

Eyes open as wide as they would go, Ghost slowly nodded. I'm not sure how he managed to convey disbelief with a single word, but as he drawled, "Okaaaay..." I got the message.

Whatever. He'd find out what I meant when it happened.

Opening his computer, the kid hit a couple of keys and like magic, the application for a business license filled the screen. While he tapped away on the keyboard, my mind started wandering back to when I'd first met him.

I'd been dating Masha for about three months before she took me to her house for the first time. That was cool by me. I had no idea how to act around kids, anyway. I mean, I knew the two of them were a package deal, but really, how hard could it be? The kid was half-grown already.

I figured we wouldn't have much interaction anyway. By the time *I* was twelve, I spent as little time inside as possible. My friends and I would go goof around in the woods for an entire day, only leaving to go home and eat, then sometimes heading back out with sleeping bags, PB and J's, and canteens filled with milk for an impromptu camping session.

Boy, did I have a rude awakening when I met Masha's kid!

When we walked into the small house she lived in with her father, Alvin sat on the couch playing video games. Excitedly, she introduced me to the zombie sitting on the couch.

"Hey, Alvin," I smiled. "Whatcha playin'?"

Just shy of being rude, the kid shot a look toward me and mumbled something just as a loud explosion came from the television.

"Thanks a lot," he yelled at the TV screen, but I knew who he was talking to. Stomping across the room to a hallway, he disappeared. A half-second later, I heard the sound of a door slamming.

"Well, that went well," I said awkwardly to my new girlfriend.

"Masha is sorry," she replied as she picked up the remote and turned off the TV.

I took her hand and turned her toward me. "Don't be sorry. I was his age once. He'll warm up to me eventually."

She slipped into my arms and we stayed that way for a while, enjoying the feel of each other's closeness.

We were still standing that way, not even kissing, when I had the pleasure of meeting Boris for the first time.

"Who is slamming door?" His voice invaded the small room like he was holding a bullhorn full of gravel.

"Ah, Papa," she pulled out of my arms, leaving me vulnerable to attack as she introduced us, "Papa, meet Ed. Ed, Boris."

I held out my hand nervously.

"Who is this?" Boris bellowed.

"Hi, sir. My name is Ed, and I think—"

Without any warning, he picked up a giant stick that had been leaning against the wall and began shouting in Russian. My tension ratcheted up a notch. Surely this guy wasn't going to hit me with that!

Backing slowly toward the front door, I held up my hands, "Look, I didn't mean to cause any problems."

Masha was screaming something in Russian, but she paused and rushed to my side. "Is okay, Ed. Masha will call tomorrow."

A flash caught my eye and I looked away from Masha's beautiful brown eyes to see Alvin giving me the bird from the hallway.

Boris began yelling again as soon as the door closed behind me, and as I made my way to my Pacer, I wondered for a split second if I wanted to deal with two very jealous men in order to keep seeing Masha. Then I pictured those soft, doe eyes looking up at me with a pureness I hadn't seen since my grandmother and I knew she was worth it.

I shook myself out of my memories to see Ghost had almost finished filling out the paper. All this thinking about the good old days had me feeling kind of- well, I promised the kid I would be right back, and headed up the stairs to find Masha. I was ready to kiss and make up.

Just like he had the first time I met him, the kid managed to flip me the bird when I left. After a particularly boisterous evening in bed with Masha, where we managed to work out most of our differences, I came downstairs the next day to find a copy of our business license application.

I scanned the paper and gave a resigned sigh. The official name of 'our' new business was Polterguys.

Chapter 9

A wave of heat rushed through my body as I angrily read the name the kid had registered my new business as, but just as quickly as it burned through me, it disappeared, and I let out a chuckle. The kid might be annoying and sarcastic, but he was smart. I mean, he fooled me, and that took a lot.

The flashing light on the answering machine finally caught my attention. I settled in at my desk to take notes for all the new clients.

The first call was a hang-up.

The second call was a wrong number.

Deflated, I punched the button for the next call.

"Yes, I'd like to speak to Ed Ward please, concerning an urgent matter. Could you please call me back at—"

Click.

I know the sound of a bill collector when I hear it.

There was one call left on the machine, and not a single new customer out of the three I'd already listened to. I hesitated before pressing the button, my shaking finger hovering in the air as I whispered, "Come on, come on, come on."

Mashing the button down as if I could will the last call into being a client by sheer force, an evil-sounding giggle filled the air, sending chills down my spine.

I pushed myself away from the desk. I needed to go upstairs and get some coffee. It had nothing to do with the fact that I was sitting in the dark basement by myself with the echo of that nasty titter still in my ears. Nothing at all.

Before I went upstairs, I went to the outside door to see what the weather looked like. Despite the fact that it should have been broad daylight outside, the rain coming down in sheets obscured any sign of the sky.

I shivered as I stared out into the darkness, the feeling of being watched creeping over my skin and giving me goosebumps. Without taking my eyes off the landscape outside, I reached one trembling hand up to check the lock on the door before slowly backing away.

As I opened the door at the top of the stairs, I smelled something burning. Shit. Masha was cooking.

She must have heard the door open, because she appeared suddenly, wrapping her arms around me and smiling up into my face. "Masha make big Russian breakfast for you. You come."

Happy she wasn't mad at me anymore, I forced a smile on my face and followed her into the dining room, where the scent of burned dill hung in the air like cheap cigar smoke.

Masha is a strong, beautiful, independent woman, but the one thing she never learned how to do was cook. I should clarify. She could cook- but it tasted terrible. And when she's happy, she makes giant, horrible-tasting meals of her home country's delicacies.

On the dining room table, a veritable feast greeted me – an unpalatable one, but a feast, nevertheless. Kolbasa sandwiches, a type of sausage laid on bread, eggs cooked sunny side up (if you ignored the blackened edges), Russian porridge, which could be made with several different types of hot cereal – this time her choice seemed to be lumpy oatmeal - and syrniki, a dumpling made with cottage cheese that was delicious when cooked correctly. And of course, sour cream. Lots of sour cream.

I don't mind sour cream. Dump some on a baked potato and I'm in heaven, but I'm not a fan of it for breakfast. Especially Masha's breakfasts. Although it does help mask the flavor of burned eggs.

Ghost stumbled in just as I sat down to eat. The horrified look on his face quickly changed to one of joy when he spotted his mother carrying more plates into the room.

"Mama! You cooked! You know how much I love your cooking!"

Masha beamed at her one and only precious, lying offspring. "Sit, Alvin. Eat. We have big family breakfast, yes?"

I exchanged a look of panic with the kid as Masha left to get drinks. "Dude," he whispered, "I can't eat this crap again!"

I shrugged. My cast iron stomach could handle it. At least, I hoped so. Leaning over, I whispered back, "Just tell her you're sick."

"Dude, no! I tried that last time! Remember? She gave me all those crazy Russian home remedies!"

I shrugged again. "Then you'll have to eat it."

With a sigh, the kid sat down next to me. Masha happily filled our plates and we manned up, mentally preparing for the giant fabrications we were about to tell.

I went first, taking a huge bite and swallowing as quickly as possible. As expected, the eggs tasted like ashy cardboard covered in dill. The oatmeal was slightly better – the lumps were at least bland. Masha hovered expectantly over us, waiting for our critiques.

"Mmm...delicious," I managed to mumble around the mush in my mouth. She shot a look at Ghost to see if he agreed. Nodding, a smile on his face that reminded me of a ventriloquist's dummy, he shoved another forkful of eggs in.

Masha beamed as she watched us cram giant bites of food into our mouths. Neither of us would hurt her feelings for the world, but honestly, the only way to eat Masha's cooking is to shove it in and swallow quickly without letting it linger on the taste buds too long. In a matter of minutes, our plates were empty, and Masha began clearing the table.

I leaned back to let the stone in my stomach roll to a more comfortable spot. While his mother was out of the room, Ghost leaned over with a glint in his eye and quietly asked, "Did you see the paperwork? I made sure to leave it where you could find it."

Nodding, I gave the kid my own evil glance. "I *did* see it. Very clever of you."

Masha came back into the room for another stack of dirty dishes, and I called out, "Masha, honey, would you like some help with that?"

"No, my big strong man. You rest." Dropping a kiss on my forehead, she left the room again. I turned my head back toward the kid. "Did I mention the reason I didn't come back downstairs last night while you were finishing up the paperwork? Or why your mother is in such a good mood today?"

"Dude, no! Gross!"

Okay, it didn't make up for his changing the name of the business right under my nose, but watching the kid stumble out of the room as fast as his long legs would take him made it a little better.

I stood up and grabbed some dishes, feeling the rock in my stomach roll as I moved. Carrying them into the kitchen, I was just in time to see Boris come through the back door. My good mood deteriorated as he hung his coat and hat on the coat rack.

Giving Masha a quick kiss on the cheek, he stole a syrniki from the platter and took a giant bite, hiding the look on his face when his daughter turned expectantly to hear his praise.

"Is very goot, Masha, my child."

"Thank you, Papa." Beaming with pride, she turned back to the sink. Boris spit the dumpling out into his hand, and with a panic-stricken look, turned around, dropping it into the deep pocket of his coat.

Narrowing his eyes, he glared, silently warning me against telling Masha what I'd seen.

I gave the old man a knowing smile and stepped up behind my wife, wrapping my arms around her ample waist and murmuring in her ear, "Masha, honey, breakfast was amazing. Best meal you've ever made."

The feeling of jubilation that shot through me when I saw Boris' scowl almost made up for having to eat an entire meal of my wife's food. And when you added in the fact that I'd grossed out the kid to boot? Well, it added up to a pretty good day, despite not having any new clients.

Between the lack of sleep over the last two days and the lump in my midsection, I left Masha happily singing something in Russian as I made my way into the living room and turned on the television.

Scrolling through the list of recorded shows, I found my favorite ghost hunting show and pressed play. Before the first frightened, "Did you hear that?" I was asleep on the couch.

It might have been the food, or it could have been the television show, but I dreamed of a motel room with faded, flowered bedspreads and generic artwork hanging on the wall. There was an undercurrent of malevolence hanging over everything as I swayed with a strange woman in the center of the room, the hem of her skirt swirling softly around my legs, and the clock radio playing a song I knew well.

David Lee Roth was running with the devil, and when my partner looked up, I realized I was dancing with one, her dull black eyes drawing me in until I was drowning in inky darkness.

I woke with a start, the dream already fading, but I still felt uneasy. The living room was black, and the black eyes in my dream haunted me one last time before they too faded and were forgotten.

A deep growl made me jump before I realized it was Boris clearing his throat.

"No power," he stated flatly.

"No kidding," I answered.

He snorted, the sound reminding me of a bear, before he said, "Time to get up."

The uneasiness disappeared in my irritation with the man. Who did he think he was to come into *my* house and order me around?

I didn't bother trying to hide the annoyance in my voice when I asked, "What time is it?"

"Is time to get up."

With stimulating conversation like that, how could I not? Grumbling, I rolled over to a sitting position.

"Where's Masha?"

Without answering, the old man walked out of the room, the tap of his stick leading him like a blind man. Since I didn't have a handy-dandy stick to ward off danger, I managed to bump into the corner of the couch with my hip and the fireplace mantle with my calf. Pressing my lips together to keep from screaming in pain, I hobbled into the dining room where Boris waited with a lit candle like he was an executioner and I was his next victim.

"Come. Sit." he patted the table like we were old girlfriends getting ready to have a bitch session.

No thanks.

I stumbled my way over to the coffee pot before I realized that without power, coffee wasn't happening. Dammit.

With a sigh, I limped back to where Boris sat patiently waiting like he had all the time in the world. Which I guess he did. He spent as much time at our house as he did the car dealership. I wondered if he would spend as much time with us if he had a girlfriend. Or even just a friend.

Sliding the chair out, I sat down next to my father-in-law.

"What do you want, Boris? And where's Masha and Gh-Alvin?"

I thought I caught a glimpse of his perfectly white teeth in the dim glow of the candle before he said, "Is goot we talk alone."

I was barely awake with no access to coffee, and the last thing I wanted to do right then was talk to the man who made it clear on a daily basis that he hated my guts.

"Why? Why is it *goot* we talk alone, Boris? What have I done wrong now?"

Ignoring my feeble attempt at imitating his accent, he flashed his teeth at me again.

"Not wrong. Not this time. Business is goot idea."

Wait, what? I was actually getting a compliment from the man? Was I still asleep and dreaming? Or maybe I'd slipped into another dimension and I was living in Bizarro World. Did that make me Superman? And I suppose that would make Boris Brainiac—

"Ed!"

I snapped back to attention. Boris smiled again, and suddenly, I felt as uneasy as a rat trapped in a glass cage with a serpent. I had no place to hide, and nowhere to run.

Dammit.

But once again, Boris surprised me. Leaning back in his chair, the stick between his legs, he said, "I give you car for business. Nice car. Will run."

Shocked and stunned, I sat there like a rock, motionlessly staring at him. What the actual hell was going on? Not only was Boris being nice, but he was offering me a car? I stared at the lit candle in front of me, trying to unscramble my brain from the stir that Boris had just given it.

"Well?" He asked the question confidently, expecting – no, certain of – the answer. I only wish I'd had a picture of his face the moment I flatly answered, "No."

Boris's mouth dropped open a little, and I don't know what he meant to say, but all that came out was a deep, "Uh."

I felt powerful! A smile crept across my face.

"Thanks, but no thanks, Boris. My Pacer will do just fine until I start making some real cash."

His eyebrows drew down in displeasure, and he growled, "Boy says car does not start."

The feeling of superiority grew. This had to be one of the most amazing moments of my life! All I had to do to keep pissing him off was deny him what he wanted!

"Boris," I tried to break it to him gently. "It's true that my car doesn't always start the first time, but it always gets me home. Besides, I don't think I could afford the strings attached to one of your cars, even if you gave it to me for free."

I stifled a squeal of joy at the look on his face. Boris, the man who rarely spoke, but still always managed to have the last word, was speechless!

As if on cue, the power came back on. I stood without another word and went to make coffee, my head held high.

Chapter 10

Boris tried one last time to get me to take a car after I proudly sat back down at the table with mugs of coffee for both of us.

Struggling to keep the anger off his face, he said, "Is advertisement for both of us."

"No."

"You lose jobs with your car."

"No."

"Is for taxes."

I slammed my hand down on the table, feeling the sting in my palm as I yelled, "Boris! I'm not taking a damn car from you! Let it go!"

Then, my father-in-law uttered the one word I'd never heard him say before. The one word I thought I would never hear coming from his lips.

"Please."

Sometimes, it takes me a little while to figure things out. Not very often, but once in a while I'm just not very smart. This might have been one of those times.

See, Boris tipped his hand when he said that one word. Those five letters made me realize my father-in-law had something up his sleeve.

For some reason, he wanted me to take his car. But why? It couldn't just be for taxes. There were lots of other, better ways to avoid paying taxes. Maybe he planned to put a tracker on the car so he knew where I was at all times? Well, not me necessarily, but the kid. Or maybe he planned on reporting it stolen so I'd get arrested and he could point his finger and tell Masha, "I told you so."

Whatever his reasons, I had no intention of taking the damn car. I was finally acting like a man, dammit! I had my own business, and eventually, I was going to provide for my family with that business!

Standing up, I puffed out my chest and proudly told him no one last time.

Then, with a smile on my face, I blew out the candle and went downstairs to my office.

The business application lay front and center on my desk. I picked it up to throw it away and felt a sting as the paper slid across my thumb, slicing it open. Another little 'screw you' from the kid, I thought, as I sucked on the wound.

With the application out of the way, my notes from the phone call with Grady lay on the table, reminding me that we had a job.

A genius idea struck. I could call Lou and ask for her and Sam's help! No, wait, her evil daughter had stuck the poor old woman in the mental hospital and put a watch on her house.

Okay, no big deal. We could handle this by ourselves. It was just a poltergeist. Although it could just be mice in the walls or something. Even if it turned out to be a real ghost, well, we'd figure it out. After all, we were the Poltergeist- ah, dammit, we were the Polterguys.

With perfect timing, Ghost's giant feet let me know that he and Masha were home. The sound reverberated through the mostly-empty basement, drumming back and forth until I wanted to scream. Pushing my chair away from the table, a loud creak made me pause.

Carefully, I stood and examined my seat. Everything was where it should be. I shrugged and went to check the weather before heading upstairs. Thunder cracked, making me jump and giving me my answer. A pale band of grayish-blue in the distance gave me hope that maybe the rain would be done soon.

A creepy, someone-is-watching feeling settled over me once again and I took a step back. Shaking off the goosebumps, I deliberately turned, putting my back to the door and standing there as proof I couldn't be scared away.

For a second, I entertained the notion of dropping my pants and giving my imagined stalker a show but stopped myself. The old Ed would have acted that way. The new Ed, well, I was a respectable business owner. Instead of mooning my voyeur, I settled for a little twitch of my ass as I walked away. Yeah, I know, kind of a juvenile thing to do, but it made me feel better.

Upstairs, things were feeling normal again. Masha and Ghost were sitting at the table drinking the last of the coffee I'd made earlier, and thankfully,

Boris had gone back to work. Or home. Whatever, he'd left, and that was all that mattered.

Masha gave me a smile and asked, "Good nap?"

I walked around to where she sat and dropped a kiss on her forehead. "Very good. I ate too much."

My wife beamed. "I make dinner soon."

"No!" I immediately felt terrible for yelling it as loud as I did, and the feeling multiplied tenfold when her face fell. "Masha, honey, I have to get to work. Why don't you make yourself something, and I'll grab a sandwich before I go."

The kid started sucking up to his mother like he was a Hoover. "I'm so sorry we can't stay for dinner, Mama. Maybe you could make something tomorrow if we don't have a job?"

The beam came back to my wife's face as she wrapped a hand around his neck and pulled him close enough to touch foreheads. "You are good boy, Alvin. Go to work. I make sandwiches for my men."

While Masha headed into the kitchen to make some – hopefully – edible sandwiches, I went to put my shoes on. When I came back into the dining room, Masha was alone, except for a giant bag.

Already winded from the trip up to the bedroom for shoes, I suddenly remembered my most important tool. Breathing heavily, I huffed, "I forgot my EMF meter."

I headed downstairs to the basement. Whose bright idea was it to buy a house with three floors? Oh, right. That would be me.

Resting my hands on my desk to try and catch my breath, I searched the top of my nearly-empty table. Nothing. Okay, I needed to backtrack. At least that gave me another second to catch my breath.

I remembered handing the meter to Ghost when we were at Lou's house, who gave it back to me in the car. Where did the damn thing go after that? I closed my eyes and pictured sitting in the driver's seat. Nothing.

Then I remembered sliding something into my shirt pocket.

Trying to race up the stairs and only managing a slow, breathless plod, I wheezed at Masha as I reached the dining room, "Honey, have you seen my EMF meter? It was in my shirt pocket this morning!"

Putting my hands on my knees, I concentrated on getting air into my lungs. I should probably put some of that exercise equipment in the basement to use. At least walk on the treadmill. Next chance I got, I promised myself, knowing I was a big, fat liar.

I could barely hear Masha's response over my respiratory distress. "What is E-M-thing?"

I sucked in a deep breath and called back, "It's a little black box with buttons and lights!"

"Oh! That! I threw in trash." Closing my eyes, I counted to three before asking, "Which trash can? And is it still in the house? I need that, Masha, honey. It's not trash, it's for my work."

"I took trash to curb before rain started."

Slowly walking into the kitchen, deliberately ignoring the gleaming new microwave on the countertop, I gently asked, "Masha, sweetie, did the trash run yet?" She shrugged at me, glancing out the window before looking down at her lap.

Shit, shit, shit.

The rain was still coming down in buckets. Ghost appeared in the kitchen just as I opened the back door.

"D- Hey, Ed! Where are you going? You leaving without me?"

"Ask your mother," I grumbled, as I plunged into the pouring rain.

After three steps, I could have soaped myself up and called it a shower. Stumbling my way to the trash dumpster at the curb, I lifted the lid. Empty. Of course.

I stood there, too wet to worry about it anymore as I tried to figure out what to do next. I could order another EMF meter online, but it would take a few days to get it.

"Okay," I announced to the empty street. "We fake it. Grady doesn't exactly sound like a Mensa candidate anyway."

I slogged my way back into the house, accidentally finding a couple of puddles on the way, and opened the door just in time to hear Masha call out, "No water on floor!"

The rain running down my face grew warmer, and it occurred to me that I might be crying a little as I stripped down to my damp tighty whiteys, bundling the rest of my clothing into a dripping ball that I clamped under my arm. Then promptly dropped.

After picking up my scattered clothes, twin grins greeted me when I entered the kitchen in my underwear. The kid's beaming face reminded me again of how much he resembled that actor – the one in all the movies. What the hell was that guy's name?

My soaked, mostly-naked body shivered like a frightened chihuahua as I stood there in my wet shorts, and I decided I really didn't give a flying fig who he reminded me of. The mother-and-son smiles were getting on my nerves, anyway.

Grumbling, I stomped wetly past the pair of grinning fools, not caring if my bare feet left puddles on the freshly mopped floor. *Alvin* could mop again for all I cared, I thought sourly as I continued my tantrum up the stairs and to the bedroom.

With clean, dry clothes and shoes, and my mood slightly elevated, I sauntered back down the stairs and into the kitchen, where Masha and Alvin greeted me with their annoying, cat-ate-the-canary smiles that irritated me all over again.

"What's so funny," I demanded as I stomped across the wet floor, slipping and almost falling on one of my own wet footprints.

"Masha is funny," my wife declared.

I took a deep breath and counted to three. I would have counted to ten but waiting that long to answer a Russian hausfrau is never a good idea.

"Masha honey, what's so funny?" I laced the words with as much saccharine as possible, trying to keep the petulance out of my voice and mostly succeeding.

Pulling something from her lap, she set my EMF meter on the table. The one I went out into the pouring rain to find. Trying my best to smile and only managing to push one side of my mouth up into the forced position, I slowly asked, "You had it all along?"

"Masha is funny, yes?"

My smile – which hadn't been much of a smile to start with – slipped a little more, and I turned away, reminding myself that I loved her, despite her decidedly unfunny jokes.

"Yes, sweetheart, Masha is a very funny woman." Keeping my fake smile firmly in place, I walked around and kissed her cheek, picking up the meter as I did.

Carefully thinking about the best way to phrase the words to hide my anger, I came up with, "I have to go, my love. Work calls."

I think she snorted when I said 'work', but then Ghost opened the door, and the rain drumming against the concrete steps made it easier to convince myself that she called out words of encouragement instead. With a quick flap of the hand, I darted out the door and to my car.

Chapter 11

Ghost, with his long legs, easily beat me to the Pacer, pulling frantically on the locked door. "Seriously, dude? Why do you bother locking this POS? It's not like anyone's gonna steal it!"

Without answering, I slid into the unlocked driver's side. I considered leaving him in the rain as punishment for not letting me in on his mother's joke, but honestly, as much as I didn't want to admit it, I was kind of enjoying the time with the kid. I unlocked the door. Well, I might have leaned over to the passenger side and yelled, "Ed is funny, yes?" through the closed window first.

While Ghost folded his long – wet - legs into the car, I started the motor. For once, my baby fired right up, although she groaned like an old man getting out of bed in the morning. Mentally promising my sweet ride an overhaul as soon as financially possible, I pulled out of the driveway, Ghost directing the way with his phone magic as we parted the night sky with somewhat-bright headlights.

"This is it," he finally announced. I pulled into the driveway and stared out into the downpour. Looked like we were getting wet again.

With a sigh, I grabbed the door handle, trying to ready myself for the second shower of the day. "Come on, kid, let's do this."

We rushed through the drizzle and onto the sagging front porch. The slight pressure of my knuckles on the door pushed the flimsy wood open a few inches. Pulling my hand back, I called through the open door, "Hello? Grady?"

A groan came out of the darkness. I needed to make a choice – either enter the dark house to check on our client or retreat and call the cops. Since I wasn't exactly in good favor with the police, by way of Riley James, I decided that bringing them into the picture probably wouldn't do me any good and might even wind up landing me in jail.

We were going in.

Fumbling for the flashlight I'd shoved into my pants pocket, I pulled it out and turned it on. A dark, paneled hallway with nothing but more darkness at the end made my butt clench a little. Of course, that's when the flashlight decided to flicker and go out. Because that's how all the best horror movies start, amiright?

Another low groan floated toward us, adding to the sense that we were in a low-grade monster flick – one that had zero budget for special effects. Summoning up my courage, I smacked the flashlight against my leg. The stupid thing left a sore spot where it landed and stayed dark. Okay, we were going to have to do this the hard way.

"Al- Ghost – dammit, I wish you'd pick one name and stick with it!"

"Mama will never call me anything but Alvin. She's the only one allowed to call me by that name, dude."

Running my hand across the dry paneling on the wall, I stepped into the darkness, feeling a splinter wedge itself under the nail of my index finger almost immediately.

"Dammit!" The pain under my fingernail made me want to scream. The splinter must have been the size of a stick because the whole end of my finger throbbed along with my heartbeat.

"Dude! What's wrong?" Ghost asked, his voice trembling a little. His fright actually made me feel a little better. Parental protectiveness washed over me, surprising me with its intensity, and I felt my nerves settle.

"Nothing a bright light won't fix. Feel for a wall switch, will ya?" I calmly coached as I tried to yank the massive branch out from under my nail. I took another step forward, using my elbow to keep in contact with the wall, and shuffling my feet along the carpeted floor, just in case there were any surprises down there.

"Okay, boss," came the sarcastic reply. I shook my head at how quickly his fear had evaporated into mockery.

Gingerly taking another step, screaming internally that every bad horror movie ever started exactly like this, and half expecting to feel an ax splitting my head in two at any second, I wondered why I'd chosen this profession.

Then I remembered. I was a loser with no marketable skills and a spotty job history. This was my last chance to do something with my life, and maybe help a few people along the way. Oh, and the money. Definitely the money.

Ghost whispered, "Dude, where you at? I can't see you."

Before I could answer, a spider web wrapped itself around my head, encasing me in sturdy strings that didn't help the fright aspect of the situation. The occupant of said domicile bit my cheek, and I yelled in surprise. Frantically brushing at the sticky web, its owner, and anything belonging to him, I smacked myself in the face with the dead flashlight.

Ghost yelped, "What was that? Dude, you're kinda freakin' me out here."

"Spider," I answered, breathless from exertion. I really needed to start working out.

Just then, a bright light drenched the hallway, blinding me.

"Uh, can I help you?"

The sound of a shotgun being racked closely followed the words of the dark figure outlined in the doorway. Good grief, was I the only person in town without a gun?

"Wait! Don't shoot! Are you Grady?"

"Uh, yeah. You Ed?"

"Yes! And this is my step-son – er, my business partner – Ghost."

"You're uh, late."

Spitting the last of the cobweb out of my mouth, I stepped into the light, Ghost right on my heels.

It was obvious at first sight that Grady worked manual labor. Large, calloused hands, with nails either worn or bitten down to the quick, protruded from the ragged sleeves of a thin flannel shirt. The faded flannel held evidence of more than a few meals on the front. Our client had jowls a bulldog would be proud of, swinging freely whenever he moved his head, and the purplish stains beneath his eyes were so prominent that I had a hard time looking up the scant distance to his eyes to see what color they were.

Settling himself down at the kitchen table, shotgun propped casually next to him, Grady picked up the book he'd tented on the table and gently inserted a bookmark into the pages. The marker immediately jerked itself out of the book and flew across the room like a cardboard bullet.

The book followed a millisecond later. Grady, his face the color of watermelon meat, threw his work-hardened hands into the air. "This is what I'm uh, talking about," he complained. "I uh, I can't do anything without this stupid uh, ghost, messing with me. He's the one that turned out the lights while uh, I was tryin' to read."

Ghost stood in the doorway of the kitchen, looking around the room with interest. "Dude, you gotta admit, that's kinda cool."

Grady gave him a dirty look. "It's uh, not nearly as cool as uh, you might think. In fact, it's uh, kind of annoying after a while."

Patting my pockets for something to write on, I realized I'd not only left my paper at home, but I'd left the EMF meter in the car. I directed Ghost to get it and asked Grady for a piece of paper.

"You don't seem very uh, organized," he responded, but he rose and crossed the kitchen, coming back with a crumpled piece of paper and a stub of a pencil.

"I promise, I'm much more organized than I look," I said while crossing my fingers behind my back to negate the lie. "It's just that this has been a rough day."

Not bothering to respond, my new customer stared at his book lying on the floor. 'Ghost Hunting for Dummies' blared the black letters across the front of the bright yellow book, and I made a mental note to pick up my own copy.

Ready to hear his story, I held pen over paper and remembering what the guys on my favorite ghost hunting shows always asked, asked, "So, can you tell me a little about what's going on? Has this entity harmed you in any way? Scratches? Are you waking up with bruises in the mornings? Anything like that?"

Grady shook his head. "Uh, none of that. But last night, I found a message he uh, left for me."

I heard Ghost's footsteps as he squeaked back into the room with wet shoes. "Dude! That's awesome! Where is it?"

Grady looked uncomfortable. "I uh, I was gonna leave it for you to see, but uh, he wrote it with uh, cereal and uh, I ate it, but I can uh, I can tell you what it said."

This guy had more uhs than a lying politician, but I tried to ignore them as best I could. After all, this was a – hopefully – paying customer. I put on my game face and continued.

"What did it say, Grady?"

"It said, uh, it said 'Leave while you uh, can.' Just like that."

Ghost asked, "It even said uh in the message?"

"Uh, what?"

"You said the message said leave while you uh, can. Is that word for word? Did the poltergeist use the word uh?"

"Uh... I don't know what you're talking about."

Ghost tried a different tactic, "Okay, can you tell us again what the message said?"

Grady furrowed his brow to think. "The message said, uh, leave while you uh, can."

I interrupted the fascinating conversation to say, "Okay, so the poltergeist told you to leave."

"Uh, yeah. I don't know why. I uh, I never done anything to bother it."

I jotted down the message and asked, "So, is this the only message you've received from him?"

Grady looked a little guilty when he answered, "Well, uh, there was sorta something' else. I uh, I think it was a message."

Ghost started wandering around the kitchen, and I did my best to stay focused on the man in front of me. Trying not to be annoyed with his partial answers, I asked, "What makes you think that?"

Grady stood, gesturing for me to follow him. I shot a look at Ghost, who looked like he'd been turned loose in an electronics store and told he could have whatever he wanted. While Grady led me out of the kitchen and into a bedroom, the kid started opening cabinet doors like he might find hidden treasure inside.

The bedroom barely qualified as one. Threadbare, dirt-colored carpet covered the floor. Bare of furniture but for a twin-sized bed and a small, metal stand with an old television sitting sadly on top, it epitomized the life of a man without a woman in his life. In fact, it kind of reminded me of my old digs before I started living in my car.

A dirty Star Wars comforter hung over the edge of the bed, Darth Vader's rumpled eyes glaring at nothing in particular. A Sports Illustrated calendar from 1996 hung on the paneled wall where the headboard should have been, the dust-covered model of August smiling out from her perfect world of sand and water.

As I looked for a message in the grimy little room, Grady cleared his throat and pointed up. On the yellowed, stained ceiling, faint letters were visible over the bed.

'GET OUT', they spelled, and I couldn't suppress the little shiver that ran down the length of my spine.

Written in a slightly darker yellow than the ceiling, the words were the color of tar that collects when a chain-smoker sits in one place to consume their coffin nails.

As I stared at the words, trying to figure out what they were written with, something touched my neck.

I spun around to glare at Grady, ready to snap at him for touching me, but he wasn't anywhere around. I turned back to where I'd started, certain it had to be some kind of sick joke and the guy would pop out of the closet yelling, "Uh, surprise!"

A cold finger touched the other side of my neck, and I jerked my head that direction. There was nothing there, but I thought I heard a faint chuckle on the air, the sound coming from everywhere and nowhere at once. Goosebumps broke out on my skin.

Fumbling for the EMF meter, I pressed the power button and stared at the blazing lights. Well, it worked, but what was I supposed to do with the information? Someone – well, I guess I should say some*thing* – smacked my hand, and my meter flew across the room, hitting the wall before bouncing onto the floor. With a squawk, the little box split into two pieces, leaving nothing but electronic components and a little speaker exposed to air that rapidly dropped in temperature.

The coldness went through me, my body suddenly filled with a trapped-in-a-frozen-maze-for-days kind of frigidness that left me unable to move.

"Wha—" The partial word was all I managed to force through numb lips. My ice-filled body began moving on its own, as though I were Charlie McCarthy with a hand up my ass. As hard as I tried, the messages I kept sending to my limbs were being intercepted as the body that suddenly felt foreign kept stiffly moving.

I could see out of my eyes, but my soul – my Ed-ness –didn't have control anymore. I'd been locked away inside my own body as someone else took over. Helplessly, I watched my own foot stomp my precious EMF meter.

I heard – through ears that weren't mine anymore - my own voice as my body walked into the kitchen after smashing the meter, even as I tried to resist the force controlling me.

"Hello? Where is everyone?" My mouth called out the question calmly, but there was something wrong with my voice.

My words had a strange tone, almost formal-sounding. If I hadn't done that television commercial recently, I probably wouldn't have noticed, but it definitely sounded like someone else as I unintentionally said, "Grady, sir, how many times must I tell you that you need to leave this house?"

Grady stared at me, his mouth hanging open like a Venus flytrap waiting for its next meal, and my mouth grinned back at him. I felt the muscles surrounding my lips widen into the smile, felt my cheeks bunch up into little happy apples, but as hard as I tried to yell out from inside my trapped body, nothing happened.

My head swung around, giving me vertigo as the room spun. My sight landed on Ghost, who stood frozen, his mouth agape in a similar fashion to Grady's. My mouth spoke again, "And you, young man, get out of my cabinets! You are all intruders in my home, and I need you to leave now."

Ghost cleared his throat and weakly asked, "Ed? Dude..."

I tried to answer the kid, but the entity possessing my body answered for me, "Ed isn't here right now. If you'd like to leave a message, please wait for the beep. In the meantime, you may call me Mr. Smith."

Grady looked terrified, and as I saw him looking around the room, I remembered the shotgun. Mr. Smith must have been able to read my thoughts, because he calmly said, "Grady, you aren't going to shoot the innocent man inside my new body, are you?"

Ghost looked like he might bolt at any second. Mr. Smith turned our gaze to him and said, "Young man, I can assure you that your father is fine inside this body. I've just taken – temporary possession – of it. Although I have to admit that it *is* rather nice to feel flesh again, rather than the empty feeling of being a bodyless spirit destined to live in this house for all eternity."

Glowering, Ghost muttered, "Dude, he's not my dad."

Grady backed up against the kitchen counter, clearly out of his head with panic. His ghost now had a face – mine. I felt it settle into a bemused look as Mr. Smith said, "Now, Grady, let's chat. Perhaps I should try politeness this time, since frightening you hasn't seemed to work."

Moving my body closer and trapping Grady against the countertop, I watched the poor man's mouth open and close like a fish out of water as Mr. Smith continued, "Sir, you are occupying my house. Squatting, if you will. I hereby request that you leave, move, disappear – whatever word suits you best. The sooner the better. I am tired of haunting you. If you would kindly remove yourself from my home so I can get back to residing in peace, I would most certainly appreciate it."

Ghost chose that moment to play ghostbuster. Tapping my – our – shoulder to get Mr. Smith's attention, he intoned, "Go into the light, dude."

The spirit turned my body around and I saw what Ghost was trying to do. Holding his phone up, the flashlight app turned on, he pointed the beam toward the ceiling. Inside my head, I rolled my eyes.

The real ghost laughed. I felt my stomach spasm as he guffawed, "You've seen too many movies. I can choose if and when I want to go to the otherworld. Trust me, I'm not going to heaven if I leave this place. I much prefer to stay right here in my little house."

He cocked one of my eyebrows and asked, "And really, must you say dude so much? It's quite annoying."

Okay, I agreed with Mr. Smith on that one. Ghost did overuse the word dude a lot, and it could get a little annoying, but hey! *I* was the dad here – sort of – and he had no business lecturing my kid.

Mr. Smith had gone and pissed me off.

Fury took over and drove me to take my body back. Too stunned to do anything before, I began pushing the issue, and I felt his hold on me begin to loosen a little. Using all the determination I could muster, I began trying to shove him out.

Of course, he fought back, struggling to keep control, but I had a secret weapon. I was married to a stubborn Russian woman. I knew how to get my way when I really, really wanted to.

Since he still had control of my mouth, I needed to improvise. Thinking as loud as I could, I began singing in our – *my* - head.

'John Jacob Jingleheimer Schmidt. His name is my name too!
Whenever we go walking down the street the people say,
There goes John Jacob Jingleheimer Schmidt.'

Over and over and over, I sang the annoying little song. Have I mentioned that I'm tone deaf?

By the fifth round, my hands were pressing against my ears. By the seventh, Mr. Smith started screaming, using my vocal cords, the bastard. "Stop it! I command you to stop!"

By the tenth time I finished butchering the little ditty, I felt the ghost's hold slipping a little more. I used the opportunity to finish shoving him out, using every cell in my body to regain control. I only knew he was gone when I felt my body flush with heat, and I suddenly understood my grandmother's complaints of hot flashes so many years ago.

The effort of pushing Mr. Smith out of my body used every bit of my mental and physical capacity, and I collapsed into a mushy pile on the floor when he fled. I might have even passed out for a second, because when I opened my eyes, I saw Ghost and Grady both hovering over me, their eyes wild with fear.

"He's alive!" Ghost crowed the words when he saw me looking at him, throwing up a hand for a high five from Grady. Our customer half-heartedly returned the gesture, looking at me with pure fear in his eyes.

"Is it really you? Or is he still in there?"

Huh. Looked like fear had fixed his little speech impediment. I gave him a tired grin.

"It's me. I shoved him out. Turns out ghosts don't like it when I sing."

"Du- uh, Ed, I tried to get him to go into the light, but he wouldn't do it."

Sitting up, I explained how I'd seen and heard everything.

Ghost nodded sagely, "We should start keeping a file with facts like that. It could come in handy. You know, in case one of us gets possessed again."

Shakily rubbing a hand over my face, I said, "I hope that never happens, but you're right. We definitely need to start keeping some kind of record."

Grady asked, "What about me? What about Mr. Smith? Did you get rid of him?"

Ghost helped me to my feet as I answered, "Grady, he's determined to stay in this house. I can't force him out. My advice is for you to find a new place to live."

Holding a thin finger over his equally thin lips, Ghost thoughtfully asked, "Wait, how did you say you forced him out of your body?"

I began singing, "John Jacob Jingleheimer Schmidt." I squinted my eyes, knowing how bad it sounded.

A crash came from the other room. Grady rushed to check out the damage, coming back with a dejected look on his already long face.

"He knocked over my television."

Ghost grinned, "Dude, sing it again."

Turning to Grady, I gave him my broadest smile and said, "If you have any valuables you don't want broken, I advise you to gather them up now and take them out of the house."

While he scurried around gathering things, I began lustily belting out the words, off-key.

More crashes came from different parts of the house, including one I'm pretty sure might have been Grady dropping one of the 'treasures' he was trying to save. Lights flickered, small appliances turned themselves on and off again, and through it all, I kept singing. Or at least something approximating singing.

I finally stopped when Ghost held up a finger, slowly turning to point at the cereal box on the countertop. After knocking itself over, spilling generic O's over the counter, the cereal began arranging itself into words.

"Please stop," the message said.

Like a conductor, Ghost's finger came down, the signal for me to start again, and I let it all out, making several dogs in the neighborhood howl in response.

The refrigerator began to shake, jostling across the floor until it reached the end of its power cord. Ghost found a screwdriver, and waved it around like a conductor's baton as he joined in singing, "His name is my name toooooo..."

The floor trembled so hard that my voice took on a new vibrato, the walls shook hard enough to make bits of plaster fall from the ceiling, and finally, just as my voice began to crack with the strain of singing so loud, an inhuman screech filled the house.

I clapped my hands over my ears and kept singing. Ghost grinned and did the same. The screech went on so long I expected to see blood covering my hands when I finally took them away from my ears, but I kept belting out the annoying little ditty.

A new sound joined in the fracas and I turned to see what the hell was going on. Grady stood in the doorway, arms full of belongings, mouth open and a hopeful look on his face as he began singing, a surprisingly operatic tone emerging from the open mouth.

"Whenever we go walking down the street the people say..."

"There goes John Jacob Jingleheimer Schmidt!"

Together, we scream/sang the last line as the cereal on the counter rearranged itself one last time.

Ghost cut off the music with a slash of the screwdriver and stepped over to look at the counter.

The cereal now read, "You win. Hell has to be better than this."

Eyes wide with wonder, Ghost asked, "Dude, did it really work?"

Our personal little Ouija board didn't move.

I grinned. "I don't think Mr. Smith's refined tastes could take our choice of song." Turning to Grady, I said, "I think that should do it. If he does come back, you know how to get rid of him now. Let's talk money."

Later, in the car, I passed half the cash over to Ghost. "Here, you've earned yourself a new video game, or whatever it is you kids buy nowadays."

The money disappeared faster than a politician's promises after election day. The kid definitely took after his mom in that respect.

"Dude," Ghost drawled, "what made you think of singing that song?"

I shot a bemused look his way as I started the car. "Don't you remember? That's what I used to sing to get you out of the room when you were younger, and I wanted some alone time with your mom."

"Dude, that's so gross."

Yawning, the kid leaned back against the seat and closed his eyes, humming the stupid song while he drifted off to sleep. I wondered if maybe I'd damaged his psyche somehow by telling him my little secret, but it was too late now.

I drove home on wet streets hypnotically glistening with evenly-spaced streetlights, hearing John Jacob Jingleheimer Schmidt playing in my head over and over. By the time I pulled into the driveway, I felt some sympathy for Mr. Smith.

The earworm wouldn't go away, no matter what I did, and I could still hear it in my head as I crawled into bed next to Masha, hoping sleep would remove it once and for all.

Chapter 12

Nope. I woke up with the stupid song still bouncing around inside my head. I glanced over at the clock on the nightstand. Almost two a.m. I snuggled a little closer to Masha, hoping maybe the movement would wake her up too, but she let out a snore and rolled over. Damn. She took one of her sleeping pills. For a split second, I toyed with the notion of going ahead and—

No, she would kill me if I tried. Or worse, she would tell her father, who would *literally* kill me with his big stick.

With a sigh, I rolled out of bed and padded through the silent house, stopping in the kitchen long enough to make a ham sandwich before quietly making my way down to the basement.

I flipped on the television, smacking the side to clear the fuzziness away just as my commercial came on the air. I shoved the last of the sandwich in my mouth as it finished playing, my mouth still crammed full of bread and meat when the phone rang.

I snatched up the phone and tried to speak. "Polthergith Guyth," I forced out around the food. That's when I realized I was going to choke. Strangling, I coughed out, "Hol' pleath."

I thought I heard something, but it might have been my own mewl of distress coming from the lack of breath. Coughing and gasping for air, I finally cleared my throat enough to rasp out, "I meant to say Polterguys. Are you still there?"

"Still here," the familiar-sounding voice whispered. "I can't stay on here long. If they catch me, they'll restrain me in my bed."

"Lou?"

The old woman started crying. "You gotta get me out of here, Ed. This is terrible! They're tryin' to medicate Sam away. I can't call my sons 'cause Riley's told 'em I'm nuts. I'm not crazy, you know I'm not!"

103

I had no idea what to tell Lou. I doubt if she knew about her daughter bribing me or that she'd personally called the chief of police to keep me away, but dammit, I liked the old woman, and she was right: I knew she wasn't crazy.

"What do you want me to do, Lou? I don't have any kind of legal authority to get you out of there."

Her whisper amplified, and I knew she must have been cupping the speaker with her hands.

"Listen, Ed. I found a security loophole. I can get myself outta here, but I need someone ta meet me and take me home."

"See, Lou, that's the thing. You daughter Riley? She kind of put a watch on your house. The cops are just waiting for me to show up. I talked to one yesterday morning."

The anger in her voice made her forget to whisper for a moment, "Don't you worry none about Riley. I'll take care o' her meddlin' ways, all right. Just meet me at the twenty-four-hour pharmacy up the road from this crazy house, okay? We'll figure it out after I get outta this joint."

"Okay, Lou, but I hope you've got the money to bail me out when they toss me in jail."

Dryly, she whispered, "I'll handle that. Just come'n get me, Ed. Please?"

How could I resist an old woman begging for help? "I can be there in fifteen minutes," I sighed.

"Make it thirty," she commanded. "I gotta do something 'fore I go."

"What's so important?" I asked, but the phone clicked in my ear.

I called Ghosty_boy69 and woke him up. "Feel up to going on a rescue mission?"

"Dude...give me five minutes."

I felt bad waking up the kid, but I needed his help. The cops were watching for me and my Pacer, but they wouldn't be looking for a kid driving his mother's pink Mercedes. Masha's car stood out, but nothing like mine did.

Sneaking back up the stairs and into the bedroom, I slipped on some tennis shoes, only pausing once when Masha groaned in her sleep. Hopefully, her pill would keep her knocked out until we made it home with her car because there would be hell to pay if she discovered it missing.

Just in case, I left a note next to the coffee pot, letting her know that a friend needed a ride home from the hospital and that I borrowed her car because mine wouldn't start.

I didn't *completely* lie in the note, just- fudged the truth a bit. I *was* bringing a friend home from the hospital, and odds were good my Pacer wouldn't start at any given time. Hopefully, she wouldn't be too mad if we were late getting back with her prized car.

I was trying to pick up her keys without jingling them when Ghost came into the room, rubbing the sleep out of his eyes.

"Dude, who needs to be rescued in the middle of the night?"

I clamped the keys in my hand and gestured him outside. Once we were inside the luxury car with soundproofing, I said, "We're breaking Lou out of the mental hospital."

Ghost's eyes lit up. Or maybe I saw the idiot lights reflecting in them when I started the car. Either way, he clapped his hands like a little kid seeing a circus for the first time, making me laugh.

"Dude! I'm glad you asked me to help you with this stuff. I haven't had this much fun in ages! Let's go rescue the old woman!"

The smile on his face as we passed under a streetlight reminded me of that actor again, the one that starred in – nope. Gone again. Why couldn't I think of his name?"

It should've only taken a few minutes to get to the pharmacy, and I outlined the simple plan as we drove toward our meeting spot. When we left the parking lot, Ghost would take over driving while Lou and I hid. He could park on the next street over from her place, and we would sneak through the backyard and into her house that way.

Easy peasy, right?

I felt pretty confident until a fire truck passed us, wailing and lighting up the night. That's about the time I caught my first whiff of smoke and felt the first tendril of uneasiness. As we drove a little closer to the pharmacy, the smell grew stronger and the night sky began to take on a strange hue. My stomach began to churn.

One last turn, and suddenly, we were facing a wall of color. Red, blue, and white flashing lights surrounded huge columns of yellowish-orange flames shooting up into the night sky. My gut echoed the chaos outside, and I felt like throwing up.

I'd planned on driving past the hospital on my way to the pharmacy, just to see if anything looked amiss. I thought maybe I'd see a few security guards with flashlights searching the grounds for a missing patient, not a blazing building surrounded by every emergency vehicle in town.

Shivering patients wrapped in blankets watched from the manicured lawn like they were giant moths drawn to the biggest lightbulb in town. I had no clue if Lou had managed to escape the fire or not, but the kid threw a whole new perspective on the scene with a single question.

"Holy shit," Ghost breathed out the words. "Did Lou do this?"

Cutting a hard left onto a side street - which didn't feel hard at all in the Mercedes, by the way - I answered, "I don't know. She said she needed to do something, but I thought she had to find her purse or her shoes, not set the damn place on fire."

Even the smaller side streets were strobed with the emergency lights as we drove through neighborhoods, weaving around pajama-clad residents who stood gawking in the streets. After what felt like an eternity, we finally came out at the cross street leading to the pharmacy.

As I pulled into the parking lot, a small figure darted in front of us, and I slammed on the brakes. Lou's pale face paused in the wash of the headlight's beams, then she was gone again, disappearing into the shadows of an alley beside the building.

Throwing the car in park, I left it running as I jumped out and went after her. The old woman could move pretty quick for her age, and my breath was coming in spurts by the time I found her. Adding 'workout' – again - to my mental list of things to start doing, I breathlessly called her name.

"Ed?" Her answer was faint and tremulous.

"Lou! Come on, let's go! There's cops everywhere!"

"Tell me about it," she grumbled, but her voice was closer when she asked, "You ain't gonna turn me in for that fire, are ya?"

"So, it *was* you?"

Still hidden in the shadows, the old woman barked, "You callin' me a firebug, boy?"

"No! I mean...*did* you do it?"

She finally crept close enough that I could see the gleam of her eyes in the dim glow of the parking lot lights. "Nope. Now, come on, let's get outta here." I wasn't so sure I believed her, but what could I do? The old woman would never survive jail time.

We'd rounded the corner of the building when I saw a cop cruising through the parking lot. "Wait," I whispered as I held my hand on her shoulder. The cop car stopped next to the Mercedes.

"No time," she whispered back. "Follow my lead."

Clutching my arm, she dragged me out of the shadows and toward the door of the pharmacy. Chattering loudly, she directed her voice toward the cop car with the open window.

"If you'd remembered to buy cat food like I asked you to, we wouldn't be in this mess. Poor Fluffy hasn't had a thing to eat since yesterday morning. What kind of son doesn't do the one thing his mother asks him to do? You're a disappointment, Levi. Why can't you be more like your brother the doctor?"

Impromptu conversations weren't my thing, so I trudged along behind Lou without saying a word, keeping my head bent to avoid being recognized. As soon as the entrance door slid shut behind us, the old woman stopped and peered between two giant signs covering the glass wall on the front of the store.

"It worked!" Clapping her hands, she stopped when she spotted the clerk coming our way, putting on a sour look quicker than I could say 'What the hell?'.

As the clerk neared, he asked, "May I help you find something?"

Pointing at me, Lou blustered, "My son here forgot to buy cat food, and now poor Fluffy is just wailing with hunger. Have you got any kibble?"

Outside, the police car lit up, the siren piercing the night – not to mention my head. As the clerk turned to see what all the fuss in the parking lot was about, I gave Lou a horrified look. We were busted. Plain and simple. Ghost let his nerves get the best of him, he told the cops we were in here, and now I was going to get thrown in jail and Boris would leave me there, and I never told the kid where the money was at so he could bail me out, not to mention the fact that he couldn't get a bail bondsman because he wasn't eighteen yet—

The cop car screeched out of the parking lot.

I thought I might faint right there in the middle of the pharmacy, but Lou grabbed my hand and started dragging me along as she followed the clerk to the pet food aisle. As soon as we reached it, she examined the shelves and announced loudly, "This won't do! This won't do at all!"

The clerk, who had been trying to sneak away from the crazy old woman looking for cat food in the middle of the night, paused at the end of the aisle and turned around. "Ma'am?"

"Don't you have any of the Purr-fect Cat Food brand? It's the only thing Fluffy will eat."

The clerk sighed wearily, probably disappointed he couldn't go back to his book, or his video game, or his nap.

"No, ma'am. What you see on the shelves is what we have."

Stomping her little foot, she glared up at me. "You'll just have to take me somewhere that carries it then, Levi. Come on, let's go. Really, can't you at least *try* to be more like your brother the doctor?"

I looked up from the spot on the floor I'd been focusing on to see the clerk giving me a look of pity. Shrugging my shoulders, I dropped my gaze back down and followed Lou's feet as she led me out of the store.

As soon as I managed to get her installed in the back seat of the Mercedes, she let out a whoop of joy. "That was fun!" She leaned forward and ruffled Ghost's hair.

He grinned, reaching a long arm over the seat for a high five. "Dude, that was awesome! I could hear you all the way over here when you were yelling at Ed. That cop totally bought it!"

Swinging the hand still in the air, she popped him lightly on top of the head. "Young man, how many times do I have to tell you that I am *not* a dude?"

"Sorry, Mrs. Woodall," he answered contritely. The words stunned me. That- that couldn't be *respect* in Ghost's voice, could it? I'd never heard it before- well, except when he talked to his mother or grandfather. This was turning into the craziest night of my life.

"Can you drive this thing?" Lou grinned as she asked.

"Du- uh, yeah, I can!"

I cinched my seat belt as tight as it would go when Ghost screamed out of the parking lot in his mother's luxury car. I might have muttered a little prayer that he didn't wreck it.

With the kid driving like we were in the Indy 500, we made it to Lou's house in record time. Luckily for us, every cop in town must have been at the fire, the one Lou assured me repeatedly that she didn't start.

Parking a street over from her house, we stealthily made our way through backyards, setting off security lights and dogs as we went. Hopefully, the cop assigned to watch her house was at the fire, too, because we were making enough noise to wake the dead.

Lou paused next to the steps leading up to the back door, stooping over and lifting a rock from the ground. A pill bottle hung from the bottom of the realistic-looking stone.

Ghost sucked in a breath and let it out with a "Whoa, that's cool, dude-uh, sorry, Mrs. Woodall."

Without remarking on the 'dude', she handed the rock/bottle combination to him. "It was my son Martin's idea. Open it. Arthritis is acting up. There's a key inside. And stop with the Mrs. Woodall stuff. Makes me feel old. Call me Lou." Ghost quickly opened the bottle and dumped the key into her waiting hand.

"I'll have to open the door," she remarked as she climbed the concrete steps. "There's a trick to this ol' thing. You have to jiggle, jiggle, turn, push." In the time it took her to tell us about the lock's idiosyncrasies, she had the door open and was inside the kitchen.

"Don't turn any lights on," I warned. "If there's still a cop posted outside, he'll see it."

I heard Lou cackle from across the room, "Honey, I've lived in this house for almost forty years. I don't need lights."

Not nearly as familiar with the surroundings, I was attempting to feel my way through the dark kitchen when I heard a crash from the other room.

"Lou! Mrs. Woodall! Are you okay?"

"Dammit, Sam! I'm here, okay? Quit breakin' my stuff!" The shout floated back to us from the far side of the house and Ghost let out a chuckle.

I couldn't bring myself to laugh, though. As soon as the cops realized Lou wasn't among the patients of the hospital, they were going to come looking for her, thanks to her daughter's connections, and this would be the first place they looked. We needed to get out quickly, or we would be right back in the same position we were in before. Worse, actually, because I would be in jail, unable to help Lou escape from her demon daughter's plans.

A door closed, and I heard mumbling coming from the other side of the house. The longer she took, the bigger the pins and needles grew as I waited for a knock on the front door. If the neighbors heard Lou talking to Sam—

With one eye on the window, I called out quietly, "Lou? We gotta go. You're not safe here. And neither are we, for that matter."

The small figure slipped back into the room, startling the crap out of me when I heard her voice coming from beside me, "I can't go without Sam."

Remembering the way Mr. Smith had invaded my body so easily, and how helpless I felt under his control, I shivered. "No. No way. Sam stays. You can come back after you've worked things out with your daughter."

Lou glared, her eyes shining up at me in the moonlight, "How long've you been married, Mr. Ward?"

The glowing eyes disappeared, and the sound of hissing gas preceded the blink of a tiny light. The tip of a cigarette glowed. She inhaled, then blew out the smoke with an almost orgasmic sigh.

"Five years."

"Do you love her?"

I shot a glance at Ghost, who stood in the shadows of the room, silently waiting to hear my answer.

"Of course, I love her!" Ghost shuffled his feet, and I thought I caught a glimpse of white teeth.

"Would you leave her alone, with no idea if – or when – you might be coming back?"

Aw, dammit. The old woman had a point.

"Fine," I sighed. "He can take over my body. But only until you can call Riley and work this out. And he has to promise to leave when I tell him to."

The glow of the cigarette grew brighter, then dimmed, and I swear I saw a Cheshire Cat smile hanging in the darkness.

Lou coughed out a laugh and said, "Let me finish this cigarette first. Sam hates it when I smoke."

A nasty thought occurred to me. "Lou, were you smoking earlier at the hospital?"

A cloud of smoke suddenly encircled my head, making me cough and giving me my answer – not to mention a few cravings I thought were long dead.

Ghost spoke quietly from somewhere in the darkness. "Dude, let me do it. Let Sam possess me."

"What? No. No way. You know what your mother would do to me if she found out?"

Ghost came out of the corner, his lanky form materializing like a real ghost.

"Look," he said earnestly, "You're gonna need to talk to the daughter, right? Right? So what if Sam went with you when you talked to her? What if some strange dude could tell her stuff about her dad that only she would know? Wouldn't that convince her?"

I wasn't so sure mere words would be enough to convince the hard-headed woman. The last time we'd met, she'd been more concerned with her husband's political career than with her own mother's welfare, but really, what other option did we have?

Lou's voice piped up through another cloud of smoke. "He's right, y'know. It's gonna take more than just your word to convince Riley. She's just like her daddy - mule-headed." She raised her voice, "Yes, Sam! They're talkin' about who's gonna let ya in! Be patient, ya mouthy old man!"

The wail of a siren grew until the sound drowned out any more conversation. Red and blue lights swept through the windows, strobing us with cold vision, and the three of us froze in place until the emergency vehicle disappeared into the night again.

"We gotta get out of here," I muttered, knowing that arguing with her would just keep us there longer, increasing the danger of being caught. "If we're gonna do this, we need to do it now. Tell him to get inside Ghost, and we'll go back to my office. I'll call Riley as soon as it's light."

Lou yelled, "Ya hear that, Sam? Get inta the tall one!"

Ghost gleefully chirped, "Dude, this is gonna be—" and then his voice changed, the timbre deepening and the tempo speeding up as he playfully called out, "Lou, baby, I'm back! Give Daddy a kiss!"

The old woman dropped her cigarette and rushed across the room, wrapping Ghost up in a hug. "Sam, y'old perv! I ain't kissin' no kid to get to ya!" Ghost wrapped his arms around her and lifted her off the floor in an enthusiastic embrace.

My stomach quivered at the thought that they might kiss. Would it be considered kiddy porn if they did? Child abuse? Ghost wasn't going to be eighteen for a few more weeks. Either way, I didn't want to see the two locking lips.

Clearing my throat, I said, "Okay, lovebirds. Let's get a move on. We need to get Masha's car back before daylight, and we've got to get out of this house before the cops show up looking for you."

Lou yelled, "Sam, grab my bag, would ya?"

Ghost grinned down at her, "I can hear you just fine with this young'uns ears, darlin'. No need to yell." Keeping one hand entwined with hers, he crossed the room and picked up the suitcase.

I could barely wrap my head around the fact that Ghost wasn't Ghost. Or Alvin wasn't Alvin. Alvin/Ghost had become Sam. Sort of. It was going to be a confusing day, to say the least. Stepping on the still-smoldering cigarette, I ground it out under my heel, my suspicions that Lou started the fire by smoking increasing as the embers under my foot disappeared.

The lovebirds were murmuring sweet nothings to each other and it was starting to gross me out a little. "Hey, Lou, don't forget that the kid is just seventeen. Don't do anything, you know, dumb."

Two sets of glares turned to stare at me.

"Young man," Ghost/Sam bellowed. "Don't you ever call my wife dumb again, or I'll be forced to take you outside and teach you a lesson in manners."

"Okay, okay, just- hush! The neighbors will hear you. Come on, the car is this way."

Feeling a little like a third wheel – or maybe a pimp - as I listened to the pair giggling in the backseat like they were teenagers again with their hormones in high drive, I drove us home, grateful that Masha had taken her sleeping pill before going to bed.

The sky was turning pink as I pulled into the driveway, and to my delight, Masha's car sat alone on the pavement. My hopes rose at the thought that we might get Lou and Sam into the basement without getting caught when a familiar navy-blue Cadillac glided to a stop behind the Mercedes. Boris. Shit.

Frantic, I turned to face my passengers, "Gh- uh, Sam, can you let Ghost do the talking for a minute?"

With a grin, he answered, "Dude! This is so cool! It's like having someone else—"

"No time," I interrupted him. "Your Ded is here. Don't mention anything about Sam, or we're dead meat." At least, one of us would be, and I was pretty sure it would be me hanging from a hook in a freezer.

Boris strolled up to the car, his ever-present walking stick banging out his approach. Opening the car door, I stepped out to greet him.

"Morning, Boris."

Ignoring me, he turned to Ghost and held his arms out for a hug, stick hovering in the air. Ghost obliged, warmly saying, "Ded, I'd like you to meet Lou, our client."

Boris swept his gaze over the woman with a look I didn't like. At all. Taking her hand, he raised it to his bent head, kissing the back gently as he said, "Is goot to meet you. Very goot. I am Boris. Alvin is taking care of you, yes?"

"Oh, *Alvin* is taking very good care of me," she piped with a grin, trying to pull her hand out of his without being rude. Ghost had a strange look on his face, and as he glared at Boris with pure hatred, I realized Sam had taken control of their shared body.

Oh, shit. This was *not* going to go well. Ghost's hands were clenched into fists. With Sam's anger issues, we weren't going to survive the morning unless I managed to defuse the situation.

Shit, shit, shit.

Chapter 13

"Alvin!" I hissed, hoping Sam would get the hint when he heard the kid's name, but the angry visage stayed firmly put. Darting a look up at the kid, Lou quickly jerked her hand out of Boris' and laid it on Ghost's forearm. The glare faded at her touch, and by the time Boris turned around to look at his grandson, the familiar dopy look of the big kid had replaced Sam's furious one.

Lou sounded just like her daughter when she asked, "Let's go inside, shall we?"

The whole situation was out of whack, with no one acting like themselves, including me. My head whirled as I tried to avoid stepping on any landmines.

Boris put his hand on Lou's elbow and started guiding her up the steps to the house. "I see you have wedding ring. You are married, yes?"

Primly, she answered, "I am widowed."

Boris smiled warmly at the answer, and I almost fell over. He was flirting! This couldn't be the same man who spent every morning at my house, could it? Maybe he was human after all.

"Boris is widower, too." I gulped at his response and shot a look over to see how well Sam took the remark.

Ghost's face changed again, flaming deep purple in the pinkish/gray light of the dawn sky. I grabbed his arm and held him back. Standing on my tiptoes in order to reach his ear, or as close to it as I could get, anyway, I wrapped a hand around his neck and pulled his head down so I could hiss, "I'm not going to let anything happen, Sam. Calm down."

He glowered for a moment longer at the pair walking in front of us. The sensation of seeing two people inhabiting the same body was nothing short of insane as I watched the angry face melt back into that of a happy, carefree teenager.

"Maybe we never left the nuthouse," I muttered. "Maybe Masha checked me in, too, and that explains everything."

Except somehow, I knew the insanity surrounding me might be my life from now on. A life I brought upon myself by deciding to start a business chasing fake ghosts that had turned out to be real.

And here we were, at my house, with my step-son possessed by the dead husband of the woman currently being hit on by my father-in-law, the possibly mob-related Russian who hated me, who was about to get attacked by his grandson, who just happened to be possessed by said woman's husband. Nope. Not crazy at all. Fuck.

I was on high alert as we entered the house, trying to keep track of any and all interactions between the three - no, wait - four people. I needed a nap. Or a drink. Or three.

Boris refused to leave Lou's side, peppering her with questions about everything from her background to her preference in perfumes. Ghost – no, Alvin - wait, Sam! It was getting confusing with two personalities and a spirit to contend with. Sam kept shooting death glares out of Ghost/Alvin's eyes as Boris continued to hit on his wife.

To complicate matters, Masha woke up and stumbled into the kitchen, blearily glaring at us. Have I mentioned that my wife isn't really a morning person? Until she's had her coffee, she's a real joy to be around. Alvin and I have learned to stay out of her way until we hear the clink of her cup hitting the sink, at which time she's somewhat her normal, cranky self.

I do love my wife, but part of the reason we've managed to stay married so long is that I've learned when to stay out of her way. Trust me when I say that you don't want a Russian woman mad at you. You might wake up in the hospital, or you might not wake up at all.

Masha narrowed her eyes and sent a piercing look around the room, her voice husky with sleep – which made it sound all the more frightening - as she asked Lou, "Who are you?"

Lou opened her mouth to speak, but Boris answered before she could say a word, "This is Lou! She is new friend to Boris and customer to Alvin." Okay, technically, she was *my* client, but I decided to keep my mouth shut. Pick your battles and all that.

Masha's eyes narrowed even more, and her lips thinned to match. Sam did the same thing in Alvin's body. We were going to have a full-out wrestling match in a second if I couldn't come up with a way to divert it. Except I couldn't think of anything. It felt like I was drowning, my lungs full of water and my head blankly bobbing in imaginary waves. I stared helplessly at the scene playing out in front of me until I realized how I could solve all my problems at once.

"Masha, honey, I took your car out last night, and I think I might have scratched the paint a little," I said the words as loud as I could without yelling, just enough to get the attention of everyone in the room.

With a furious screech that sounded like a hawk bearing down on its prey, Masha began screaming endearments at me in Russian, her father joining in and completely forgetting about his new love interest. Lou sat wide-eyed and still at the table while my wife and her father stormed outside to see the damage.

Waving a hand at my guest – guests? - I urgently whispered, "Come on, they'll be back in a second!"

Lou hurriedly stood and made her way over to me, followed by Gho- Alv- dammit! - Sam.

Rushing Lou over to the basement steps, I heard Masha and Boris coming back inside, still grumbling in Russian. I eased the basement door shut as quietly as I could, flipped the light switch on, and gestured Lou down the rickety steps.

"Did you really wreck her car?" Lou whispered the question as we carefully made our way down and over to my office.

"Nah," I casually threw the word out there. "But it got their attention off you. And Sam. Speaking of which—" I turned to Ghost/Alvin/Sam. "You promised you would let Alvin take over in front of his family. You have to stop throwing dirty looks at Boris."

Alvin's body pointed a finger in my face, but the words coming out of his mouth were definitely Sam's, "You listen here, young man, if you think I'm going to let that Commie hit on my wife—"

I could feel my temper rising. I tried to be polite, but before I could stop myself, I hissed, "First of all, Commie is incredibly racist. Second of all- you're dead, Sam! Lou has every right to date if she wants to, although—"

Lou broke in, both hands held up in the air as she tried to defuse the argument, "Listen up, boys, none o'this is doin' us any good. Sam, you're my one and only love. I got no interest in that man upstairs, so just get on over your macho bullshit. Ed, I 'ppreciate everything you're doin' for me, but I think the sooner we get holda Riley and get this situation taken care of, the better."

The room went silent long enough for me to hear Masha and Boris still speaking heatedly in Russian upstairs. Hopefully, they didn't actually find anything wrong with the car, or I was going to have to move down here.

Running my hands through my hair, I said, "Okay, okay, you're right. Here's what we're gonna do. Lou, go call your daughter. No, wait! If you call her from my phone, she'll know where you are, and she'll send the cops to arrest me. I'm going to have to go buy a burner phone."

Behind me, I heard, "Dude! I got this! Hang on!" He pounded up the stairs, slammed a few doors that, incredibly, stopped the shouting up there, and pounded back down a minute later. Shoving a small flip phone at me, he said, "Here, use this one."

Narrowing my eyes, I asked, "What is this? Alvin, are you selling drugs? No one needs a burner phone unless they're selling drugs."

Rolling his own eyes back at me, the kid flipped me off. "Dude, you watched Breaking Bad, didn't you? I'm not a fucking idiot. I don't do drugs, and I don't sell them."

Hoarsely, I whispered, "Then why do you need a second phone? Huh? And- *language*!"

To my surprise, Ghost laughed. "Dude, I'm a hacker. I use burner phones for when I need an anonymous phone number."

Feeling slightly – but only just – mollified, I didn't bother apologizing. That's the parental thing to do, right? Instead, I made a mental note to ask someone what a hacker was and handed the phone to Lou.

"Here, call Riley. Let's get this settled."

"Maybe I should talk to her," said Sam.

"NO!" Lou and I both shouted the word together like we'd been practicing for a chorus.

Putting a hand on Ghost's arm, Lou explained, "Sam, honey, you know how Riley is. She's not gonna believe either one of us. She's got her mind made up, and that's just the way it is. So, here's what we're gonna do..."

Drawing us all closer, the old woman explained how we would handle her headstrong daughter.

My stomach fluttered when I heard Riley's phone start ringing. I had no desire to talk to Mrs. James again, but I liked Lou, and for her, I would do it.

Ever have one of those epic psychic moments where you feel the future unfolding in front of you before it actually happens? A kind of reverse déjà vu?

That's how I felt when Lou's daughter answered the phone. I felt every emotion, every word, a split second before I heard them. I knew Riley would screech with happiness when she found out her mom made it out of the hospital safely, then let out a burst of anger immediately after. I knew she would demand to know where Lou was hiding, and whether she started the fire or not.

I knew my name would come up, and then the subject of the money would be next. The money I hadn't told Lou about yet.

To be fair, in all the excitement, I kind of forgot about it.

So when Lou turned around and glared at me, her daughter's screeching rivaling that of Masha's when she thought I damaged her car, I felt like the world's biggest heel. I held my hands up in self-defense, the only defense I could come up with as I backed slowly away from the furious, silent woman holding the phone and the seething voice coming from the receiver.

Ghost grabbed my arm, and Sam asked, "What did you do? Why are they so angry? I can't hear what they're saying."

"I- I- I forgot. I forgot Riley gave me money to stay away from Lou. But then Lou called, and the fire, and the cops, and you, and- I just forgot!"

Surprisingly, Sam didn't sound mad when he asked, "How much?"

Still in my confused state, I had no idea what the question meant. "How much what?"

"How much did Riley give you?"

"I – I never counted it, and she didn't say. Just shoved the envelope at me. Sam, I swear, I tried to give it back to her."

The old man inside the teenager's body laughed, which confused me more than ever.

"Let me explain the dynamics of women to you, Ed." Sitting down on the staircase, he patted the riser next to him. "Sit. They'll be on the phone for a while."

Feeling awkward taking orders from Ghost, even though I knew it was Sam driving his body, I gingerly sat down next to him, wondering just exactly what he wanted to tell me.

"Listen, young man, one thing I've learned in all my years of being married is not to get between a mother and daughter when they're fighting." Waving his hands over the teen's body, he continued, "You're lucky. This fine young specimen will never have the kind of strife with his mother that those two women right there have." I wasn't so sure about that, but I let it go as he continued lecturing.

Nodding at Lou, who stood with her back to us, he said, "You see, those women are just alike, right down to the way they brush their teeth in the mornings. They don't see it, because they like to think they're different, but they are identical in spirit."

The confusion in my head wasn't clearing up any. What the hell did the mother and daughter fight have to do with the money?

I finally managed to choke out, "I don't- I don't understand."

"They're each tryin' to protect the other. Lou called you because she wanted proof I was real. See, I haven't shown the kids I'm back, not because I'm afraid of scarin' them, like Lou told ya, but because of what it might do to Randall's run for mayor. Lou don't agree, said they need to know so Riley's got all the facts and can defend herself against the accusations that her mama's crazy. See? Tryin' to protect her baby. Of course, Riley, not knowing I'm back, thinks you're taking advantage of her mama, so she tried to pay you off to protect Lou."

"Wait, are you trying to tell me that you set this whole thing up? That you knew all this would happen?"

Ghost's familiar grin popped onto his face, and I had just enough time to realize his eyes looked different as Sam said, "I ain't admittin' nothing. I will say that that dang fire was a stroke of genius, although it got outta hand."

"You convinced Lou to call me when you saw the ad. You *knew* Riley would send Lou to the hospital when she told someone else about you. And you knew Riley would try to keep it under wraps because of her husband running for mayor."

Sam sat silently, smiling while he waited for me to put the rest together.

I mulled what little I knew over and over in my head. Why was it so important for Riley to give me money? Why did Lou need to be out of the house? What did Sam know that Lou didn't?

As Lou finished up her shouting match and hung up the phone, a thought popped into my head. It couldn't be that simple, could it? I looked over at Ghost/Sam and the gleam of satisfaction in his eyes and suddenly knew without a doubt that I was right.

"I was already tryin' to find ways to get her – and hopefully me along with her – out of the house. Since I died, she's been coopin' herself up, not going anywhere or doing much of anything besides puttering around with those old figurines she's got stacked everywhere."

As Lou started coming our way, anger oozing out of every orifice on her tiny body, he dropped his voice to a whisper, "Just play along, okay? You like Lou, I know you do, or you wouldn't've rushed out in the middle of the night to save her. So save her from herself. Give her something to do, a reason to live."

Lou stormed up to stand in front of us and asked, "Riley gave you money? Where is it?" I stood up, sidling my way out of arm's reach. I'm not going to lie, even though the woman barely reached my shoulder and only weighed about a hundred pounds soaking wet, I was a little afraid of what she might do to me.

"I'll get it. I didn't touch it, Lou. I didn't even count it. I swear I was going to give it to you."

"Just give me the damn money," she snapped.

I heard Ghost/Sam speaking to her quietly as I made my way over to the heater vent where I'd stashed the envelope. Snatches of conversation floated my way, although I couldn't make out what they were saying.

Yanking the vent cover off, I immediately dropped it on my foot when something landed on my head and scurried in circles, pulling out a few strands of what little hair I had left as it looked for an escape route.

"Yaaaah!" I'm not sure whether the scream was for the pain in my foot or the giant rat on my head, but either way, my hands went up while my body went down, my teeth clacking together as I hit the concrete floor. Clutching my hair, the rat went along for the ride.

Ignoring the pain while frantically brushing at my head, I felt the rodent jump onto my arm and my eyes involuntarily closed. I didn't want to meet its beady little eyes, couldn't stand the thought of seeing the monstrous little vermin with its germs and bacteria all over it.

The weight of the feet barreling down my bare arm told me the thing must be a full-grown rat, one that would do some serious damage when the inevitable bite came. The bite that would send me to the hospital for rabies or maybe worse.

I swatted blindly, hoping for some kind of Jedi magic trick to help me knock it away. I could hear faint laughter coming from the area of the stairs, making me redouble my efforts to get rid of the giant rat that would most likely drag me away and eat me while they laughed and pointed. What did they know? They were safe and sound on the other side of the room, next to the escape route.

Something touched my shoulder and I screamed again, jerking myself away so hard that I fell over and hit my head on the floor. When the stars cleared, I finally opened my eyes to see Ghost standing over me.

"Dude, you scream like a girl," he laughed, and with one of the freakiest things I've ever heard, the laughter changed, and Sam chuckled, "You really do."

Breathing heavily, I felt my head for blood while looking around for the mutant rat, but it was nowhere to be seen.

Lou appeared next to Ghost. "Are you okay? I know it's startling when a baby mouse jumps out at you. One time when we first moved into our house—"

I interrupted her trip down memory lane, asserting stiffly, "That was *not* a baby mouse. It was a rat. A giant rat. I think it bit me."

The two (three?) of them burst into laughter again as Ghost held out his hand. A baby mouse sat shivering in the center of his palm, staring up at the three of us – or four of us, whatever – in fear.

Before I could stop myself, I snapped, "Well, do something with it then. Don't wait for Mama Rat to come out to take him back! And while you're at it, grab the envelope out of there." Crossly, I gave my head one last rub and hauled myself to my feet. I needed a drink.

While Lou and Sam pulled the money out of the envelope and started counting, I headed for one of the only other hiding spots I had in the house – a cardboard box with a picture resembling my car on the side.

Masha hated my Pacer and hated when I worked on my baby even more, so when I'd ordered a new alternator for her, I stashed the empty box and began using it to hide a few things I treasured in there.

I knew Masha wouldn't open the box for fear of getting grease on her hands, so honestly, the mostly-empty box sat on a dusty shelf against the wall, hidden in plain sight. Lifting the flaps, I pulled out an equally mostly-empty bottle of Jack and took a swig.

Fire burned its way down my throat and into my belly. Hot breath burned my neck. I turned to see Ghost/Sam leaning over my shoulder, eyes gleaming with desire.

"Is that- is that whiskey?" Sam almost panted with want as he eyed the bottle. I started to hand it to him, but then remembered he was in the kid's body.

"I'm not giving this to you!" Visions of being beaten bloody, Boris smiling triumphantly while standing over me with his stick, flashed through my head. Or worse – the image of Lou cradling her shotgun as she stood over my bullet-riddled corpse. "You're in the body of a teenager!"

As I glared into his eyes, I saw them change color – just a little, but enough for me to understand that my step-son was speaking.

"Dude," Ghost laughed. "I've had alcohol before. I'm not a nerd."

"Oh yeah? Good to know. I'll be sure to monitor your breath from now on."

The face turned sullen as he muttered, "You're not my fucking dad, Ed. Quit trying to act like you are. Just give the old man a drink. I'll chew a piece of gum or something before Mama and Ded see me."

My face settled into an obstinate mask. "Language. And yeah, I know I'm not your dad, *Alvin*, but I'm the closest thing you've got besides your Ded. And I'm not going to be the one that gives an underage kid alcohol. Riley is looking for any reason to ship me off to jail to get me away from Lou. You think giving my seventeen-year-old step-son whiskey won't get me tossed? I know you can hear me in there, Sam, and you know I'm right."

The eyes changed color again. Just a few shades from hazel to green, but Sam was back, his face sad. "I understand. Maybe another time."

Lou made her way over when she heard the ruckus and stood there silently listening to my lecture.

"Samuel Loren Woodall!"

We froze. That tone- well, you didn't argue with it. Ever. It represented the attitude of a woman so furious that she would just as soon brain you with a cast iron pan as look at you. That tone meant you were in the deepest trouble of your life and arguing might just end it right then and there.

The three names were a way of presenting the rage that resided in a tight little ball inside the female body, a ball with the potential to explode, leaving your guts splattered over the wall and your brain disarticulated into tiny bits of worthless goo.

I knew that tone. I'd heard it from my mother as a kid. I'd heard it from my grandmother as a teenager. I'd even heard it from my own wife over the years. And no matter how many times I heard it, no matter what woman was speaking, it always sent a bolt of pure, icy fear down my spine.

"Are you seriously suggesting that you're willing to compromise the integrity of a teenage boy for your own wants? Is that what you're doing?"

Slowly moving closer, she emphasized each word with the click of her heels on the floor, "I. Will. Send. You. To. The. Afterlife. Myself."

Any man who tells you he isn't afraid of his wife when she's as furious as Lou was is either lying to you or just plain stupid. Sam wasn't a stupid man.

"I'm sorry, sweetheart. I wasn't thinking clearly. Of course, you're right."

I was busy memorizing the phrase that magically calmed Lou down when she said stiffly, "I'm not an idiot, Sam. I don't have time to deal with this right now, but rest assured, this isn't over. When we get home, well, let's just say you may regret decidin' to stick around."

Wisely – again – Sam kept his mouth shut. Lou turned to look at me and I saw a twinkle return to the gray in her eyes. "Well, Ed, looks like you might be the only man here with any sense."

Taking the bottle of whiskey from my hand, she unscrewed the lid, wiped the mouth of the bottle off with the side of her hand, and took a long pull.

She was slightly breathless when she finally recovered from the fireball that hit her. "I rarely drink, Mr. Ward, but Riley can bring the desire to lose my senses in a glass to the forefront in an awful damn hurry."

While the two – three – of us goggled at her, she pulled a pack of cigarettes out of her shirt with a flourish, blatantly watching Sam/Ghost as if daring one of them to say a word while asking in my direction, "Someone give a poor old woman a light?"

I patted my pockets, even though I knew without looking that I didn't have a lighter. I'd quit smoking right after I'd married Masha – not completely willingly, but I wanted to make my new bride happy, and seeing her face scrunch up in disgust every time I lit one had seemed a good enough reason to quit at the time. Now, however, as I looked for a light for Lou, the agonizing desire to smoke along with her struck me for the first time in years.

Hazel eyes momentarily met mine as Ghost pulled a lighter out of his pocket and lit the old woman's cigarette. I started to ask what he needed a lighter for, but before I could, Lou started recounting her conversation with Riley.

"I didn't tell her where I was hidin', but I think she knew. Mosta my friends are either dead or in a nursin' home, and this is really the only place I coulda gone."

She took a drag off the cigarette and blew the smoke my way. The addiction pangs grew stronger.

"Anyway, I managed to convince her not t'call the cops. Least, not yet. Instead, I'm gonna meet her at a coffee shop, and you, Mr. Ward, are gonna go with me, along with your sidekick here."

I glanced over to see Sam's green eyes gleaming with satisfaction. I couldn't really blame him. Who among us would be content living as a ghost, stuck in the same four walls for eternity? Who could sit by and watch as their wife slowly lost her zeal for life before your very eyes?

I thought about how I would feel if I could only watch Masha from a distance, never able to touch her, not able to feel her warm body next to mine ever again, interacting with an invisible division of worlds between us until she died. I wouldn't want to see her dead. I would want her to go out, see the world, and be happy.

So, yeah, I understood. I made a couple of decisions right then and there. Lou and Sam were going to be a part of my life in some fashion. We could work out the hows later. I would be more attentive to my wife, try harder to make her happy. And I promised myself I would try and live my life to the fullest. Meanwhile, I turned to Lou and asked, "You got another one of those smokes?"

Without any hesitation, she shot back, "You got more'a that whiskey?"

While Sam glared, we each took another shot and a cigarette to prepare ourselves for the meeting with Riley. I'm not embarrassed to admit it, I needed the whiskey to bolster my nerves.

The cigarette didn't taste nearly as good as I remembered. After coughing and hacking my way through half of it, I finally gave up and dropped my fond memories into the empty whiskey bottle, lightheaded and nauseated.

Lou gave a little jig when we reached the bottom of the stairs, then lost her balance on the first step. With a giggle, she let me set her back to rights, then bounded up the rest of the steps like a white-headed kid. I liked seeing this side of her, and even though Sam/Ghost grumbled with each step he took, he wasn't fooling me. He enjoyed seeing his wife with that sparkle in her eye again.

When we reached the top of the staircase, Masha and Boris were nowhere to be seen. I have to admit, I was a little disappointed. I'd wanted to start my new resolutions right away.

On the bright side, Boris wasn't there to relentlessly hit on Lou, and that made things infinitely easier. I didn't have the time or the energy to deal with Boris' newfound libido and Lou's alcohol-reduced inhibitions, not to mention Sam's jealousy. One devil at a time, and right now, Riley was our target.

We met at the same coffee shop I'd met her at before. She was already sitting at a table, one of those tall pub ones that made her look even more haughty. Dressed to the nines, every hair in place, a ring on her finger that looked like it might be the big brother to the Hope Diamond, she remained every bit the Ice Queen – and I don't mean the Disney version with the happy ending. I wondered how I'd ever thought her beautiful.

The ice on her finger didn't compare to the coldness in her eyes when she saw us come in, though. She gave Lou a pass on the dirty look, although the almost-mayor's wife cringed when she saw her mother stumble and giggle after attempting to skip across the room. Ghost – or maybe Sam – caught her before she fell and gave her his arm for balance.

Riley's lips thinned even more than they already were when she saw Lou lean into Ghost/Sam for support. If she hadn't been wearing the perfectly applied lipstick, I might have thought she didn't have lips at all.

I tried to stand tall as I walked in, but *you* try when laser beams of hatred are shooting at you from a glacier. Resolutely, I made my way over to Riley without curling up into the ball she wanted me in.

"Hey, I'm married to a Russian, your steely gaze doesn't affect me."

That's what I wanted to say, anyway. Instead, I stepped in front of her, held out my hand and politely murmured, "Nice to see you again, Mrs. James."

She finally moved, but it wasn't to reach out for my hand. Instead, she let her eyes drop to where my hand hung in the air waiting, then brought them back up to show me the frozen landscape of her irises. She really was a bitch.

I thought I saw a tiny softening around the Ice Queen's eyes when Lou climbed up into the seat across from her, but I might have been wrong. The frosty voice matched her stare when she stiffly greeted the old woman, "Mother."

Lou grinned foolishly. Drunk on freedom rather than alcohol, she was giddy with happiness. Speaking too loud for the small shop, she said, "What? It's Mother now? You called me Mommy when you were three, called me Mama 'til you were fifteen, then switched to Ma when you heard all your friends callin' me that. I guess I should just be grateful you aren't callin' me Louise."

The words seemed to have their intended effect. Riley dropped her eyes to the coffee cup on the table, caressing the waxed surface like it was a restless child in need of calming. The blood-red nails on her hand matched Lou's, I noticed, and inwardly, I laughed. Sam had hit the nail on the head. Mother and daughter were a lot more alike than either stubborn woman wanted to admit.

When she finally looked back up, some of the iciness had slipped off her face, although the hands gripping the coffee cup tensed until the cardboard almost crumpled under the pressure of her fingers. "Mama," she said, her tone a little softer, "You know how important this mayoral race is to Randall. You can't go burning down hospitals and shouting to the world about ghosts."

Lou sat up a little straighter in her chair. The words from her daughter seemed to have sobered her up. Leaning forward, she snorted, "Because it's all about you, isn't it, Riley Ann? It's always been about you. Never you mind that I'm a widow woman livin' all alone, her kids too busy to come'n see her 'cept at Christmas – and that's only 'cause it's a good photo op for your fancy-dancy Randall! Would it be any wonder if I went a little nuts? Rattlin' around alone in that little house – you remember it, dontcha, Ri? The one you were raised in, the one where we had lotsa laughs and good times? And now it's as empty as a walnut hull tossed to the ground by squirrels, and just as useful."

Riley had the good grace to blush at her mother's words. She took a sip of coffee to avoid looking at Lou. I noticed the cup trembled a little when she set it back down on the table.

"Mama, please—" she started, but Ghost interrupted her. Well, Sam did, but she had no way of knowing that.

"Hey, Pumpkin, do you remember the time I took you out of school early and we went ice skatin' – just the two of us? I made you swear not to tell your mom. Did you ever tell her about that?"

Riley's eyes widened until I could see white all the way around the irises. Her voice shook when she said, "How- I never- how do you know about that?"

Ghost/Sam continued talking as though she hadn't said anything, "How 'bout when I taught you how to ride a bike? You remember that day, dontcha? You cried and said you were never gonna learn, that you weren't even gonna try anymore. Do you remember what I told ya?"

Riley froze again, but this time, it was from fear and astonishment. "You said quitters never win and winners never quit. But how do you know all this? Who are you?"

"Riles, it's me, Daddy."

As the ice began to melt, water started leaking onto her face, and yet she sat in place as though the slightest movement might shatter her frozen body. Her voice fluttered with emotion as she said, "No, you aren't my dad. My dad died. I don't know how you know these things—"

She stopped mid-sentence. I could almost see the thought process change her emotions as her eyes narrowed. Turning to face her mother, she asked accusingly, "*Oh my god*, Mother, did Price Sterling's people pay you to discredit Randall? How much did they pay you? I can't believe you would do this to us!"

Lou sighed and looked over at Ghost/Sam. "I told you she wouldn't believe the truth."

Turning her fury on me, Riley asked, "Or is it you, scamming my mother? You found my dad's journal or something and you're using it to get money from her. Or are you trying to get more money from me? What I gave you wasn't enough? Fine, I'll double it."

I thought about saying something, but honestly, I had no clue what might convince Riley James of the truth. Instead, I stayed silent, watching to see what Lou would do. In response to her daughter's accusations, she primly pulled the envelope out of her purse and slid it across the table. "It's all there," she quietly told her daughter. "All ten thousand."

Ten thousand dollars? Ten grand? And she gave it back? I felt a little sick as I tried not to think about all the things I could buy with that much money. A new starter for the Pacer, a real desk, real business cards!

Before I could start crying at the thought of all the lost money Riley so casually stuffed into her purse, Ghost took the wheel of their shared body, "Dude – uh, sorry, I mean, Mrs. James – I know you don't believe us, but I think I can prove we're telling the truth."

The beautiful face twisted into a haughty sneer, marring any resemblance to her mother. "Oh, you think so, huh? And how exactly do you think you can do that?"

Straight-faced, as formal as I'd ever seen him, I realized the kid wasn't a kid anymore when he said, "By letting your father possess your body for a minute. He's willing, and promises to move right back into my body once you see we're not lying to you."

I wanted to face-palm myself. Such a simple solution, and it took the kid to come up with it. Okay, maybe he *was* earning his part of the money. Oh wait, never mind. We had no money. Well, if we ever earned any more money, I'd be sure to give him his cut.

Riley looked at her mother and the disbelief on her face cut poor Lou like a knife. "Let me see if I've got this straight. You want me to allow my dead father to possess my body so you can prove to me that his ghost is still hanging around and haunting you? Are there some hidden cameras somewhere? I need to be sure they're getting my best side."

Lou gently asked, "What've you got to lose? If we're lyin', nothin' happens. If we're tellin' the truth, well, least you'll know. I'm not tryin' to ruin your husband's political career, Riley. Surely you know that. Please," she pleaded, "for my sake, please say you'll do it."

Riley rolled her eyes so hard I'm pretty sure she caught a glimpse of her brain at the top of the circuit. "Fine," she muttered. "I can't believe I'm agreeing to this. I've never heard of anything so ridiculous in my—"

Once again, the ice queen froze, but this time, her perfectly-made-up lips twisted into a wry smile. Sam spoke through the ruby stain, "I think she believes us now."

Things progressed quickly after that. Sam didn't stay in his daughter's body long, his presence enough to convince her of the truth. As soon as the spirit slipped back into Ghost's body, Riley slumped in her chair and closed her eyes, tears streaming down her face along with the mascara she'd undoubtedly put on with care that morning.

I thought about suggesting she switch to the waterproof mascara that Masha sold, but bit my tongue.

When she finally opened her eyes again, most of her queenly demeanor had disappeared. "Oh, Ma," she cried. "I'm sorry I didn't believe you! I'm sorry I put you in that terrible place!"

Lou smiled, and with the haughty look gone from the daughter's face, the similarity between them reappeared. Reaching across the table, she placed a hand over Riley's trembling one. "I understand," she said quietly. "Took me a while to convince myself I wasn't losin' my mind when your dad first came back."

Relief trickled down my spine. The threat of jail that had been hanging over my head like the sword of Damocles? Gone. At least, I hoped so. I cleared my throat to ask, but Sam beat me to it, "So, Pumpkin, does this mean everything is okay now? No more puttin' your mama in a nut ward or sendin' Ed here to jail?"

I knew how she felt as she looked into Ghost's pimply face and answered her father. "Yes, Daddy, everything is fine. Well, mostly fine."

With a single breath, the insecure woman turned back into a political demon. "I need you all to understand something, though. I can never speak of this to anyone else, and neither can you."

She pronounced 'neither' as 'nyther', giving me another reason to dislike the ice queen act. And it was all an act, I knew that for certain now.

"This race for mayor is very close, and if Randall's opponents find out that I believe my dead father is haunting my mother's home, well, that could look bad – not just on Randall, but on all of us."

With her free hand, she retrieved the envelope from her purse and pushed it toward me. "Keep this. Consider it hush money, if you must, but promise me you won't ever tell a soul about any of this."

Something about her words sounded- off, but I ignored the little voice that kept telling me to push the issue and find out more. Instead, I glanced at Lou, who gave me a tiny nod. Snatching the money off the table, I shoved the envelope into my jacket pocket. "Mrs. James, I give you my word that I won't tell a soul."

What I didn't mention was the fact that I intended to ask Sam and Lou to help me on some jobs. Everybody won. Sam and Lou could get out of the house, I would have a ghost employee – and who could spot a ghost better than another ghost? – and last, but not least, having the unconventional couple on board meant we had an in with some of the elite of the town.

By the time we left the coffee shop, mother and daughter were smiling and holding hands. We watched the pair from the comfort of my car as they hugged goodbye, a smile of satisfaction on Ghost/Sam's face.

"Now, let's talk about the money," Sam said, after the women pulled apart and continued talking. "I want you to hire Lou."

"You read my mind," I laughed.

Sam wasn't laughing when he leaned over the console, eyes still fixed firmly on his wife and daughter.

"You were right earlier when you said Lou has the option to date now that I'm dead, but I want your word that you'll keep that Russian bastard away from her. He's wearin' a skin that don't belong t'him."

"What does that mean – wearing a skin that doesn't belong to him?"

Sam shook his head. "I can't explain any more than that. Just, keep Lou away from him."

As Lou began trotting toward the car, looking ten years younger, I promised, even as my mind raced with possibilities.

But Ghost had undoubtedly heard the conversation.

Shit.

Chapter 14

The lack of sleep the night before had worn me down to my core, and I could barely keep my eyes open on the way home. Despite my exhaustion, I remembered my promise to myself when we walked in and I saw Masha sitting in the kitchen watching her afternoon shows.

I gave her a kiss on the forehead, trying to show my love and affection, but apparently, all I managed to convey was spit. Wiping her forehead angrily, Masha asked suspiciously, "Why you lick Masha?'

"Masha, honey..." the rest of the sentence eluded me. I was simply too tired to explain my newfound philosophy to her. Instead, I stumbled to the bedroom, where I found Boris stretched out across our king-sized bed fast asleep, his stick propped against the wall.

I stared at him for a second while I considered taking his stick and smacking him with it, then shrugged my shoulders and crawled into the bed beside him. In seconds, I relinquished my exhaustion to sleep.

I woke up at ten that night. Masha had replaced her father in the bed, the tinkly little snore that belonged to her alone making me smile. Giving her a quick kiss, I slid out of bed and headed for the shower.

Clean and somewhat awake, I made coffee and got down to business. Carefully making my way down the basement steps to avoid spilling a single drop of the precious coffee, I gave a little sigh when I finally sat down at my desk. I needed a little alone time to think things through, and it looked like I might finally get a few minutes of peace.

The answering machine light kept winking at me like I might buy it a drink, but I ignored the messages. I needed my coffee in blessed silence before I dealt with anything else. A little boost to the psyche, so to speak.

The tick-tick-tick of the water heater, the sound of the air conditioner kicking on – those were the only noises in the house, and that feeling of solace I wanted settled around me as I lifted my mug for that first taste of liquid energy.

The same sip that went all over my desk when Ghost popped out of the shadows and said, "Dude! I've been waiting for you!"

"Alvin! What are you doing down here? You scared the shit out of me, dammit!" I looked frantically for something to wipe spilled coffee off my precious sheets of paper before I remembered we were rich. Sweeping the whole shebang into the trash, I looked at Ghost expectantly, waiting to hear why he felt the need to scare ten years off my life.

The kid just grinned, not even bothering to look ashamed of himself. "I had an awesome idea, dude! We need a website, and who do we know that can make the best one in the world? This guy!" Pointing both thumbs at himself, his grin increased wattage, which only served to irritate me more than I thought possible.

"Why do we need a website?" I pointed at the answering machine blinking away. "We're doing pretty good without one."

With a sigh, Ghost said, "Dude, how long do you think you'll keep getting business from that commercial? It's supposed to run – what, another couple of days? Not to mention the fact that it airs at two in the morning. If we have a website, people can find us twenty-four seven."

I shrugged. "So? Word of mouth is the best way to get new clients. My uncle never once advertised his HVAC business, and he never lacked for customers."

The kid sighed again. "Dude, you are so tech ignorant. Everything is online these days. Everything. You're going to have to move into the twenty-first century. Besides, you won't even have to do anything, I'll handle that part of it."

Crossly, I lifted the mug of coffee again. "Do what you want. I'm going to drink this coffee and answer these messages from *real* people."

Ghost produced his laptop from behind his back with a flourish. "I was just waiting to get the okay from you, dude."

Opening it, he showed me the website that popped onto the screen. "Polterguys" read the giant red letters across the top. "The people to call when something goes bump in the night."

It was impressive. It was perfect. And it pissed me off something terrible. The kid had managed to come up with a perfect website *and* the perfect tagline. It got your attention and held it. Hell, *I* wanted to call the number on the screen.

Dammit.

Grudgingly, I muttered, "It's pretty good, I guess."

Holding his finger over the keyboard, he asked, "Dude, you can't trick me into thinking you don't like it. I've lived with you for five years. I know all your tells."

"My tells?"

"Like in poker. You know, when someone always raises an eyebrow when they have a good hand, or when they subconsciously tap their finger on the table before they fold. Haven't you ever played poker?"

I laughed a little at the kid's enthusiasm. Shaking my head, I asked a question of my own, "In the last five years, have you ever seen a group of men here smoking cigars and drinking beer while we play cards?"

Ghost laughed, and just like that, my irritated state disappeared, and for the first time since I'd met him, it felt like we had a real connection. Maybe this parenting thing wasn't all bad.

With a smile, I gave him the go-ahead to make the website go 'live', whatever that meant.

Still feeling that fatherly emotion, I gave him a stern-ish look and said, "Shouldn't you be in bed? You've got school in the morning."

Ghosty_boy69 rolled his eyes. "Dude, it's Saturday night. There's no school tomorrow." I guess that explained why he'd been able to go with me all day. Maybe I wasn't as good at the parenting thing as I thought.

"Okay, let's see what kind of calls we have tonight." I rubbed my hands together and picked up my pen. Then I remembered I'd tossed all my paper in the trash. I snagged the least coffee-stained one I could find and with a flourish, set it in front of me. With the press of a single button – the most technology I wanted to deal with – a masculine voice filled the air.

"You're a fucking idiot. Suck my—"

I hit the erase button before he could finish.

The next message was slightly better.

"You honestly believe in ghosts? The bible says—"

Erase.

Message three filled the expectant silence with nothing but the sound of someone breathing. We listened to see if anyone ever spoke, but after a full minute of nothing else, I hit erase on that one as well.

Then we hit the jackpot. A feminine voice that sounded like she truly needed help said, "Mr. Ward? I need your help. There's an evil presence in my house."

Now we were cooking with gas! As I tightened my grip on the pen, I heard a giggle. The speaker's voice muffled as if she pulled the phone away from her mouth and she said, "I can't do this! You do it!" She giggled again, then I heard a click as the call disconnected.

I almost didn't listen to the last message. After all, it was most likely the teenage girl's friend calling back. I finally hit play, figuring it would stop the damn blinking light if nothing else.

A deep, masculine voice with the hint of a southern drawl spoke, "Yes, my name is Harrison Harris. Yes, I know it's a strange name, and yes, I've spoken to my parents and they named me that on purpose. Now that we have that out of the way, I'd like to talk to you about an issue I'm having. I don't really feel comfortable talking about it on the phone, so if you could please come to my house, I can pay you mileage on top of your going rates. The address is 545 Wildwood Lane and...aaaaahh...I'll be up all night, so don't worry about waking me."

I'd been so certain the last message would be another crank that I hadn't bothered to pick up my pen. I hit play again, this time ready to take notes. The voice sounded familiar somehow, but I didn't know anyone named Harrison Harris. That's the kind of name you remember, y'know? Shrugging, I jotted down the information and looked at Ghost to see if he was paying attention.

Shades of black and red from the computer screen lit his face, reminding me once again of that actor whose name I couldn't place. You know who I'm talking about, right? The guy who's in all the movies? He was named America's Sexiest Man by People Magazine once, not that I pay attention to that stuff.

His name was right there on the tip of my tongue, and then Ghost coughed. His face changed back to that of a gangly teenage kid with a giant zit on his forehead. Back to square one.

Just to see if he could hear me through the new headphones he wore, I made sure to call him by the hated surname when I asked, "Hey, Alvin, going with me? This one sounds promising."

Pulling one earpiece away from his head, the kid asked, "Dude, you say something?"

"Yeah, I asked if you were going with me."

"Where we goin'? Never mind, I don't care. Let's roll, Holmes."

"Who's Holmes?"

Ghost gave me a sideways look. "Dude, it's nobody. It's like saying 'Bye, Felicia.'"

I furrowed my brow. "Who's Felicia? Who are these people?"

With a tiny shake of his head, Ghost slipped the headphones back over his ears, laughing quietly to himself as he tapped away on his phone. Probably texting his friends to tell them how dumb I was. Oh well, at least I'd been upgraded to stupid. Only a year ago, he'd been telling them I was dead.

Ghost stayed in his little musical world until we were in the car heading out of the city. Pulling the headphone away from his ear, he asked over the noise trumpeting from the earpiece, "Where are we going?"

Keeping my eyes on the street signs as we passed them, I absently answered, "Wildwood Lane."

"Dude! Stop! Pull the car over right now!"

I stomped on the brakes, almost throwing us both into the windshield with the force of the stop. Anti-lock brakes weren't a thing in the seventies, just FYI. Breathing heavily, I asked, "What? What's so important?"

"What's the address on Wildwood Lane?"

"545. Why? What's going on?"

"Dude, don't waste your time. That's another cemetery."

I threw my hands up into the air. Sarcastically, I answered, "*Dude*, our first case was in a cemetery, remember? What makes you think this one's any different?"

Ghost pulled the headphones back and let them rest around his neck. The music stopped suddenly, leaving an uncomfortable void. Leaning across the console, his face lit only by the dash, I could see fear in his eyes.

"Look, Ed, this cemetery- well, we used to come here to party. Please don't tell Mama. The only reason we stopped using this place is because all this weird stuff started happening. I don't mean like the things we've been dealing with this week. I'm talking evil-type stuff. Especially when we were close to one area in particular."

A sneaking suspicion crept through my mind like a cat burglar on the prowl for an unlocked window. "Let me guess – you were near the grave of one Harrison Harris."

Eyes shining like they were lit from within, Ghost nodded fearfully, "How did you know- never mind. Dude, there's some seriously bad stuff going on out there – like demons and shit. I'm talking girls getting felt up when no one else was around, invisible fingers running down your arm – or worse, your spine – and *hearing* things.

Once I walked away to go pee, and I could hear someone whispering in my ear, telling me that my friends were plotting against me and that I should use the shovel leaned against the tree nearby to make them pay. There wasn't anyone else around me. Dude, I would have peed my pants if I didn't already have my junk hanging out.

And the craziest part is that it would all just kind of fade away whenever we'd leave the cemetery, so we'd go right back the next time and it would start all over again. The only reason we finally stopped going out there is because one night I wrote everything down on my phone whenever something crazy happened. When I showed it to the others the next day, it was like somebody turned on a light or something. All of a sudden, we could remember everything, even though every single one of us had completely forgotten it again. Then, when you said the name of the cemetery just now, it all popped back into my head. It's like there's some kind of spell or something that makes you forget what happens when you're there."

The confession gave me chills. Ghost looked away, unwilling – or maybe unable – to meet my eyes after letting me into his fear. The sound from the headphones started up again, then grew louder, and he settled them back over his ears as though the music might drown out his bad memories of the place.

I sat and thought about what he'd said for a minute, trying to decide whether to continue on or not. The rough idle of the Pacer's motor and the faint, rhythmic thump of bass coming through Ghost's headphones kept distracting me, so with a sigh, I put the car in gear and started driving again.

I shot a glance at the kid to see if he was going to say anything else, but he sat stiffly in the passenger seat, staring at the empty road like he expected Harrison Harris to jump out of the darkness and onto the windshield at any second.

I felt bad for him. No matter how well he'd handled himself over the last few days, he was still just seventeen. I didn't blame him for being scared. Hell, *I* was kind of frightened after what he'd just told me, but something kept urging me to keep going.

With the money from Riley James in my pocket, I convinced myself that I could afford to be altruistic – at least, this one time. Besides, the message on the phone had aroused my curiosity. I wanted to figure out why the stranger's voice had sounded so hauntingly familiar. Hauntingly. I giggled a little at the unintended pun. Not because I was nervous. Not at all.

I stopped the car at the gates of the cemetery. Not because I wanted to, but because the gates were closed. Har-de-har. Two good ones in as many minutes and I couldn't even share them with the headphone-wearing kid.

Turning to Ghost, I poked him in the ribs and yelled loud enough for him to hear over the noise he called music, "You can stay here if you want. I'm going to go see what's going on. I want to make sure there's not someone hurt out there."

I saw the kid girding up his loins, so to speak, and he pulled the headphones down before he answered, "Nah, I'm coming. I know the area. I can take you to the spot where we used to party. But dude, I'm warning you, if I see or feel anything like the stuff that used to happen, I'm outta here, and I'm dragging your sorry ass with me."

The bravado he used to hide the fear sent another chill down my spine, and a feeling of dread began to snake its way through my gut. I swallowed hard and tried to keep my tone somewhat normal-sounding when I said, "If you're sure you want to go, then let's do this. The sooner we go, the sooner we get back."

Ghost muttered something as he opened his car door. I think he said, "Famous last words," but I didn't ask him to repeat it. Asking to hear that particular phrase a second time in the setting we were in seemed like it might be asking for trouble.

The double gates were loosely chained together. Ghost squatted under the metal links and slipped his skinny body through the gap without any trouble. Easy peasy. Lying down on the asphalt and rolling over on one side, I put my arms through the gap between the gates and wormed my way forward until my head was through the hole, feeling the metal gates move along with me.

No problemo. I hadn't gained *that* much weight since high school. I could do this! I planted my elbow on the driveway to help pull my weight, wincing at the feel of gravel pushing into the bone, and shoved my heels down against the pavement outside the fence. With a solid push, my chest moved easily through the gap in the gates.

I repositioned my elbow, bent my legs, then dug my heels in and pushed as hard as I could. If the kid could get through, then so could I.

My paunch met the metal bar on the edge of one gate, stopping me with a jerk like I'd hit a speed bump doing eighty. Stuck halfway through, unable to shimmy forward or backward, I felt like a magician's assistant right before he pulls the boxes apart to prove they aren't connected anymore.

I might have started to panic a little as I pictured myself stuck there until I starved.

Common sense disappeared as I frantically, desperately tried to free myself from my self-made trap. I wiggled. I writhed. I pushed, and I pulled. I pushed and pulled at the same time. Nothing changed. Visions of my lifeless body being found and eaten by vermin made me struggle that much harder, but no matter what I tried, nothing worked.

The metal fencing crashed and rang like a death knell each time I moved, like it was building up a crescendo for the fat man's final song.

My shirt worked its way up around my chest, and the skin on both sides of my midsection began to burn from the friction of rubbing against solid metal posts. I stopped to rest, feeling the poles pushing into my skinless gut with each breath.

This was it. This was where I was going to die. The panic receded as acceptance began to take over. I could even picture the headline in the paper: 'Local Man Dies Stuck in Cemetery Gates, Step-son Watches, Clueless'. Wouldn't *that* burn Boris' ass!

Oh, no.

I wasn't about to give Boris the joy of my dying. I had plenty of things to live for, and pissing him off made the number one spot on my top ten list of things that made me happy. I started fighting with the gates again, sucking in my gut and squirming like a snake stuck under a pitchfork.

Ghost whined, "Dude, come on!"

If I could have reached him, I would have smacked him.

Fixing an image in my head of the kid's face disappearing under my fist, I growled, "Shut up and pull."

Ghost grabbed me under my armpits and yanked. I sucked in my gut and shoved my feet against the ground at the same time. The gates pulled taut against the chain as we worked together to free my stomach, and just when I thought I would have to give up and let Boris happily live the rest of his life Ed-free, I popped out of my trap, the metal making enough noise to wake the dead.

While Ghost shook his head and groaned something about his arms hurting, I rubbed my burning belly and stared up at the dark, starless night, relieved to be free of my prison. After a few minutes of catching my breath, I scrambled to my feet, feeling a sense of foreboding like I'd never had before.

Too late. We were here, and I wasn't about to leave.

With nothing but a thin blade of yellow streaming from my flashlight, we stumbled our way around gravestones and over questionable mounds.

I tripped over something once, landing on my ass in the wet grass that was overdue for a cut. I expected the kid to laugh at me, but he just shoved a hand down to help me up. His breath was strained, like he expected zombie hands to start breaching the ground at any second.

I was breathing hard too, but for once, it wasn't from exertion.

The farther we walked into the cemetery, the worse I felt, almost like a morbid déjà vu that only grew as we neared the center of the graveyard.

We kept walking, stumbling over markers and ledgers until Ghost suddenly stopped, grabbing my arm to keep me from moving any farther.

As I played the light over the headstone in front of us, the kid's pointing finger began trembling. His voice shook even harder than the finger when he asked, "Dude, what is *that*?"

At first, I had no idea what he meant. The kid's eyes were sharper than mine, but after a second (and some squinting), I saw it. Behind the gravestone that read 'Harrison Harris – Yes, it's my real name' a black silhouette hovered, a hole darker than the night air surrounding it.

The blackness inhaled every form of life surrounding it, leaching the cells of every living thing near it, and leaving nothing but skeletal husks behind. In return, the form exuded pain and suffering that multiplied tenfold as it grew. I could feel the pull of its magnetism, and I let the light drift toward the ground as I lost the will to examine my end.

Ghost backed up a few steps, and I knew I had to stop him, or he would chew up the grass with his long legs on his way back out of the graveyard. I grabbed his elbow, telling myself it was to keep him from hurting himself, but really because I didn't want to be alone in the dark with the emptiness that radiated malevolence.

"Wait a second," I growled, taking a step back and shaking off the lethargy that filled my body. "Let's find out what it is."

Ghost whimpered, "Dude, can't you feel that? It's pure evil. We gotta go, and *now*."

His words just strengthened my determination. No way was I going to let a kid tell me how to do my job, even though I had no idea how to do it myself. How would I learn, though, if I didn't stick around and figure it out?

I took a step forward, still holding onto the kid's elbow, and called out, "Mr. Harris? It's me, Ed Ward. I believe you called?"

A chilling laugh rang out across the silent cemetery. Before the echoes completely died away, a voice that seemed to come from the center of the blackness responded, "You're quite prompt, Mr. Ward. I do appreciate that quality in a man."

I thought about telling him promptness wasn't exactly one of my best virtues, but the feeling of familiarity swept over me again. Before I could figure out why the voice seemed so - well, familiar - he spoke again, "You don't remember me, do you, Ed? I'm pretty sure your little friend here does, though. Hello again, Alvin."

I heard the kid whimper, but my body refused to let me check on him. Mesmerized, I shook my head at the black hole behind the headstone. Almost as though the voice's owner had the skies under his control, the full moon appeared, and the darkness bled away.

Faster than my eyes could process the transformation, Harrison Harris appeared in front of me. He wore a black pinstripe suit with a blood-red handkerchief folded neatly in the jacket pocket. For some reason, the handkerchief drew my attention, and I stared unblinkingly at it.

"My eyes are up here, Ed," the man laughed gently. The joking tone didn't stop cold fear from crashing through my bones as I wondered just exactly what kind of force we were dealing with.

This guy couldn't be a ghost. Harrison Harris didn't resemble Sam in the least. Sam was just your average bored spirit looking for a little adventure. This guy exuded evil. He could manifest himself without a host body, unlike Sam or Mr. Smith. Did that make him a demon? Or worse, the devil himself?

What had I gotten myself into? When I'd first hatched the idea to start a ghost hunting business, I'd thought I could have a few laughs while setting a couple of mouse traps before declaring the 'haunted' homes spirit-free. I didn't actually *believe* in supernatural beings.

Then, with my very first job, I'd discovered ghosts and goblins and witches were real, and they could be more frightening than anything ever written in a book.

But this- this wasn't like anything I'd encountered in my short time working in the field, and the knowledge that truly malevolent entities existed in our world scared me in a whole new way.

Harrison Harris emanated evil like the devil himself, and I suddenly understood why Ghost had been so frightened at the thought of encountering him again.

When I finally dragged my eyes away from the red handkerchief and looked into the dark eyes above, the magnetism in them drew me forward, even as my brain screamed at me to stay put. This time, it was Ghost's turn to grab my elbow. If he hadn't, I most likely would have walked right into the stranger's arms without any apprehension at all.

Grounded by Ghost's touch, I came back to my senses a little, averting my eyes from the man who smiled so engagingly at me. "Who are you? Why should I remember you? And what do you want?"

I shot the questions at him like bullets from a machine gun. It was the only way to get them out before my throat closed with fear again.

This time when he spoke, the words evoked a fuzzy memory that began to emerge from the depths of my cerebral cortex. An image so deeply hidden that it refused to form completely, no matter how hard I tried to force it into focus.

"Really, Ed? Think about it for a second. It's in there, deep in that reptilian brain you humans are so proud of. If you'll let it come to the surface, you'll remember we used to have some entertaining times, you and me. You don't remember the night we picked up the two sisters at the bar and took them back to my motel room?"

Feeling a little hypnotized, a barrage of drunken images began parading through my head. The bar I used to frequent in my drinking days, the words 'He's Not Here' flashing in red neon behind the counter. Below the sign, the snake tattoos on the bartender's bald head coming alive with color. The smell of stale beer and sawdust. Drinking every night until standing on my feet became impossible, then scream-crying at the bartender from the floor after he cut me off.

Crying into my beer every time someone played the song on the jukebox that reminded me of how inconsequential we all were. Sleeping in my car because my keys went missing, then finding them in my lap when I woke up the next morning, thanks to the snake-headed bartender checking to be sure I was alive and safe as he went home for the night.

The memories kept coming. Hitting on women every night and having drinks flung into my face. Drunkenly stumbling across the dance floor with my mug of beer, the only partner willing to dance with me. Being tossed out of the bar by the unofficial bouncer who got paid in free drinks. Drinking harder to numb the fact that I was all alone in the world, that not a soul on earth cared about me.

Then the images changed, became more upbeat. A new regular began coming in. Harry was as charming and handsome as they came. He wore snazzy suits with a fresh red rose in his jacket pocket every night. And the best part? I finally had a friend who drank as heavily as me. The casual acquaintance bloomed into friendship after seemingly endless nights of drunken confessions and laughter.

The night of getting lucky with my new friend and the two sisters finally appeared in the procession of memories. The night things finally went my way. I was already pleasantly buzzed and chatting with my new friend when two women walked into the bar.

Women who claimed they were sisters and took an unusual interest in the two drunk men who awkwardly tried to flirt by acting like skittery-eyed idiots. Sisters who became friendlier and better-looking as I bought round after round of drinks for the four of us. Laughing at everything and feeling like nothing could stop me.

Once I remembered the night of the two sisters, the images came faster. Drinking in a cheap motel room with no idea how we'd arrived there, the rum tasting stronger and the sisters becoming more affectionate with each cocktail until we broke apart into couples and danced. I remembered falling onto the stained, faded flowers decorating the coverlet on the nearest bed, pulling my 'date' along with me as we proceeded to – what? The images faded away into the blackness born of too much alcohol.

I thought the images were in my head, but when I opened my eyes, I realized they were scrolling across the man's eyes like a bad movie made by an addict. I heard Ghost sigh, "Whoa..."

The realization that the kid could see parts of my life that I didn't particularly want to remember myself brought me out of my daze, and through sheer force of will, I shouted, "Stop it!"

With a single blink, Mr. Harris' eyes changed to a blank darkness that unsettled me more than the pictures had. "You remember me now, don't you, Ed? We had a lot of fun that night. At least, it looked like you were having fun from where I stood."

"You called yourself Harry. Harry- ugh, what was it? Something so corny it had to be true."

Smoothly, he finished, "Harry Angell. I used that one a lot in the eighties and nineties. I had a lot of fun back then."

Pulling up the knees on his perfectly-creased suit pants, he sat/sort of leaned on the gravestone bearing his name. At least, the Harrison Harris name. At that point, his identity seemed to be the least of my problems.

"Now that you remember me – and our fun night together – do you remember what else happened that night? Before the fun started?"

Shaking my head, I thought maybe I *did* remember – and suddenly, I didn't want Ghost around to hear any more.

"Put your headphones on," I commanded. "Or go back to the car. Or both."

Ghost whined, "Dude, it's just getting good! I wanna hear what happened!"

Harrison Harris raised one hand and the kid disappeared.

Panic flooded my body and I yelled, "What did you do with him? Bring him back!"

Sighing, he answered, "Which is it, Ed? You want him here to listen to your sordid tales, or do you want him in the car listening to that racket he calls music? You can't have it both ways, you know. In fact, if I remember right, I've told you that before."

With that, everything came back in a flood of images. I closed my eyes to keep from screaming. Every vivid little detail became as sharp as if I were sitting in that run-down bar again.

My new friend Harry drunkenly pointing out the two women sitting in the corner and betting me he could convince them to come with us for a good time. Meeting them and buying rounds of drinks until we could barely walk, much less perform any 'fun' acts.

The motel room that smelled of cheap air freshener and unhappiness, where we turned on the clock radio and danced like fools – all while continuing to guzzle the rum drinks Harry made from a supply that never seemed to end. Making out with the shorter sister, Cindy, who had become the most beautiful woman in the world. Collapsing into the bed with her and passing out before we could do more than clumsily remove our shirts and laughingly toss them aside.

Then I remembered/saw myself waking up the next morning, the only sound in the room the jungle drums playing in my head. The sisters lay quiet and still beneath the flowered bedspread, and the thought crossed my mind that they were sleeping like the dead before I realized Harry was gone, leaving me alone in a strange motel room with the two women.

I grabbed my shirt and snuck out. I didn't want to be there when they woke up with the same pounding headache as me. I didn't want to engage with women who were still virtual strangers, rehashing foggy events from the night before as we tried to piece together what happened.

But mostly, I didn't want to admit to myself that I was drinking too much and avoiding responsibility.

I caught it on the news that afternoon, from the television behind the bar.

When the next occupant of the Sleep-EZ Motel room entered, he told the police he was just looking for a place to rest his weary head. Instead, he found the bodies of two dead hookers.

The manager on duty presented the motel's logbook to reporters, showing no one registered to Room 6 the day before. He claimed he knew nothing about the women's presence, hurriedly going on to emphasize the motel's safety and cheap prices before the young reporter cut him off.

The news story went on to inform the public that there were no fingerprints in the room other than the women's, no sign of a struggle, and most importantly, no way of telling what caused the women's deaths. It was like they had just entered the room, crawled into the beds, and died.

The reporters called it a mystery.

Except it wasn't.

I went back to the bar again that night, expecting to see Harry, and half-frightened he'd show up. We sat in a booth in the back, our whispered conversation not attracting any attention in the bar full of working men and women. Country music blared over the speakers, giving us that much more of a cloak over our decidedly uncomfortable conversation.

"What the hell happened?" I wasn't really sure I wanted to know the answer, but I had to know at the same time.

Sitting across from me in the booth, my friend's face devoid of all emotion, he blithely answered, "I don't know. They were fine when I left. Did you do something to them?"

"No!" The word came out louder than I meant it to, but no one glanced our way. "I mean, I don't- I wouldn't—"

"You sure about that, Ed?" Harry adjusted the collar of his dress shirt. "I mean, you drank quite a lot. Maybe you did something and just don't remember."

"I would never- I couldn't hurt a woman. How do I know you're telling the truth, and that you didn't—" I whispered the dreaded word, "*kill* them before you left?"

Ever casual, Harry lifted his drink and gave me a little salute with the glass, winked, and said, "You don't."

"We should turn ourselves in." The idea made me sick, and I took a sip of the water I'd ordered. Right then, I didn't care if I ever touched another drop of alcohol.

"You're welcome to turn yourself in if you want, Ed, but I have no intention of doing so. In fact, you might look a little silly when you try to tell the police about your friend who helped you pick up two women in a bar, magically whisked you into an empty motel room with no one noticing and then left you alone with two dead hookers after he disappeared. Do you really want to spend the rest of your life in prison, Ed? Because that's what would happen. Meanwhile, I'll be out here living the high life."

"But- we have to tell them we were there! We can't just walk away from it!"

"Can't we?" He asked the question while flicking away a piece of invisible lint on his perfectly-ironed shirt.

Back in the present, I opened my eyes and stared at Harrison Harris, aka Harry Angell, who wore a look of amusement on his face.

"I think you're refusing to remember the most important part of our conversation that night, Ed."

I closed my eyes again, more to avoid looking into those dark, soulless eyes than to remember.

Back in the bar, Harry smiled at me. "Don't worry, Ed. I can make this go away."

"What- what do you mean?" I wasn't sure I could trust Harry anymore, but I knew I hadn't killed those two women, and the thought of spending the rest of my life in prison for something I didn't do wasn't exactly appealing.

The smile on Harry's face increased and the dark brown of his eyes turned black. My 'friend' leaned over the table as he said, "Consider it a favor. One of these days, I might need a favor from you, and you can repay me then."

"What kind of favor? I'm not sure I'm comfortable with that."

Harry leaned back in his seat and examined his fingernails. "You can't have it both ways, Ed. You can go to prison, or you can forget about all this and repay my kindness sometime. Your choice."

Feeling like I'd been backed into a corner, I agreed. And then, Harry Angell walked out of the bar and out of my life. The mystery of the dead hookers faded away as quickly as he did, and somehow, I forgot about all of it. Until now.

Opening my eyes and daring to look into his, I asked with a sigh, "Okay, Harry. What is it you want from me? And bear in mind – the kid stays out of it."

"Don't worry," he said with a grin as evil as anything I'd ever seen, "It's simple. You just have to deliver a little package for me."

"What kind of package? And why?"

"It's just an envelope. I wouldn't put you in any danger. I mean, nothing like leaving you in a motel room with a couple of dead hookers."

Feeling a lot like a marionette dangling from the ends of the puppet master's strings, I knew with certainty I'd been played – and played well. I didn't know exactly what the end game was in Harry's little scenario, but I had a feeling it wouldn't work out well for me. Even that wouldn't have bothered me so much if it weren't for the fact that it felt like Harry orchestrated the whole thing for his own amusement.

"Well?" He grinned at me after a moment of silence on my end. "What'll it be, boy? Yes or no?" The words brought back a last flashing scene of dancing with Cindy in the motel room, Meatloaf wailing about teenage love while we fumbled and bobbed around the tiny space we laughingly, drunkenly called the dance floor.

But in the present, I was older and sober. A glimmer of an idea formed. Feeling trapped, I figured I had nothing to lose, so I went for it.

"Can I ask you a question first?"

"Sure," Harry said confidently, the certainty of victory in his tone.

"Are you a demon?"

Raising an eyebrow, Harry Angell tipped his head. "Why, Ed, look how smart you are when you're sober. Yes, I am a demon."

"So, are you a Crossroads demon? Like on the television show?"

Harry let out a laugh, a bellow that set dogs howling in the distance. At least, I was hoping they were just plain old dogs. "There's no such thing as a Crossroads Demon, Ed. No, you can think of me as a used car salesman, only

I buy and sell souls instead of lemons. The difference is that with *me*, all sales are final."

I ran a hand over my head, wincing a little at the feel of the thinning hair under my fingertips, then forcing myself to focus. "So, technically then, you have to offer me something in order to ask for something in return."

With a lingering chuckle, Harry asked, "What is it you want, Ed? My protection from life in prison isn't enough for you?"

I waited a second to answer. I wanted to be sure I phrased the words just right, crossing the t's and dotting the i's. Otherwise, the whole thing would be in vain.

Harry grew impatient, tapping one Italian-leather-clad foot as he waited. I let him stew. My ragged old tennis shoes were tiptoeing through a minefield of his making. He could wait as long as I needed him to.

Meanwhile, my mind raced, trying to decide the best way to get out of this. A tiny glow at the perimeter of my vision gave me some small comfort. Ghost, the typical rebellious teenage boy, hadn't stayed in the car but had crept to a spot nearby to watch, despite his fear.

Harry hadn't locked him in the car!

That small mistake proved Harry wasn't infallible, that he *could* screw up, and I felt a small surge of confidence flow through me. The kid's little rebellion might be what saved my life.

Harry was beyond impatient now. His warning sounded ominous when he said, "Ed, I've been patient with you, but really, I have other things to do. There are other souls than yours on the line, and I really need to get back to them."

And just like that, I knew how to reach the other side of the minefield safe and sound.

Shaking my head sadly, I answered, "See, the thing is, Harry, I never asked you for your protection. You *offered*, and I accepted, but since I technically didn't *ask* for the favor, you can't really force me to do something in return. I mean, it's not like we signed a contract or something."

The heat of his anger flowed toward me, and for just a second, I thought maybe I knew what the outer edges of hell felt like.

His voice shifted, changing into a deep, booming, rage-filled tone a normal man would have been afraid of, but after five years of marriage to

Masha, well, I'd grown immune to shouts of anger. After all, my wife was all
threat and no action, and I was pretty sure that without a pact for my soul it
would be the same with him.

"I'm warning you, Ed, it won't be pretty if your DNA turns up in the
evidence box for those women!"

His face finally resembled what I'd always imagined a demon would look
like, what with the deep, cooked-lobster shade that crept up into his scalp,
but I shrugged away the tingle of fear trying to creep over my own pasty skin.

Smiling, I said, "Go ahead. How are they going to prove after all these
years that I killed them? And how did I kill them? And that's assuming the
cops decide to open up a cold case on two hookers. There was no sign of
any wrong-doing at the scene, no poison found at the autopsies." Smugly, I
continued, "Admit it, Harry, you screwed up. You assumed I would be so
afraid that I would do whatever you asked without question – or without a
contract for my soul."

The demon began quivering with fury, and a sense of pride went through
me as I finished up, "If you'd asked me to do something for you back then, I
would have done it out of fear. But I'm older now, I'm married to a woman
whose father has been looking to make me disappear for years and hasn't
been able to figure out a way to do it. If a man in the Russian Mob can't
do it, I doubt you can. Turns out being a schmuck is a great way to protect
yourself!"

And then I forced a laugh as Harry disappeared in a puff of smoke,
leaving nothing to show he'd ever been there except for a little red goo
splashed on my face.

Ghost stepped out of the shadows, his face pale in the glow of the moon
that was rapidly disappearing behind a cloud, "Dude! That was awesome! I
tried to look up ways to send him back to hell, but I couldn't find anything
useful online."

With a grimace, I wiped the demon snot off my face and looked at the
kid. "Thanks for sticking around. Gotta admit, I was a little worried there for
a minute."

With a grin, Ghost said, "So, turns out you just have to piss a demon off
to get rid of them?"

I shrugged, "I guess so. I was playing it by ear."

We started walking back to my Pacer when the kid brought up the one thing I'd worried he overheard.

"Uh, Ed? Is it true what you said? About Ded being in the Russian Mob, I mean?"

Well, shit.

Chapter 15

In the few short days since I'd started this business, we'd fought off a witch, a spirit, a ladder-climbing politician's wife, and a demon, but none of those things scared me as much as talking to this kid about his grandfather.

"Look," I explained, while keeping my eyes locked on the road, "I don't know that. I was just throwing stuff out there to scare Harry off."

"But you believe it. I mean, Sam said something the other day about Ded wearing a fake skin, or something like that."

"Alv- Ghost, your Ded doesn't exactly open up to deep, heart-warming conversations about himself – especially with me. If you want to find out the truth, you're either going to have to do some research or ask him yourself. I honestly don't know for sure one way or the other."

The kid silently slid the headphones back over his ears. My shoulders relaxed a little at the lack of any more questions. After dealing with a demon, I didn't really feel up to telling tales of a human monster – or, you know, something like it.

In the darkness, with the headlights of my Pacer the only thing illuminating the area, something small and dark landed on the hood of my car, then just as quickly disappeared. Nerves already stretched to their breaking point, I slammed on the brakes in shock. My poor baby promptly died with a shudder.

Immediately, something hit the roof with a thud so loud Ghost pulled his headphones off to ask, "Dude, did you hit something?"

Shaking my head, I debated how to answer him. There were too many things it could have been. Was Harry not done with me? Maybe the witch Lou shot had a sister from the West who wanted revenge. Maybe Mr. Smith changed his ghostly dwelling and we were trampling on his new territory. Geez, we were making a lot of supernatural things mad lately.

I had just enough time to wonder if I should rethink this whole ghost hunting thing when a bullet hit the window next to my head, leaving a perfectly round circle in the glass and making me shriek like Little Miss Muffet when she saw the spider.

Ghost stared at the hole and I think he asked, "Dude, did someone shoot at us?" just as the bullet began buzzing his head. The thing that definitely wasn't a bullet let out a screech that entered one ear, circled my skull long enough to give me a headache, then exited the other ear, leaving me feeling like my eardrums were leaking brain matter onto my shoulders.

I sat there in my dead car, my head pounding and my ears feeling like someone chewed a tunnel through them when my hearing returned enough to hear a whirring sound. Ever have a bee buzz your head so close that you could hear their wings moving a million flaps a second? Multiply that by a hundred. Visions of giant, killer bees appeared behind my pounding eyeballs – and not the funny John Belushi kind – making me instinctively straighten my hand into a human fly swatter.

The thing moved fast. Too fast to focus on the blur and tell for sure what it was. I knew next to nothing about guns, only what I'd seen in video games and movies, but the one thing I *did* know was that bullets don't swirl and swoop and turn like this thing. That only left one option.

"Bee!" I began swatting at the empty air, hoping for contact since I couldn't see the damn little kamikaze.

Have I mentioned that I'm terrified of bees?

Squirming in my seat, I swatted and smacked and swung at every little dust particle swirling around, feeling the sting of my hand every time it came in contact with the cheap interior of the car.

Ghost scrunched down as far as his legs would let him and yelled, "Dude! What *is* that thing?" as it buzzed and whirred its way around and over us.

"Get out of the car!"

Escape was our only option, and I sent up a quick apology to Pops for having to abandon his car and let it rot on the side of the road after so many years.

As the kid reached for the handle to open the door, the bee attacked his hand repeatedly until he finally let go, pulling the wounded appendage to his chest for protection.

"Ah! That hurts!"

I reached for the door handle, ready to leave the kid behind if that's what it took to get away from the angry buzzing sound. Four stings, each one a bullseye on my knuckles, made me drop my hand in shock.

As I pulled my hand to my mouth to suck away the pain, the bee flew to the dashboard and settled down.

"Now that I have your attention," a tiny voice said, "we need to talk."

What the hell? Since when could bees talk?

Squinting, I could just make out a miniature female form backed by butterfly-like wings as big – or maybe even a little bigger – than the body. The wings were in constant movement, making it difficult to tell what they looked like. This thing was no bee.

"What are you?"

The winged creature looked so delicate that it shocked me when she said, "I'm a fairy, dumbass. You know, if you're going to mess around with things you don't know anything about, you should at least do some research first. Fucking idiot."

Well, I wasn't about to sit there in my own car and be insulted by something the size of a moth. I began slowly raising my hand up, planning to swat the thing into fairy dust, but before I moved it more than a couple of inches, she disappeared from sight. Something burned the back of my moving hand, and before I had a chance for the pain to register, I felt a matching sting on my forehead.

"Don't be a moron," she taunted, as she hovered in front of me. My eyes crossed trying to focus on her, and she darted at my face again, stinging the end of my nose before I knew what was happening.

"Hey! Stop that!" I swatted at her anyway and felt the sting of three more bites on my face and neck.

"*You* stop," she threw back in my wounded face, not even winded after her attack. "I promise you, I can keep doing this all night. When you're ready to talk like a civilized person, let me know."

As an aside, she spoke to Ghost, who had hold of the door handle again, "That goes for you too, big boy. Move that door handle even a *centimeter*, and I'll rain pain down on your big, stupid head."

I swear I heard him mutter, "Bitch," but he pulled the hand back to his chest and began massaging the wounds she'd already left.

"Now," she settled back onto the dash, patting her hair into place and slinging glitter everywhere. "Are you done? Ready to talk?"

"What do you want?" I grumbled. The bites she inflicted hurt even more now, like the tips of her teeth were covered in poison, and as hard as I tried not to touch them, I kept finding myself rubbing at the sore spots.

"I came here to give you a little intel, but if this is how I'm going to get treated, screw you both."

This was how she wanted to help? By attacking us and tearing up my classic car? My blood boiled at her tactics.

Ghost kept it together a little more than I did. Keeping his voice calm, he asked, "What kind of intel? And why did you attack us if you're trying to help us?"

Yeah! I thought silently, too afraid to say it out loud and risk getting bitten again by the poisonous little mosquito.

"Listen, chumps, I had to get your attention somehow. I mean, look at me compared to you big, bumbling jackasses." She preened, flinging glitter everywhere as she put her hands on her hips, then cocking one like she wanted to show us her best side.

Ghost held his hands up in the air so she could see them. "I'm going to turn on the light so we can see you better. Is that okay?"

Slowly, so she could see what he was doing, the kid reached up and turned on the overhead light while she hovered above the dash, ready to bite him again if needed. Once his hands were back in his lap, she started talking again.

"Look, humans aren't exactly at the top of the 'Let's be pals' list with us. I mean, yeah, we live in the same world and all, but somehow, most of you manage to avoid seeing us. Hell, most of you humans won't even admit we're here!"

Someone needed to be defending the human race, so I stuttered out, "I-we didn't know until a few days ago."

The kid muttered, "I heard some rumors, but until that witch tried to kill us, I never saw anything. How were we supposed to know?"

The fairy held up her hands to shut us up, lifting off the dashboard again to make doubly certain we were paying attention.

"Oh, shut up. It doesn't matter. What does matter is that you two have done more damage in the last week than most humans do in a lifetime. The council told me not to talk to you at all, but—"

Putting her hands back on her tiny lips, she rubbed her wings suggestively, dropping more glitter on the dash, "—I'm a bit of a rebel."

"Council? There's a council?" I asked the question – stupidly, I guess - because she sneered and floated above the dash like she was preparing to dive-bomb me again. I flinched, and the sign of fear seemed to be all she needed because she settled back down.

"Of course, there's a council, dumbass. Can you run your society without a government of some kind? No, of course not. Fucktard." She spat the last word out with venom. No, really. Venom. My dash began to smoke a little where it landed.

"Quit tearing up my car! This is a classic!" Getting the dash and window fixed was going to cost a fortune. I waved goodbye to my share of the money from Riley in my head.

The fairy laughed, a mean little chuckle that sent shivers down my spine. Have you ever heard a fairy laugh? It's evil, not the tinkling, happy, bell sound that movies and books make it out to be. And I'd heard it before.

"Classic? Let me guess, you think the BeeGees are classical music, too? You know, as the first humans I've ever talked to, I was really hoping to find more intelligence, but I guess I should have known better."

I was really getting tired of being insulted.

"Could you just maybe tell us what you came here for?" Ghost saved the day again as he kept me from throwing out a string of curse words and probably getting stung in even more vulnerable places.

"At least one of you seems to be somewhat smart," she simpered, as she turned to Ghost and smiled. What a bitch.

"I came here to let you know that the witch's coven isn't happy about you guys shooting Marzipam."

"Who?" The word slipped out before I could stop myself, earning me another sting on the tender part of my earlobe.

"Ow! Stop it!"

The evil little mosquito flashed me a grin before turning serious again. "Marzipam. AKA Pammy. The witch you shot. She worked for the WCPD."

"What the- what's the WCPD?"

The fairy rolled her eyes, speaking slowly like I was an idiot, "The WCPD. Witch's Coven Police Department. How could you not know they have a police department? Have you done *any* research?"

Ghost mumbled something, but I couldn't make out the words. The fairy, however, must have caught it, because she answered, "Exactly. The WCPD has been trying for years to take out a sex trafficking ring involving young witches. You sick fucking humans pay big bucks to sleep with a witch. You know, like a fetish. The problem is that they force these young women to use their magic to help cover their tracks. The word on the street is that Marzipam might have gotten a little- overzealous in trying to track down the humans involved."

Ghost asked, "So, she's just enticing men by placing ads, then torturing and killing them when they answer? How does that stop the sex traffickers? And how do you know all this?"

With a sharp look in my direction, the fairy explained, "Well, at least one of you is asking the right questions. I'm pretty sure Pammy is – was – trying to slow down the process by taking out the customers. And for the record, I know all this because I open my ears and listen, rather than just stumbling around like you two morons are doing."

I opened my mouth to say something, then closed it again with a snap, worried I would only be inviting more bites. The pain factory looked my way and sharply asked, "You got a question, too, dumbass?"

I clenched my jaw at the insult. Speaking through gritted teeth, I asked, "Why did you say Pammy *was* trying?"

With a sigh that included a flap of her wings, glitter flew everywhere. I was never going to convince Masha that I hadn't taken the kid to a strip club if she ever looked inside my car.

"I said *was* because Marzipam has been MIA since the night she met up with you two bumbling idiots."

I had no clue how to react to her statement, and I'm guessing Ghost must've felt the same way, because we both sat without saying a word while she got comfortable, crossing her legs and leaning over with her chin resting on the palm of her hand.

"Now, the reason I came here to warn you – at great personal risk to myself, I might add - is that I think you're well-meaning, in spite of the fact that you're giant, bumbling jerks.

So, here's what I'm going to do for you. I'm going to give you the number for the WCPD's chief of police. She's very interested in chatting with you. It would be in your best interest to call her before she tracks you down – and she *will* track you down. She's incredibly good at her job. *However*, when you do call, you can't tell her I sent you. I'm a rebel, but I'm not a stupid rebel."

My eyes widened. "It was you that called us that first night from the cemetery church, wasn't it? I heard you giggling before we went in. You put the picture of the hairy jerk on his phone. You wanted us to stop Marzipam before she hurt him."

It had taken me a little while to put it together, but it was the only thing that made sense. There was no way the phone calls had come from the witch, and Heavy Breather hadn't known what we were talking about when we asked him.

The fairy gave me a surprised look. "Call it a test of sorts. I wanted to see how you handled things. You handled it, all right! Don't get me wrong, Marzipam needed to be stopped, but man, oh, man, talk about overkill!"

I tensed my hand up, thinking about trying to swat her again while she didn't expect it, but remembered the stinging on my face and the smoking dash and let the hand fall back on my lap.

With a fake cough that almost covered his laugh, Ghost asked, "Who are you anyway? And thanks for the heads up."

With a preen and a suggestive smile directed toward the kid, she said, "You can call me Tinkerbell."

And with that, she flew back through the bullet-sized hole in the window and disappeared.

"What the—" I stuttered, as Ghost let out a "Dude—"

Tinkerbell left a tiny little card on the dash of my car, blank but for something sparkly scrawled across it. Ghost tried to pick up the scrap of paper without success.

"Let me try," I said, as I reached my own sausage fingers up to the dash. Finally slipping my nail under the card, I lifted it carefully in the air, only to drop the damn thing into the darkness of the passenger floorboard.

"Fuck," the word slipped out before I realized it, and with a grin, Ghost reprimanded me with my own chastisement. "Language, dude!"

Tired, frustrated as hell, sore from fairy bites, and still off-balance, I barked out an unexpected laugh. The surprise of it after the night's harrowing adventures made me laugh again, and then all bets were off.

I started chuckling.

Then I giggled a little.

Before I realized it, I was howling with laughter, sitting in my car in the middle of the road, just outside the cemetery where I had been threatened by a demon, then attacked by a hateful little fairy that called herself Tinkerbell.

Ghost stared at me for a second before joining in. We spent the next ten minutes crying and laughing, holding our stomachs at the hilarity of everything that had befallen us over the last week.

Finally, I managed to reign in the near-hysterical laughing, wiping my cheeks with the bottom of my filthy, graveyard-dirt covered shirt, only to look over at Ghost and start all over again.

The laughter relieved some of the stress from being pulled in so many different directions and it kept me from crying. It was easier to sit in my car and chuckle at the insanity my life had become than to actually deal with any of it.

The little break with reality needed to end, though. Like it or not, my life had been thrown a curveball. The job I'd started just so I could tell my wife I was working at something had turned into a real job, something I thought I might actually be good at – eventually - and I knew I needed to finish what I'd started.

"Okay, Alvin. Time to get to work. See if you can find that card with the number on it, and let's get home." Surprisingly, the kid didn't argue with my use of his given name, just pulled out his phone.

While Ghost fumbled around the floorboard, using the flashlight on his phone to light up the carpet worn shiny with use, I tried to start my car. Nothing. Of course.

We'd been sitting on the road with the engine shut off, the dome light on, and the headlights shining down an empty road for almost a half hour. The battery was as worn out as Ghost's security blanket, and my wallet was lighter than Tinkerbell's wings.

"Uh, small problem," I moaned. Ghost looked up, face red from being bent double, and said, "Dude, seriously, time to get a new car."

"This is a classic," I snapped, feeling the lie even as I said it. I could have told the kid the truth, I guess, but the promise I made to Pops was between the two of us. No, this car wasn't going anywhere. Not anytime soon, anyway. Besides, the only way I could afford another car was to take Boris up on his offer, and I already knew I couldn't afford his payments.

With a sigh, Ghost punched a few buttons on his phone and leaned back in his seat. "Help is coming," he murmured, closing his eyes. With nothing else to do but wait, I followed suit.

The combination of flashlight shining in my eyes and a tap on the broken window woke me up with a start. "Mr. Ward?"

"Wha- yes? I'm Ed Ward."

"You wanna pop the hood and let me take a look at your engine? I'm from Henry's Towing."

I shot a look at Ghost, who nodded. Rolling the broken window down slowly while praying it didn't shatter, I squinted up into the man's face. "Pretty sure I just need a jump," I said.

His face expressionless, he responded, "The hood, please?" As soon as I pulled the lever, he walked to the front and lifted the hood. A minute later, he poked his head around the metal flap and shouted, "Try it now!"

The car started with a cough, then grumbled its way back to a smooth-ish purr. The tow truck driver came back around to the window, his face blank as he shoved a piece of paper at me.

"How you wanna pay for this?" Leaning toward him, I fumbled for the wallet in my back pocket, knowing full well I had nothing but cobwebs in there. Before I could clamp my fingers on the thin leather, Ghost leaned over and said with a smile, "Hey, Henry, can you just charge this to my account?"

"Mr. Bykov! Sir! I didn't see you over there!" The dull face turned deferential as he leaned into the window. "No charge, sir. Your father is a great man. I'm happy to do this for him."

I swelled with pride at the compliment before I realized the tow truck driver meant Boris. Deflated, I opened my mouth to correct the mistake but closed it again. It wasn't worth the effort. When I turned back to look at the kid, he was deep in thought, headphones forgotten around his neck.

"Maybe he *is* in the Russian Mob," he muttered. "So many things make sense now." Without another word, he slipped the headphones back over his ears and turned to stare out the window. I watched helplessly for a minute, trying to decide whether or not I should try talking to him, but he steadfastly refused to look away from the darkness outside.

I put the car in gear and drove us home.

When I pulled in the driveway, the sky was turning that shade of gray that comes right before the sun lifts her outer covering and shows her pink underskirt.

Ghost hauled himself out of the car without even a "dude", pausing long enough to hand me the tiny slip of paper the fairy had given us before heading inside to his room.

I wanted to talk to him, but really, what could I say? 'Hey, it's okay if your grandfather is in the Russian Mob,' didn't seem right, and neither did, 'It's okay, at least your dad is – insert famous actor name here that I still couldn't remember.'

I finally let him go without saying anything. Maybe he would come to me when he wanted to talk. Maybe not. Like it or not, I wasn't his dad. He'd made that very clear over the years.

However, that brought me back to who his father was: it seemed day by day, the kid looked more and more like that famous actor – the guy I'd just seen in an advertisement for a new movie. What was his name?

I pondered the question as I stretched out on the leather couch in the living room.

As I drifted off to sleep, the name finally popped into my head. Alvin's father was – unconsciousness swallowed his identity, along with everything else.

Chapter 16

The sensation of something touching my cheek woke me up. Immediately thinking of Tinkerbell and her nasty bites, I swatted at the air as I opened my eyes. Surprisingly, I connected with something – my wife's arm.

Rubbing at it, she looked at me with shock on her face. "Why you hit Masha?"

"Masha, honey, I'm so sorry! I thought you were- you know what, never mind. You wouldn't believe the things I've been dealing with this week."

Swinging my legs around to sit up, I glanced at the giant clock on the wall. Noon. I still had no idea why we needed a clock that took up half the wall, but Masha said it was fashionable. At least I could read the time even when my eyes were still blurry with sleep.

Grinning at my wife, I patted the seat beside me. "C'mere. Let's pretend we're teenagers again and make out on the couch."

Giggling, she waved my suggestion away and left the room. A minute later, the sweet scent of coffee beans wafted throughout the house and I smiled. The woman knew how to make me happy.

I pushed myself off the couch with the intention of heading into the kitchen, stopping to look at my football trophy on the mantle. Wiping a miniscule bit of dust from my name, my shoulders straightened a little. Maybe with this job, I'd finally found the thing in life that would make me as proud as that football win had.

With a little more confidence in my step, I made my way into the kitchen, where Masha waited with my coffee. Taking it, I set it on the counter and pulled her in for a long, lingering kiss that she responded to with passion. Yup, our marriage cycle was definitely on the upswing.

"Eww...sick!" Ghost's elegant statement startled us apart. My wife turned red, and wiping her lips, she turned away and began loading the dishwasher.

Meanwhile, I leaned on the counter and grinned at the kid, feeling manly. I was bringing sexy back, if you know what I mean.

Pretending to stick a finger down his throat, Ghost made gagging motions, which only increased my smile. Coffee in hand, I swaggered into the dining room to sit down and enjoy my brew. And maybe my victory over making the kid nauseous.

A minute later, Ghost came in with his own cup of coffee. I could hear Masha puttering around in the kitchen, and life seemed right for once. Until the kid had to open his mouth and ruin the moment.

"Dude," Ghost leaned toward me and whispered, "Did you call the WCPD?"

I shook my head. "Fell asleep. I'll call in a minute."

Opening his mouth to say something else, he closed it again with a snap when Masha came back into the room.

"We spend day together, yes? Like old times? Maybe we go see movie."

"Masha, honey—" I started to explain that we had work to do, but her thick, dark brows immediately drew down in displeasure. Glancing over at Ghost for help, he looked just as helpless against his mother's burgeoning anger.

I smiled charmingly at my wife, and gave her the only answer she would accept, "Of course, my dear! Just let me get a few things out of the way, and we'll go. I'll even pay!"

The brows lifted, and the threat of storm clouds left her eyes. I felt guilty suddenly. I couldn't remember the last time we'd left the house together, much less with Alvin along. If watching a chick flick at the movie theater made her happy, then that's what we would do. I'd even spring for an extra-large popcorn!

"Go get cleaned up, Ghost- uh, Alvin. We're going out for the day."

"Why you call him Ghost?"

The kid stepped up to bat. "It's like a nickname, Mama. Just something Ed likes to call me."

"But is not your name."

Giving her a warm smile, he said, "Mama, you always said you wanted us to be closer. The name – it's like a joke between us – you know, ha-ha?"

I could tell she was still confused, but at least I didn't have to worry anymore if I slipped up and called him Ghost in front of her. Besides, the name had kind of grown on me. The tall, gangly kid with the pale skin did resemble a ghost, kind of.

Just like the one that actor played in the movie. The actor Ghost reminded me of so much. What the hell was his name?

And then it happened.

Masha smiled fondly at her son and answered all my questions about his parentage with one fractured sentence.

"Maybe we see new Vinny Stephens film today, yes?"

That was it! The name of the actor that had eluded me for so long! The man Alvin Vincent Bykov resembled, right down to the cleft in his chin.

My jaw dropped open in shock and I let out a little gurgling sound.

Two sets of eyes met mine, and thinking quickly, I closed my mouth again and gave a wry smile. "Sorry."

Masha wrinkled her nose in disgust, then turned back to her son and asked, "Yes, Alvin? We see movie today?"

"Sure, Mama. Let me help Ed get this work out of the way, then we'll go. You want to look up the movie times while we do that?"

Masha lifted a section of newspaper lying on the other end of the table and waved it at us. "We go at three o'clock."

Young Vinny Stephens looked at me questioningly. "Yeah," I choked out, "We'll be done in plenty of time to go."

As soon as we hit the stairs leading to the basement, the Mama's boy persona faded away and Ghost asked, "Dude, what the fuck? You looked like you saw a ghost up there. I mean, you know, a real one."

I shook my head without answering, not even bothering to get onto him for his language.

Almost certain now that I knew who the kid's father was, it opened up a whole new can of worms. What if I slipped up and accidentally told him? Should I just go ahead and tell him what I knew? I mean, he had to be curious, right?

No, it wasn't my place to say anything. Masha must have had a good reason to keep the identity of Alvin's father a secret all these years. Besides, I didn't know for sure. Alvin Bykov bore a striking resemblance to the man.

So what? Maybe they were doppelgangers. People were always spotting other people that looked like someone they knew. It happened all the time. That had to be it. I was stressing out over nothing.

I waited until we reached the bottom of the stairs to say, "Let's call this police chief and get out of here. I think we've earned a day off."

I felt kind of bad for leaving the kid's question unanswered, but if that was the worst thing I ever did, then I wasn't doing too bad as a stepfather. At least, that's what I kept telling myself as we settled in at the desk.

Holding the tiny slip of paper out at arm's length, I squinted but still couldn't make out what it said.

With a sigh, Ghost held out one hand, palm up. "Dude," he said, shaking the hand. Dropping the paper into his palm, I watched as he took his phone and pressed a few buttons. The camera flash went off, and a second later, he held a zoomed picture of the card in front of my face.

The numbers were written in gold sparkle that, even enlarged, were hard to read against the white cardstock.

"Is that a five or a six?" I asked, squinting as I leaned away from the phone.

"Dude," he said again, and I wondered if I should be worried that I was beginning to understand his one-word vocabulary.

Punching the numbers into his phone, he handed it to me just as I heard ringing coming from the hidden speaker.

The feminine voice answering the phone reminded me of the old movie actresses from the forties. You know what I mean. You can see the bun in their hair and the perfectly pointy-tipped lips just from the way they speak.

"This is Chief Beatrix Martin. To whom am I speaking?"

Oh, great. Another odd name and a grammar buff, to boot.

"Uh, okay, so, this is Ed. Ed Ward. I was told I should call you about the witch hurt in the line of duty?"

I don't know what I expected, but I can say with certainty that it wasn't the shriek of rage that reached out and slapped me – not to mention deafened me - through the phone line.

"Yooooooouuuuuu!"

Jerking the phone away from my ear – which had been rendered useless by the sound of her screech – I stared at the handset spewing curse words like a Marine who discovered all the crayons were gone.

Even though I could only hear the threats out of the one ear, the voice on the other end made it quite clear that if she ever saw me in person and had her way, I would be left hanging upside down by a *very* personal piece of my anatomy in a very public place, then slowly cut down one razor blade slice at a time in that same personal area before being fed to some ravenous demon-goats she knew.

I cringed a little at the imagery but let her finish the angry rant. The only reason I stayed on the line was the hope that she would eventually let me tell my side of the story.

When she finally stopped to draw in a breath – damn, she must have been practicing or something, because that rant had lasted five minutes or more – I said, "Beatrix, Madame Chief, Mrs. Martin, however you want to be addressed, I didn't shoot your officer."

Icily – how was she not even winded after all that? – she asked, "Then who did?"

That was the sticky part. I wasn't about to sell out Lou and Sam, but at the same time, I needed a scapegoat – not to be confused with the demon-goats previously mentioned.

"It's uh, kind of a long story. Is there any way we could meet in person?" I figured at the very least, that would give me time to come up with a story that made sense. Worst case scenario, she wanted an answer that instant, in which case I decided I would just hang up and then dodge any return calls until I could figure something out.

I held my breath until she wearily answered, "Fine. Meet me at three down at the old bus depot. But I warn you, if you don't show, I'm going to hunt you down and string you up. With dental floss."

I held the phone away from my face to keep her from hearing my gulp, but I guess she did, anyway. "Be there," she demanded. "This is your only chance. You don't know me, but I promise you - I always keep my word."

She slammed down the phone and I almost smiled despite the pain in my injured ears. She got it. There really wasn't any better way to show how mad you were than smashing the receiver down on an old-school phone.

When I gently punched the end button on the kid's phone, he asked, "So what's it going to be, dude? Piss off your Russian wife or a witch who happens to be the chief of police for the local coven of crazy witches?"

I shuddered. Neither option sounded pleasant.

"There's no way around it. I have to meet Chief Martin. She didn't leave me much choice in the matter."

Ghost sat for a moment in thought, twiddling with his too long hair, and just as I thought he was going to wish me farewell and good luck in my next life, he gave me a look of triumph. "I got it! I know how to get you out of the movie with Mama."

After all the stunts he'd pulled on me over the years, I wasn't sure if I believed him, but honestly, we'd been getting along better than we ever had since we started working together, so what did I have to lose? Masha would be mad at me whether he screwed me over or not.

"Okay," I sighed. "What's the plan?"

"Dude, I just have to give her a better option is all."

I waited, head in hands while he pounded up the stairs. Strains of conversation floated through the open door, but I didn't hear Masha screaming in rage, so there's that.

Minutes later, Ghost came pounding back down. "Done deal, dude. You're set."

Curious, I asked, "What did you tell her?"

Plopping himself down on the bar stool next to me, Ghost grinned like a kid getting cake and ice cream for breakfast. "I told her you were getting on my nerves 'cause we'd been spending so much time together lately. Asked if just the two of us could go. She almost cried from happiness."

Okay, not gonna lie, that kind of hurt my feelings. It must have shown on my face because the grin slid off his. "Dude, uh, Ed, I didn't really mean it. I was just making sure you could get to your appointment with the old witch."

I forced a smile. "I know. The last thing we need right now is for Chief Martin to come looking for us and meet your mother instead."

With a laugh, Ghost barked, "Dude! That would be epic!"

I had to laugh along with him. The thought of the two alpha females in the same room together *was* pretty epic. Well, if you weren't married to one and in hot water with the other, that is.

"If this meeting doesn't go well, we'll just sic your mother on Chief Martin," I grinned.

"Throw Lou into the mix, and you could sell it to pay-per-view!"

The thought of Lou sobered me up in a hurry. How could I keep the WCPD from finding out that the old woman shot her officer? Assuming the chief hadn't already figured it out, I'd have to do some fancy dancing to keep the old woman safe.

"Okay," I sighed. "Go keep your mom out of the way while I get the witch out of our hair."

Ghost snapped off a sloppy salute that *almost* made me laugh again. Almost.

Picking up my office phone, I called Lou. I needed to let her know what was going on. Just in case Chief Martin already knew she was involved in the shooting.

I should have known better. Lou insisted on going with me. Sam too. Without Ghost to act as a host for her husband, I told Sam no. I knew he wouldn't hand over the controls if I let him possess my body, and I wasn't about to let the two of them go meet Chief Beatrix Martin alone.

Man, being responsible and shit really sucks sometimes.

Lou argued, "You have to take me, at least. I'm the one that shot her, for heaven's sake! I won't have your family bein' put in danger 'cause of somethin' I did."

"Fine," I sighed. "I'll be there in an hour. Be ready to go."

When I pulled up in front of the house, the old couple had a surprise for me. Sam jumped into my body before I could do anything about it – although I'm not sure what I could have done to prevent it. To make matters worse, Lou brought her shotgun along for the ride, tucking the stock neatly into the floorboard, where it rested against her leg.

Lou asked worriedly, "You remember how to drive, Sam? It's been a while."

Sam's voice came out of my mouth, "I got this, baby! Let's go take care of this problem for Ed!"

And *that's* how a ghost and an old woman kidnapped me in order to go talk to a witch.

Chapter 17

I thought about trying the John Jacob Jingleheimer Schmidt thing with Sam, but I had a feeling the old couple would just join in singing until *I* was the one trying to escape my own body. Besides, I couldn't concentrate enough to remember the words. Sam was scaring the hell out of me with his driving.

"Sam!" Lou screeched his name every few seconds. "Watch out for that car! Sam! Red light! Sam!"

By the time we reached the old bus depot, my nerves were jangling like a set of those chattery teeth on a bed of loose steel shot.

It wasn't difficult to pick out the chief. The image of an actress from the forties disappeared in a flash as I – we – looked across the room at her. Then again, she didn't resemble the wicked witch stereotype with a wart on her horribly long, hooked nose and a greenish skin tone, either.

The chief of police was a decent-enough looking woman about my age. Wearing an official-looking uniform and a gold badge on her chest, she watched the room expectantly with razor-sharp eyes that took in everything and missed nothing.

Secondly, she was the only other person there. Well, except for a few homeless people that were doing their best to stay invisible. Mostly from her, I assumed. She exuded a power that I could feel all the way across the empty building and in my numb, possessed body.

I'm not sure if it was the power of her position, or her power as a witch, or maybe it was the two combined, but I understood why the homeless people in the room were doing their best to stay out of her line of sight. Sam, however, seemed to ignore the authority coming at us in tangible waves as he barreled my body straight across the room to the waiting cop.

I kept fighting and struggling to make myself heard over Sam as he neared the woman dressed in black, her equally dark hair hanging in a loose braid over one shoulder. So much black. Even her eyes looked black in the shadows of the room, matching the look thrown our way when Sam neared her.

"Mr. Ward." The chilly voice echoed against concrete walls as she stated, rather than asked, my name.

"Sorta," Sam replied.

The answer didn't seem to surprise her. I had the feeling not much did.

Sliding her cold gaze over to Lou, who held her shotgun cradled like a baby, she asked, "And you are?"

"I'm Lou. I'm the one you're lookin' for. I shot your deputy." For a split second, I was almost glad Sam had control over my body so I couldn't quip, "But I did not shoot your sheriff."

The smart comment faded quickly as I helplessly watched the cop reach out and pluck the shotgun out of Lou's arms. Pulling out a set of handcuffs, she began giving the old woman a warped version of the Miranda rights.

"You have the right to be seen before the grand judges of the coven, who will determine your guilt. You have the right to be kept alive until such time as your fate is decided. You have the right to –"

"Hey, wait!" Sam's angry yell hurt my ears.

"Easy, boy," I muttered, hoping the shout wasn't the final straw that did permanent damage to my hearing.

"You listen here, you, you – witch! We came here to talk to you, to explain what happened! You can't just take my wife away –"

"Oh, yes I can," the cop smoothly interrupted. "She just confessed to the attempted murder of a police officer. It's perfectly within my rights to arrest her."

Murder? Yeah, Lou shot her, but the screaming meemie was still alive when she disappeared into thin air. I needed to talk to Chief Martin myself.

I knew Sam's hotheadedness would get Lou – and me - in deeper water than we were already in, so I began a silent litany of begging Sam to let me take over for a minute. Finally, after watching the chief clamp the handcuffs over Lou's wrists, Sam shut up and let me speak.

"Hey, listen, okay? I'm Ed. You've been talking to the ghost of Lou's dead husband, Sam, but I have control of my body again – at least for a minute. Can we please talk about this?"

Shooting me a strange look, the witch asked, "Possessed? Or is this a ploy? I can arrest you as an accessory, you know."

Look," I pleaded. "Do whatever you have to do, but at least let me explain what happened first. It was self-defense. I mean, I think so. Just- just let me explain. Please."

Up close, now that I could see her myself, I realized her eyes weren't black at all. In fact, they were a gorgeous shade of silvery/gray like nothing I'd ever seen before. They were mesmerizing. They were—

"Hey! What are you trying to do? Hypnotize me? Stop it!"

The witchy woman almost smiled. Almost. The corner of her mouth twitched before settling back into the grim countenance she'd been wearing since our arrival.

"You have your tricks, I have mine," she said smugly, not sorry at all.

"This isn't a trick," I pleaded. "Please. Let me explain what happened."

"You have two minutes," she said, as she hefted Lou's shotgun over her shoulder.

"Okay, okay," I said, doing my best to keep Sam back down where he belonged. The display of his gun on the cop's shoulder set his temper off, and I could feel him struggling to take back over.

"Look, I don't know how much you know about what happened that night."

"I know one of my officers was shot in the line of duty. That's all I need to know."

"Yeah, but see, Lou didn't kill her. I mean, yeah, she shot her and all, but unless she turned into a splotch of grease on the driveway, she was still alive when she left Lou's house."

Beatrix Martin cocked a hip and raised an eyebrow. "Pammy's been MIA since that night. We received a transmission from her stating that she had been injured in the line of duty. We traced it to your friend's house, but no one has seen or heard from her since. I can only assume she died of her injuries."

Stumbling to get the words out before Sam's rage boiled over, I said, "About that - I'm not sure she was on duty so much. We interrupted her doing something crazy to this guy in a little church. I don't know what your methods are, but I find it hard to believe you would allow one of your officers to tie up and torture some guy, even if he *is* a pervert."

"What are you talking about?" She asked the question suspiciously, and I realized that maybe one of her officers had gone rogue without her knowing about it.

I pushed on, "We started getting phone calls from this guy who could barely speak. We traced the number to a cemetery. When we got there, we found a church, and inside, a guy tied up to a chair, wearing nothing but some tiny little underwear."

I shuddered – okay, gagged - a little at the memory of the overweight guy in the barely existent banana hammock. The cop had a thoughtful look on her face, so I kept talking as fast as I could shove the words out of my mouth, before I lost my chance.

"The guy said he'd answered an ad for some fun times with a witch, but when he showed up at the meeting spot, the woman tied him up and left. She told him she was coming back to torture him. When we tried to cut him loose, she showed back up and went nutso. She kept trying to attack us. Ghost took a picture of her with his phone, and she disappeared. Then she reappeared outside the church and came after us again. She even followed us to our next appointment at Lou's house. We didn't know she was a cop, I swear! We didn't even know she'd followed us until we pulled into Lou's driveway and she started coming after us again."

Lou took up the story. "I looked out my window and saw some crazy woman attacking the two guys in their car. I'd called them to help me calm down my husband, Sam. Well, when I saw her going after them and screeching at the top of her lungs, I grabbed my shotgun and shot her."

The witch cop's mouth hung open like a dead fish by the time Lou finished talking. As if she finally realized what she must look like, she closed it with a snap, then blinked a few times before asking, "Are you telling me that Pammy was using entrapment to lure victims to their torture and death? Then lost her mind when you let one of them go?"

I nodded emphatically. Maybe too emphatically. I felt something in my neck pop, giving me an instant headache.

Suspiciously, the chief asked, "You have any witnesses for this supposed illegal activity?"

I nodded again, more carefully this time to avoid doing any more damage to my neck. "My partner Ghost will tell you the same thing. He's got the picture on his phone for proof! And I'm pretty sure he wrote down the victim's name. You can ask him yourself."

The chief of police thought for a minute before she said, "Assuming your story is true, your friend here would still be held liable for the death of an officer. However, if I can confirm your story that Marzipam went rogue, well, that's an entirely different set of circumstances. I would need to talk to the council before I could make any decisions."

Desperate, I pleaded, "I called you from Ghost's cell phone. Call him back. He'll tell you. Can't he send the picture of Marzipam to you somehow?" As she pulled out her phone, I remembered, "Oh, I forgot to tell you. Ghost is a nickname. His real name is Alvin. Alvin Bykov."

She looked up at me, and I swear I saw fear flash through those silvery eyes. "Bykov? As in Boris Bykov?"

Confused as to why a witch would know my father-in-law, I carefully answered, "Yes, that's his grandfather."

Before I realized what was happening, the chief witch of police quickly uncuffed Lou and said, "You're free to go. Don't let me see you again."

Lou rubbed her wrists and stepped away from the cop. "What just happened? Do I get my shotgun back?"

Chief Martin waved her questions away with a single flap of her hand. Reaching into her shirt pocket, she pulled out a card and handed it to me, a new hint of respect in her voice, "Please ask your partner to send the picture of Marzipam to me at his convenience. And if you should run into any more of my officers in the future, Mr. Ward, please call me. I'll be happy to help with anything – difficult – you need help with."

Totally dumbfounded, I made my way back to the car with Lou beside me. Sam popped back out before I could stop him, threw my arms around his wife, and planted my lips on her forehead. "We did it, baby!"

Pushing my body away, she laughingly said, "Oh, no, you silly old man, Ed did it. Well, technically, I guess Ghost did, somehow." Giving me – well, Sam – a stern look, she said, "And don't think you're drivin' us home. I'd forgotten how bad a driver you are. Now, you just get back down in there and let Ed take us home."

I could hear Sam grumbling as he settled down inside me somewhere – I refused to let myself think too hard about where – and I slid into the Pacer. Which wouldn't start. Again.

I popped the hood and hauled myself back out of the car. Sam kept yelling that he knew how to fix it, but I held him firmly in place. Before I could get around the car, a sleek black Cadillac SUV pulled up beside me.

The tinted window rolled down, and for the first time, I saw a bemused look on Beatrix Martin's face. Without the perma-scowl, she looked almost pretty.

"Car trouble?"

I rolled my eyes, careful to keep my head turned so she couldn't see it.

"I don't know what's wrong with her."

Hopping out of her SUV with an ease and grace that hinted at a lot of gym time, she came around to the front of my car and raised the hood. With barely a glance at the motor, she pointed at the battery. "There's your problem."

I squinted at the area she pointed at, but nothing looked out of place. Rolling her eyes, she reached in and adjusted something, then said, "Now try."

A little miffed that *she* rolled her eyes at *me*, I did what she said, mentally crossing my fingers that her little trick wouldn't work. The car started right up.

Dammit.

Strolling over to my window, she leaned down, her eyes glinting as she said, "Let Mr. Bykov know I did you a solid."

With that, she gracefully stepped up into her giant SUV and rolled silently away. Once again, I had my father-in-law to thank for getting me out of a jam. I couldn't help but wonder just how far his tentacles – uh, I mean, fingers – dipped into the world I was now involved in.

Sam had been unhappily silent during the whole interaction with the cop/witch, but I didn't want to take the chance that he would get us arrested after we'd just been handed a Get Out of Jail Free card. I drove to their house, listening to him grumble somewhere inside me the whole way.

When I pulled into their driveway, Lou invited me inside to have a cup of coffee.

I started to tell her no, but after she'd offered herself up for slaughter to the cop, so to speak, I kind of felt obligated. Once we were sitting at the kitchen table, and Sam was mercifully out of my body again, she asked, "So, what exactly happened back there? Why does Boris hold so much esteem in the witch's community? Because I gotta say, that was crazy."

Speaking of crazy, I noticed her talking to her dead husband had begun to seem normal when she turned and shouted, "Yes, dear, I'm *asking* him about it now!" She paused, and when she spoke again, her voice took on the tone of a woman trying to keep her rage under control. "What was that?" Pause. "You did *what*?"

It might have been entertaining under other circumstances to listen to the old woman berate her dead husband, but things were getting stranger by the minute and I needed to know what was going on. At least, I thought I needed to know. As things turned out, I wished she'd never told me. Or at least, I wished I hadn't asked.

When the one-sided conversation paused, I saw my chance.

"What's that all about?"

Lou gave me a quick, sharp glance that instantly made me nervous. Picking up her purse from where it hung on the back of her chair, she pulled out a pack of cigarettes and lit one.

"Yes, I *know* how much you hate it when I smoke, Sam! Why do you think I'm doing it right now? If you hate the smell so much, then don't let the door hit ya where the good Lord split ya."

I kind of wanted to laugh, but at the same time, my instincts told me to keep my mouth shut. The old woman was perturbed, and I'd seen firsthand how she handled things when she was upset.

"Lou?"

Taking a long drag off the cigarette, she spoke while blowing smoke out, "Seems Sam here didn't bother mentionin' that your father-in-law helped out Riley's husband Randall awhile back.

"Wait, are you telling me that Randall James works with Boris? Doing what exactly?"

Holding up two fingers, cigarette clamped firmly between them, she clarified, "No, I'm telling you that Boris did some work a few years ago that

– well, let's just say that Randall's name never came up, although by sheer coincidence, some things happened that directly benefitted him."

I don't keep a very close eye on politics, especially local stuff. It never matters who's in office, things don't change for the every-guy like me. But even I had heard of a certain scandal that happened a few years back. A scandal that was truly – well, scandalous.

Seems a certain man running for city council had been discovered in a hotel room with a very handsome – or would it be pretty? – transgender person. This certain politician was found dressed in clothes that better suited a hooker, for lack of a better word.

Those two factors might not have damaged his campaign in this day and age, had said politician not been running on the platform of bringing traditional values back to our city, values that *didn't* include wild sex in a cheap hotel room with someone who wasn't the stay-at-home mother of his children.

Add in the fact that the other person in the hotel room was technically neither he nor she at the time of the discovery, being only halfway through the transformation of changing from female to male, and things turned ugly fast.

The older, conservative constituents who had been happily rallying around said politician's battle cry weren't happy with the idea of having the cross-dressing, possibly gay, and *definitely* adulterous councilman representing them and their traditional values.

Now, don't get me wrong. I don't care what anyone does in their private life. If they think they're trapped in a body of the wrong sex and they have the money to change that, well, more power to them, I say. However, it seemed fortuitous that the incident in question just *happened* to have been discovered one week before the city council election. One short week, during which time Randall James jumped to the forefront of the polls faster than a jones-ing heroin addict in line at the methadone clinic.

I knew my father-in-law could be lax with his scruples. Money ruled his world, and it reigned supreme. But would he go so far as to set up an innocent man for the right price?

Yes. Yes, he would.

Now I just had to figure out what to do with this new information. Even though I had no evidence of Boris' involvement in the scandal, Sam's word was good enough proof for me. After all, I'd shared my body with the man. If you can't trust the guy who possesses you, who can you trust? And- it explained some of Sam's anger toward my father-in-law. You know, besides the fact that he was hitting on his wife.

"Look," I told Lou, who sat calmly smoking her cigarette and ignoring the figurines breaking in the other room, "don't say anything about any of this to Ghost, please. He just found out yesterday that his grandfather is possibly in the Russian mob. This is the last thing he needs to hear coming on top of that."

Waving her smoke away, Lou grinned, "Cross my heart, Ed. But mobster or not, you need to find out what the hell your father-in-law has on that cop. I don't wanna wake up in shackles to find myself being burned at the stake."

"I'm pretty sure you've got that backward," I grinned, "but I'll see what I can do. In the meantime, I need to get home and spend a few minutes with my wife."

By the time I left Lou's house, the sun was going down. I made a quick stop on the way home and bought a bouquet of flowers for Masha, trying to keep my promise to myself to be more husbandly.

The driveway was empty, and the house dark when I pulled in. Strange. Masha always tried to avoid coming home after dark. She said it creeped her out to walk into a dark, empty house. That 'they' took advantage of the dark to hide. She never told me who 'they' were, but I figured it had something to do with growing up in Russia. Or maybe just from growing up with Boris as her father.

Either way, I walked into the house and turned on the kitchen light. Bam! Boris Bykov sat at my kitchen table, gently stroking his wooden staff like he was – well, let's just go with petting a kitten.

"We talk," he said, but the timbre of his voice made it hard to hide the tremor that swept over my body. Have you ever talked to someone so far beyond anger that they've come full circle to calm again? That was the feeling I got coming from Boris. Fury that he'd compressed and rolled up into a little furry ball of dead.

Speaking of dead, I was pretty sure I wasn't going to be seen again, and I couldn't think of a single way to point my murder at Boris. I just hoped he completed the job before shoving my feet into a pair of concrete boots and sinking me in the nearest lake.

"Sit," he ordered.

Trying to avoid my imminent death for a few more minutes, I began rambling, "I think, uh, I kind of want some coffee. You want some? I don't mind making enough for both of us. It's just as easy to make some for two as it is—"

The gruff voice commanded. "Sit."

Helpless, I did as he instructed. Boris was finally getting me out of his daughter's life. He only needed to kill me to do it. I just hoped Ghost would be okay.

Wait, was that a fatherly instinct thing? Worrying about the kid instead of myself? I almost patted myself on the back, and it took everything I had to control the smile of pride that kept trying to creep onto my face.

Boris kept yammering on about something, but I wasn't listening. I didn't care to hear the details of my gruesome death or why. I was still coming down off the glow of parental pride when I heard him say, "So you tell her for me?"

Wait, what?

Oh, I meant to say that out loud.

"Wait, what?"

"You will call Lou. Arrange, uh, how you say, date?"

Holy shit. I'd totally misread his mood. He wasn't mad at all. This whole thing was about the old man getting laid. A sense of relief flooded through me like cheese on a fondue fountain. Then it hit me.

Boris had no idea Lou was connected to both his co-conspirator and the politician who gained office due to their meddling. I needed to let him know, but how could I tell him without letting him know that I knew about his part in the scandal?

I opened my mouth to say something – what, I'm not sure – but before I could, the kitchen door opened. Ghost and Masha walked in together, laughing loudly and carrying bags.

"Papa! You're here!" Masha dropped the packages on the counter and came around to give her father a kiss on the forehead. Ghost followed closely behind her, giving the old man a quick, one-handed hug and a muttered, "Hey, Ded."

Shooting a look across the table to me, he mouthed, "We have to talk" over Boris's head.

Oh, great. They'd gone to the movie and he'd seen the resemblance himself. The kid had figured out who his dad was. Now I'd have to deal with that, too. Before I could say anything, Masha yanked my chair back, almost spilling me to the floor in the process.

Plopping down on my lap and kissing me on the lips, she murmured, "Beautiful flowers" as she looked in my eyes. I felt a switch flip inside me. My wife loved the flowers so much that she was giving me that look. The one that meant she wanted some sexy time with her main man. Unless... she *did* just spend the afternoon with her son and his father. Well, okay, not really *with* Vinny Stephens, because he was on the movie screen, but still...

Nope. Not going there. Masha loved the flowers. That had to be it.

Wrapping my arms around her waist, I kissed her neck and felt her shiver a little. Holy crap! I was gonna get lucky tonight! That was twice in one week! Well, if I could get rid of the kid and the old man. Masha solved the problem for me.

"Papa, please to go home. I wish to make love to my handsome husband."

Retching sounds came from behind me, and I turned my head to see Ghost pretending to stick his finger down his throat.

Boris pushed his chair back and stood up. "Alvin, come with Ded. Has been long time since we shared night together."

Ghost didn't waste any time. Heading straight for the back door, he paused to grab an apple from one of the grocery bags, then headed out into the darkness. Boris followed, his face grim, until I yelled after him, "Hey, Boris, I'll see what I can do, okay?"

Masha nuzzled her nose against my neck and asked, "What will you do for Papa?" Standing up with my wife in my arms, I berated myself again for a half-second about needing to work out before I remembered that sex burned calories. Close enough.

"Not near as much as I'm going to do for you," I growled, as she giggled and kissed me again.

Chapter 18

By three a.m. I was awake, lazily watching Masha sleep in the wash of moonlight. She barely moved when I crawled carefully out of bed.

At least until I stubbed my toe on the footboard, but even that barely elicited a response. With a groan and a shift, she rolled over and went back to sleep while I limped my way downstairs.

The light on the answering machine was flashing, but I left it while I nursed my broken toe. Musing, I tried to decide if I could come up with enough money to get health insurance for all the injuries this new job entailed, but after the throbbing dropped to a dull ache, I put insurance out of my mind and checked my messages.

Another call from a religious nut, threatening me. I deleted it. The second call caught my attention enough that I played it a second time to be sure I'd heard correctly.

"Hello, I'm hoping I've reached the correct number. I'm trying to reach the Poltergeist Guys. Uh, I guess if this isn't them, just ignore this message. If it is, however, I need to speak to you. I don't like to talk on the phone, so if you could meet me at my house, the address is- oh, wait. I don't want to give that out over the phone in case someone is listening. Could you please meet me at the park on Elm Street when it gets light out? I'll wear a hat so you know it's me. Crap. No. You wear the hat. I don't want to make myself obvious. Yes, that's it! *You* wear a hat and I'll find you."

I leaned back in my chair, which promptly groaned. Freezing, certain the old wood had finally reached its breaking point, I let out a breath when my seat stayed put. That was the catalyst it needed. With a crack, the legs gave out and dumped me to the concrete below.

Now my toe *and* my ass hurt.

Pulling myself up by grabbing hold of the table, I sent up a little prayer that it held my weight. For once, something went my way and I made it to my feet without anything else breaking. With plenty of time to kill before meeting my mystery client, I decided to make a list of everything I knew about my father-in-law. Maybe seeing it in writing would help to connect the dots.

Bent over the table, I started.

Boris was possibly in the Russian mob.

Somehow, he knew the chief of police of the witch's coven police department.

He had been involved in the scandal that put Lou's son-in-law in office

He hated me but was willing to overlook that in order to get a date with Lou.

He hated me.

Okay, I know I repeated that last one, but I really felt like I couldn't stress enough how much he disliked me. Lately, his demeanor had mellowed some, and I wondered if maybe Ghost had been talking me up to the old man.

Seeing the words on paper didn't help much. I would have to do some detective work if I wanted to figure out the real story. Normally, I would have asked Ghost to do any computer research for me but considering the touchy subject of it being his grandfather, I decided maybe I'd better look somewhere else.

I briefly considered Ghost's friend Inkspot - what kind of a name was that, anyway? - but they were friends, and he would probably tell the kid. The only other option at my fingertips was Beatrix Martin.

But - and it was a big but – if she was as cowed by Boris as she seemed to be, how much could I possibly learn?

No, I needed to find someone who wasn't connected to my father-in-law at all. And in the small-ish town we lived in, that might be a tall order. Especially since everywhere I turned lately, his name kept popping up.

Pushing the thought to the side momentarily, I folded up the list and shoved the paper into my pocket. It wouldn't do for Masha or Ghost to wander down here and see my thoughts. I might as well paint a target on my back.

I picked up the pencil again and started a new list, one that made me smile as I wrote. Things I Could Finally Buy, I labeled it. That made me remember I hadn't ever split up the cash from Riley. Now, where did I put it?

I checked all my hiding spots, even the rat house. Then checked them again. Then a third time for good measure, hoping my eyes were playing tricks on me and the torn envelope full of money had appeared in one of the dusty hiding spots. Nothing.

Panic took over. I paced the floor, kicking at the remnants of my chair, getting my foot caught in the jacket that had been hanging on the back, tripping myself, and managing to stomp on my sore toe. Once I could think about something besides the pain, I tried to go step-by-step through the last time I'd seen the money.

I wanted to slap myself in the head. Who loses ten thousand bucks - twice? Me, that's who. I started over again. Riley gave us the money back and I put it in my jacket pocket. What did I do with it after that? I tried to force the memory, but it wouldn't come out and play.

As a last resort, I picked my jacket up from the floor, knowing the money couldn't possibly have been in the pocket the whole time. It felt heavier than normal, and my heart lifted even as my nose wrinkled from the scent of sulfur still clinging to the fake leather.

In the pocket, I found the envelope. I'm man enough to admit that I kissed it. Maybe I danced around the room with it, maybe not. I contemplated stripping down and rolling around naked on it but stopped myself.

Then, for the first time since Riley gave it to me - again, I counted my moolah.

Sitting precariously balanced on Ghost's stool, I pulled the neatly stacked wad of money from the envelope and counted out ten thousand dollars in cash. I was rich! Okay, not rich, but definitely better off than I'd been for a while.

Once I came down from my cash cloud, I carefully counted out three thousand, four hundred dollars. I figured I could be generous enough to give Ghost a bonus on his share. Then I counted out another thousand to go toward fixing my car.

Tinkerbell would pay for the damages she did to my window, I decided, but until I could find her again, I needed to be the adult and take care of it myself.

The early morning sun peeked its golden head through the basement windows when I hid the rest of the money in the heater vent – after carefully checking it again for rats. Time to go meet my new mystery caller.

I debated taking Ghost with me, but he had class and I didn't want him to miss any more school this close to graduation. Silently, I congratulated myself. I really was getting better at this parenting thing!

Slipping on my jacket, I headed up the stairs to meet my mystery date.

Ghost sat at the kitchen table, one arm wrapped around a giant mixing bowl full of cereal.

"Dude, where you going?" Tiny bits of sugary flakes and milk flew out of his mouth as he mushed the words around the food.

"Meeting with a mystery client. I'll let you know how it goes after school."

Swallowing hard, he pushed the chair away from the table and stood, bowl in hand.

"I'm going with," he announced.

As the parental figure in the room, I sternly shook my finger and pronounced, "No, you have school today. I'll fill you in later this afternoon."

Obviously impressed with my skills as a parent, Ghost snorted as he carried the bowl over to the kitchen sink. "Dude, it's senior skip day. I'd rather meet a client than go drinking with the rest of the immature idiots in my class. Well, except maybe Inkspot."

Grabbing his jacket from the coat rack, Ghost slipped it over his shoulders as he walked to the door.

I tried one last time. "I just don't think—"

"Dude, I'll stay in the car while you meet with him. You never know, maybe it's that demon dude again, trying to trick you."

I thought about what he said for a minute before finally admitting to myself that the kid might be right. What if something happened to me? We hadn't exactly made a lot of friends since we started doing this.

"You're telling the truth about skip day?"

His eyes lit up. "Cross my heart, dude."

Without access to truth serum, I figured his word would have to suffice, so I gave the kid the okay, with the caveat that if he was lying to me, I wouldn't stand between him and his angry mother.

At the last second, I remembered the hat. Snagging the fisherman's cap Boris had left behind during the rainstorm, I dropped it on my head and swaggered out the door.

The park was empty when we pulled into the parking lot. Well, unless you counted the lone dog taking a crap. We watched as he scratched grass over his turds, then proudly trotted away.

After the dog disappeared, I glanced over at Ghost's lanky body, his head skimming the roof. Part of me was kicking myself for not taking Boris up on his offer of a new car. The Pacer's openness, while an advantage in some situations, was definitely not built for surveillance – or concealment.

"Scrunch down," I encouraged the kid. "Try to make yourself invisible."

"Dude, unless you picked up an invisibility spell from that witch, there's no way I can hide in this rolling aquarium."

"What if you laid down in the back seat? You could stretch out a little. At least until I find this guy."

Looking between the bucket seats, Ghost looked over at me with a grimace. "Have you ever once cleaned up back there? I mean, Dude, there's trash from the eighties in the floor. No way I'm going to fit."

"Well, you have to do something. If he sees you, he's not gonna show."

With a bunch of unnecessary groans and complaints, Ghost slid down a little further in his seat and leaned his head over the gearshift. "Better?"

I looked down on his blonde hair, gauging how much showed from the outside of the car. "A little. Okay, I'll be back in a few to get you. Hopefully, this guy isn't as paranoid as he sounded on the phone."

But he was. He was so much more paranoid than he sounded on his message.

Chapter 19

Settling the cap back on my head, the too-big hat promptly slid down over my eyes. I tilted it into a jaunty position on the crown and sauntered my way over to a concrete park bench.

It wasn't until I sat down that I realized the dark bench was not only freezing cold, but wet with dew, too. Just my luck. I felt the chilly water soaking into the back of my pants. Hoping the guy showed soon, I sat and shivered on the wet bench, feeling the cold creep up and hug places that shouldn't ever be that cold.

It felt like I sat there forever. In reality, it couldn't have been more than thirty minutes before I saw a flash of something in the trees on the other side of the park. Squinting, I watched the spot where I thought I'd seen it.

There it was again! It almost looked like someone was using a mirror to direct sunlight into my eyes. With a sigh, I stood up, the wet spot that had finally started to warm up instantly freezing my personal space again as the light breeze hit it.

I started through the dew-ridden grass, freezing my ass off – literally – and cursing. I wanted to check over my shoulder to see if Ghost was watching, but I worried that if Mr. Paranoid noticed I had someone with me, he would disappear like the smoke from one of Lou's cigarettes.

Then again, maybe that wouldn't be a bad thing. I was starting to get some really bad vibes about this guy. Really, *really* bad vibes. I mean, really, who was this paranoid?

As it turned out, he was.

When I reached the tree line, I heard a bad bird call. Like, not even remotely sounding anything like any bird I'd ever heard before. I stopped and did the only bird call I could think of in return – a duck.

"Quack!"

The hat slid down over my face again. I felt like a fool. To my surprise, a whispered shout came back, "Mr. Ward?"

I dropped all pretense of covertness and said in my normal voice, "Yeah? You my client?"

"Shhhh! They're listening!"

"Who's listening?"

"The aliens! The ones who work for the government!"

Whoo boy. This was going to be one for the books, I could already tell. I decided to play along for a minute. Worst case scenario, I could always run back to my car. Maybe I'd get a good laugh out of it later.

Whisper/shouting back, I asked, "Why are they listening to us?"

"Oh, like I'm going to tell *you*," came the quick reply. "You could be one of them for all I know!"

I was getting a little annoyed, and I snapped, "You called *me*, remember?"

The man stayed silent for a few seconds and I debated going back to the car.

"Hey, buddy," I finally called over to the man I still hadn't seen. "You gonna tell me why you asked me to come here, or not?"

Flapping his hand, he demanded, "Step a little closer."

I did as he asked, not really frightened of the wary freak, although in retrospect, I should have had a healthier respect for his paranoia.

He fumbled with something – a bag of some sort, and you know that little niggle of fear that you get in your gut sometimes? The one that says, 'Yeah, I know everything *looks* fine, but it really, really isn't'? That little niggle started nudging my stomach. Then it began kicking and screaming when the guy pulled out a gun and pointed it at me.

Well, shit.

Chapter 20

Psycho Guy herded me through the woods, poking the stupid gun into my back every time I stumbled. I'm not gonna lie, I almost peed myself a few times. Plus, he wasn't trying to be gentle when he shoved the barrel into my flesh. There were going to be little black and blue polka dots all over me when this was over. I could only hope I'd be alive to complain about it.

Boris's too-big hat fell off my head and when I tried to stop and pick it up, he gave me another poke, so I left it there in the dead leaves.

The scariest part of the whole thing was that the mystery man refused to speak while we worked our way through the brambles and roots. His silence instilled a fear in my gut deeper than the sight of the gun had.

"Hey, where are we going?"

If he was taking me somewhere to kill me, at least I wanted to know where my remains were going to be left. I mean, I could end up as a ghost, haunting the woods and scaring kids who wandered away from the park.

No answer from Paranoid Guy. Great. That didn't bode well for my future existence. I just hoped Ghost hadn't fallen asleep in the car or gone into one of his musical-eyes-closed-hypnotic trances.

If Ghost *had* been paying attention, if he saw me disappear into the woods, maybe he followed us. Maybe. There were a lot of them running around my head while I walked. Maybe's, I mean. On the bright side, at least I could count all the walking as cardio.

I figured I'd try talking to the guy one last time. If nothing else, if Ghost was following, he might hear my voice and have an idea where we were.

I tried to sound as jovial and business-like as possible as I wheezed, "So... what made you call Poltergeist Guys- oh, wait, I mean Polterguys?"

The barrel of the gun made another bruise on my back.

Well, that just pissed me off. Here I was, being forced to walk through the woods of a park in the early morning hours with a crazy man who kept

poking me with his gun and I was *still* trying to be a decent human being –
and he couldn't be bothered to say a word?

Nope, if I was going to be killed, then it might as well be right here. I
stopped walking and turned around to face him.

He looked kind of surprised for a second, then his face flushed red.
"Keep moving," he barked.

"No. Either tell me what's going on, or I'm leaving. You can shoot me
if you want, but I'm not going one step further until you let me know why
you're making me traipse through the woods."

He heaved a sigh and lowered the gun. "Look, I've got a little place out
here. It's not exactly um, legal, but I've been off the grid for a while."

I took a step closer. "Okay, now we're getting somewhere. Why are you
staying off the grid? And what's your name? If you're gonna kill me, I'd at
least like to know the name of my killer. Oh! And why!"

To my surprise, he grinned. Then he laughed, holding his hands over his
mouth to stifle the sound.

I thought about grabbing for the gun while he was distracted with
laughing at me, but he seemed pretty comfortable with the weapon –
meanwhile, I'd never touched one before - and I wasn't quite brave enough
to try.

Finally, he straightened himself back up. Still smiling, he asked, "If I tell
you my name, will you go with me?"

I pretended to consider his offer. Like I really had a choice. I was pretty
well stuck. I'd never done the boy scout thing, and I had no idea where we
were or how to get back to my car. Unless Ghost popped up from behind
a tree, I pretty much had to go with Crazy Man and hope he didn't kill me
when we reached - wherever.

"Alright, fine. You've kind of got me at a disadvantage here, you know,
what with the gun and all, so yeah, you have a deal."

"You can call me Dante."

"Dante? Did your mother hate children or something?"

Wrong thing to say. He lifted the gun and pointed it at me. "I answered
your question. Now move."

Grumbling, I turned and started walking again. I called back over my
shoulder, "You never did tell me why."

"You'll find out soon enough. See that big oak up there? Turn left just past it."

Like I said, I never did the Boy Scout thing. I didn't know an oak from a hole in the ground, but I kept walking, figuring he would let me know if I went too far.

As it turned out, it was pretty self-explanatory. The tree was giant. Its girth was bigger around than my arms and it looked to be at least a few hundred years old. I took a left as instructed, then stopped when he growled, "We're here."

Looking around in confusion, all I saw was a mound covered in leaves and sticks. "What are you talking about?"

"Look straight in front of you. That's the door."

Feeling like I was looking at one of those crazy, jumbled-picture kid's books that Ghost used to love as a kid, I stared at the confusion of leaves and sticks in front of me. Then I squinted my eyes and suddenly saw a perfectly straight gap in the foliage. Following it, I traced a semicircle in the hill.

A door. But what did it lead to?

As I reached out to grab the stick being used for a doorknob, I heard Dante smugly say, "Pretty camo, right?"

Oh, yeah. Pretty camo. No one would ever find my body. Awesome.

Pulling the door open, I sucked in a breath. Two steps made of logs led down into an underground room lit with battery-powered lanterns. For being a rabbit hole, it was even kind of nice.

Astonished at the homey little scene before me, I asked, "How long did it take you to make this?" He answered with another poke in my back and I ducked down to enter the hole, Dante following on my heels and closing the door.

Crap. Even if Ghost did follow us, he would never spot the place. It took a full minute of me staring at it to find the door. The kid never was very good at those dumb books.

Inside, I stopped thinking about anything except the room. Carved out of the earth, I expected the hole in the ground to be moldy-smelling and dank, but instead, it kind of smelled like – I took a deep breath – sawdust.

Pieces of salvaged tin covered the walls. The flooring consisted of planked wood of various lengths that looked like they'd been lifted from a dumpster at a construction site. Not a single board was more than six inches long. Carrying them through the woods a few at a time, it would have taken months just to lay the floor. This was not a hastily-constructed hideout.

There was enough room for the two of us in the little space that kind of reminded me of a hobbit house or a rabbit's burrow, although we couldn't quite stand up straight. Bent at the waist, I shuffled my way in a little circle until I could see Dante.

"What is this?" Without a word, he pointed to a crudely made sign on the wall.

'The Hideaway', it said.

"Well, that answers all my questions. Thanks, Dante." I didn't mean to be sarcastic, but really, what else are you gonna do in a situation like that?

Pointing at a small chair-like thing constructed of branches, he said, "Sit down and I'll explain."

Again, I had no choice but to do as he said. I was totally and completely screwed if he decided to shoot me and leave me in the little den. All I could really hope for was that he wouldn't want to mess up the homey little place he'd worked so hard on.

I wiggled my way into the little chair and waited while he settled onto a crudely-constructed bench near the door.

"My name isn't really Dante."

Considering his behavior so far, that wasn't much of a stretch to believe.

"You don't say."

Putting the gun into a little cubby next to his head, he took off his jacket and shifted on the wood bench to get comfortable.

"Thanks for coming with me. I'd heard you were dumb, but following some strange guy into the woods, well, I never thought it would work. In fact, I figured I'd have to get to you in your house."

Suspicion began to form, and I asked, "Are you the one that's been watching me at home?"

Dante – or whatever his name was – grinned. "You caught that, huh?"

"Uh, yeah, I caught that! Why? What possible reason would you have to watch me?"

The psycho shrugged, "I like to scope out my victims before I do anything."

Wait. Victims?

Dante giggled, a decidedly feminine sound. "I've already placed the ad for you and everything."

I had no clue what he meant. What ad?

"You still haven't figured it out, have you?" Pulling something out of the cubby, he tossed it at me. Instinctively, I caught the small, soft – underwear? What the hell?

Letting the G-string panties dangle from one finger, I finally put two and two together.

"Marzipam?"

Without looking, he reached into the little cubby in the wall and pulled out a stick, reinforcing my suspicions. Still, it was hard to take the man – woman, witch, whatever – seriously when their weapon was a small branch.

"Strip!" Marzipam pointed the stick at me, which only gave the opposite effect of what she wanted – I let out a chuckle at the ludicrousness of it.

"Whatcha gonna do with that?" I asked, trying to keep a straight face. "Spank me into submission?"

Dante backed himself against the wall. He waved the stick, and suddenly, Psycho-Man disappeared. In his place stood Marzipam, missing witch extraordinaire. She ordered, "I said strip!"

The stick wasn't nearly as funny when being held by a witch who presumably knew how to use it to her advantage.

Suitably frightened, I yanked my shirt over my head, smacking my hand against the ceiling, then yanked my pants off. Standing there in the middle of a hidden room deep in the forest next to a public park, I gave a bent-over pirouette in my tighty whiteys.

"Shorts too!" The witch's words coincided with the sound of something rarely heard – my cell phone ringing. I froze in surprise.

Marzipam jerked and screamed out a single word when the shrill sound of my phone went off, the stick turning back into a gun before my eyes. Pointing it at my chest, she muttered angrily, "This is all your fault. No one was onto me until you showed up at the church. Now I've had to go into hiding and everything I've done to stop these sex traffickers has been for nothing."

At least, I think that's what she said. My phone kept ringing, drowning out her words while she accused *me* of being the bad guy. When it finally stopped, she took a deep breath and screamed, "I said strip!"

Slowly, Marzipam raised the gun until the barrel pointed directly at my head. I closed my eyes, waiting for the bullet to hit my skull. A single tear rolled down one cheek. This couldn't be happening. I wasn't ready to die. I'd just discovered my life's work!

The boom of the weapon in the tiny, enclosed room deafened me. My eyes popped open. I was alive! Bits of dirt and leaves fell to the floor around me. Ears ringing, I watched her lips form the word, "Strip!"

I jerked at the waistband of my shorts to get them off before she shot me for real. I kicked them away while putting my hands against the low ceiling, my fingertips touching the hole she'd created.

Marzipam said something, but all I heard was a big, fat nothing. Her lips kept moving, but the words dissipated as they left her mouth. The gun wavered between me and the front door, and all I could think about was that I was going to die right here, in some stupid hobbit bunker built by a crazy witch, and no one would ever find my body once she closed the door and left.

Her lips kept moving. I couldn't hear anything, how could she? Slowly, her back pressed against the tin wall, she rose to a tall squat, keeping the gun leveled at my chest the whole time.

Just when I was starting to wonder how long the witch was going to make me stand there in the nude before she got tired of talking and shot me, a thin beam of light stretched across the room, growing wider by the second, and dousing me in warmth and indignity.

The gun started swinging toward the door as it opened, and like magic, Marzipam turned into Dante again. His finger moved the tiniest bit on the trigger just as I recognized the kid standing in the doorway.

"Noooooo!" I screamed like the madman I had become in the last few minutes of my life and threw myself at the other madman – mad witch-woman? - in the room. Tackling him, I felt something hard press into my bare belly and then I felt it catch fire.

The last thing I saw was Ghost mouthing the word, "Dude," before I lost consciousness.

Chapter 21

I woke up alone in a hospital room. Images of Ghost standing in the doorway of the crazy witch's lair filtered through my head like one of those movies with alternate endings. In the first one, he ran for help, coming back with Chief Martin and rescuing me. In the next, Marzipam shot him.

I shut that one down pretty quick. My eyes began watering a little at the thought. I mean, they were watering from the dryness of the room. I wasn't crying, okay?

After my little session of not-crying, some semblance of logic finally began to return to my scrambled brains. Ghost had to be alive, or I wouldn't be in the hospital. I mean, someone rescued me, right? And it sure as hell wasn't Marzipam.

In the movies, they always show the person who sleeps in the chair next to the bed until their injured loved one wakes up. Slowly turning my head, I checked the chair, hoping to see Masha – or Ghost - sleeping peacefully, but the only thing in the seat was a discarded rubber glove.

Just then, my stomach began to burn. We're talking Olympic-sized torches marching across my midsection. I peeled the sheet back slowly, afraid to look, and afraid not to.

I could move my arms and head, so that was good, but what about my legs? Oh man, I couldn't feel my legs! Marzipam must have shot through my stomach into my spine! I was going to be in a wheelchair the rest of my life, and just when I finally started my life's work, and holy crap, would Masha even want to be married to a man that couldn't walk?

Oh, shit! Speaking of Masha - did my wiener still work?

Once I managed to shove the blanket below my belly button, I tried to see the damage, but the bulge of my stomach hid it from me. If my legs weren't paralyzed, I was going to start working out when I got out of here.

Running the tips of my fingers gingerly over my fat – I mean, muscled – abdomen, I had just reached the area below my belly button when Masha walked into the room, followed by Ghost and Boris.

The kid was alive! I didn't have time to celebrate before Masha grabbed my hand and lectured, "Ed! Not to do in hospital!"

I was completely and totally confused about what she was talking about until she reached over, took my hand, and placed it on my chest. She then pulled the sheet up over the hand, scolding me all the while.

"Is not nice to do such things. Keep hands up top, please."

It slowly sank into my brain what she meant. She thought I was going to- the thought of doing that in a hospital room was just- did she think I was some kind of sex-deprived animal that couldn't go more than a few hours without pleasuring myself?

"Masha, honey, I was just trying to feel my wound. How bad is it? Will I be able to walk again someday? Don't spare my feelings. I can handle it."

It was her turn to be confused. Turning to look first at Boris, then Ghost-er, Alvin, she asked, "What is meaning?"

Oh geez, it was worse than I thought! I was going to be in a wheelchair for the rest of my life! I looked at Ghost, the only one of the three I knew would give me a straight answer. He was too busy laughing to meet my eye.

Wait, why was he laughing? Being wheelchair-bound for the rest of my life was nothing to laugh at!

The kid walked over to the bed and slapped my leg. Hard. He hit me so hard that I felt the sting of each finger where they touched my leg.

Wait a minute... I felt the sting!

"Dude," he laughed, "You're such a hypochondriac. The bullet grazed your stomach, then you rammed your head into the wall when you tackled Marzipam. They brought you in to be sure you didn't have a concussion."

The laughter stopped, and his face settled into a more somber one. "I just wanted to- I mean, what you did- well, I just wanted to say thanks for saving my life, uh, *Dad*."

Okay... I had to be dreaming, right? Or hallucinating, or having a vision, or something. Had to be. Because there was no way that after five years of living with the kid that he just called me Dad for the first time. I shot a look at Masha to see if she heard it too.

My wife stood next to Ghost, her face beaming with love and joy. I knew for sure it was real, though, when I saw the disgruntled look on Boris' face. Holy crap. The kid called me Dad!

I reached up and took the kid's hand. Weakly shaking it, I said, "Any time, kid. Any time." Dropping my hand back to the bed, I asked, "Can someone please tell me what happened? How the hell did you find me, Ghost?"

I heard Boris muttering, "Who is Ghost?" but I ignored his question and Masha's quiet explanation as I locked eyes with my son.

"Dude, when you disappeared into the woods, I tried to follow you, but I don't know any of that Indian tracking sh- uh, stuff." After a quick glance to see if his mother caught the slipup, he continued.

"I remembered seeing you slip your phone into your pocket when you got out of the car, so I pulled up the carrier's website on my phone and ran a GPS on yours."

I had no idea what the kid was talking about, but hey, I could always ask questions later.

"I knew I was heading the right direction when I found Ded's hat on the ground. Then, when your phone stopped moving, I knew you were right there somewhere, so I called your phone. I finally found the door to that crazy bunker. If I'd known she had a gun, I might not've opened the door."

Eyes shining, he finished, "Then you took a bullet to save my life! No one has ever done anything like that for me before! So, I took an example from your bravery and rushed in. You knocked the gun out of her hand when you tackled her, so I reached under you and yanked it out – sorry if I did any more damage to your belly – and held it on her while I called Beatrix."

I wasn't sure how to respond. Grateful that he had saved my life, I felt like a fool for letting myself get into that situation in the first place. With a weak grin, I finally managed to spit out, "Thanks for saving *my* life, *dude*. That witch was a serious fruitcake."

I glanced over at Boris to see what he thought about all this, only to be greeted with a look that could have burned holes through the atmosphere.

A rustle of movement behind my family and Beatrix Martin appeared, looking as grim as usual. Ghost explained, "Oh, yeah, the witch cops want to talk to you. After that, we can take you home."

Masha stepped forward and took my hand, her warm fingers pressing against my cold palm. "We take you home after. And then we talk about crazy job, yes?"

With a grin, I answered, "We will talk. Yes."

I knew I couldn't give this job up. Despite being shot by a crazy witch, I felt more alive than I had in years. Demons, ghosts, poltergeists, witches, crazy, enraged fairies- there was a whole world out there that I was just starting to learn about, and for the first time in my life, I felt like I'd found what I was meant to be doing. No more floating through life looking for meaning. I had discovered it, and now that I had, nothing was going to stop me from my mission.

With Alvin, aka Ghost, doing the technical work, Sam and Lou helping with the spiritual side, and Tinkerbell as a confidential informant – assuming I could convince her to keep working with us – we made a team that could defeat anything.

And Boris? Well, we were going to have a talk, the two of us. I was going to find out the truth about him, with or without his cooperation.

I beamed as I watched my family shuffle out of the room, ready for anything Chief Beatrix Martin could throw at me.

The End?

I was sitting in the office when the kid walked in with a smirk on his face. Knowing that usually meant nothing good – for me at least – I asked, "Why do you look like the cat that ate the canary?"

"Dude, I have no idea what that means," Ghost answered. "But I have good news."

"Good like winning the Publisher's Clearing House prize? Or good like a cigarette after playing Pizza Boy and the Princess with you mother?"

"Ew, gross," he said, twisting his face up in a familiar look of revulsion.

I mentally patted myself on the back for grossing the kid out.

"Dude, check this out," he said after swallowing hard a few times. "There's gonna be another Polterguys book."

"Yeah, right," I said, leaning back in my chair. "Like anybody wants to hear about us."

Ghost shrugged. "Whatever, dude. Guess you'll see around the first of October."

Wait, maybe the kid was serious. "Really? This year?"

He nodded. "October, 2019. Better start getting ready for it now."

Shit. He *was* serious.

Polterguys 2 was coming.

Don't miss out!

Visit the website below and you can sign up to receive emails whenever Sonia Rogers publishes a new book. There's no charge and no obligation.

https://books2read.com/r/B-A-KWTD-CXUY

BOOKS 2 READ

Connecting independent readers to independent writers.

Also by Sonia Rogers

Polterguys
Polterguys

Zombie Baby
Zombie Baby

Zombie Club
Zombie Club
Zombie Club 2
Zombie Club 3

Standalone
Zombie Mom

About the Author

Sonia Rogers isn't afraid of ghosts and goblins. At least, not in the daytime with all the lights on.

At night, though, it's a different story. That's when the ghoulies come out and whisper their stories into her ear.

It would be remiss of her not to write them down.

Wouldn't it?

Besides, they've threatened her with her life if she doesn't.

So please, if you can, leave a review and let the ghoulies know she's doing her job.

For heaven's sake, I'm begging you!

Made in the USA
Monee, IL
26 July 2021